A NOVEL

ELI WELLINGTON

Eli Wellington/Dystopian Publishing
Post Office Box 401170
San Francisco, CA 94140
info@dystopianpublishing.com

R / Eli Wellington. – First Edition.
ISBN 978-1-959656-07-4 Print
ISBN 978-1-959656-08-1 eBook

This novel is dedicated to Nitin Garg,
who got me to start again when I was stuck,
and to Sağnak Taşırlar
for getting me over the finish line.

Publishers Note: This is a work of fiction with themes of White supremacy and other racial issues in the United States. There are varying opinions on the appropriate ways to reference Black and White. This novel adheres to the guidelines established by the Chicago Manual of Style (CMOS), which dictates that each is capitalized.

PREFACE

The shepherd always tries to persuade the sheep that their interests and his own are the same. – Stendhal

CHAPTER 1

"Citizens and Patriots, I can no longer stand by as a silent observer to the events happening behind the scenes of our great country. Our democracy is at risk. Trust me when I tell you that I am an insider to our government with a security clearance that gives me insights into the wrongdoings that are not being reported to you, the nationalists that need to know. I cannot post everything at once, but I promise you I will share complete and accurate information about the secret tribunals that are being conducted to preserve our society. I am not alone in the fight to preserve the Constitution that was put in place by our forefathers generations ago. Respect the word! You are being misled! More tomorrow. – R"

It didn't take long to read the post, and as R clicked on the button that pushed the message live for the world to see, there was no turning back. It was time.

■

Tony Williams slipped behind the wheel of his silver F-250 Ford truck and eased into traffic. As he drove by Sam Houston Park, he bristled. They'd removed the Spirit of the Confederacy statue from the grounds, which still annoyed him." Don't forget who you are and where you come from," was his motto, taken from F. Scott Fitzgerald. He was a fifth-generation Texan and proud of it. The statue had been moved to an outdoor space at the Houston Museum of African American Culture. *Why did it end up there?* It was his history and commemorated the efforts of the Confederate Army. The inscription even read: "To all the heroes of the South who fought for the Principles of States Rights," not anything to do with African American culture.

The country was going downhill quickly when the Black Lives Matter rioters were winning. They should be thrown in jail for causing a disturbance, not rewarded with the removal of a piece of Texan history. Why didn't *his* life matter? Blacks said they were marginalized, yet he was the one who was being told he was guilty of sins just because his skin was white. He didn't have privilege. He'd just finished twelve hours of grueling work as a plumber. Crawling under houses, snaking out drains, and literally dealing with shit most of his days wasn't glamorous. *White privilege, my ass.*

Tony pulled a pack of Marlboro Reds from his shirt pocket, flipped open the box top, and extracted a cigarette. His girl-friend, Erica, had tried to get him to switch to a vape pen, saying it was healthier for him, but he enjoyed the feel of the paper-wrapped tobacco in his hand. The acidic smell of the sulfur from the match as he inhaled to light the tip felt comforting and tactile. The vape pen created a billow of vapor, but it wasn't the same as his cigarettes. He exhaled smoke toward the opened crack of his driver's window and turned onto the road that wound toward his neighborhood. He was looking forward to getting home. He hoped Erica was in the mood for sex. He wanted something to distract him from his frustrations from the day.

■

The president of the United States, Dominic Coronet, looked at the expanse of lawn outside the Oval Office and smiled. A businessman with no political ties and a broad social following had taken advantage of a splintered party that couldn't agree on the level of conservatism of their candidate. With a playing field of ten candidates, he'd slid into the position as front runner with more moderates splitting the primary votes between them and allowing his far-right views to tally the most votes.

As soon as he'd won the primary, he'd known that he would be the next president. His opponent didn't have the same level of celebrity as he did by appearing on national television each week as the reality TV star of *Mega Mergers*, a show that gave entrepreneurs a chance to pitch their ideas to the billionaire in hopes of merging ventures for profitable gain. Dom was the pillar of the show and often chastised applicants for their limited business acumen, stupid ideas, and lack of foresight. Viewers loved the show because of the glimpse into a world most of them could not even dream about. Each week, The Coronet Company would display their venues and successful businesses to highlight the flaws in the applicant proposals. The fact that he'd declared bankruptcy multiple times, was named in numerous lawsuits, and had dubious credit was never broached and was downplayed whenever it came up externally.

He wore a heavy, diamond-encrusted Super Bowl ring for when his team had successfully taken home the coveted title. With fifty pounds of extra weight, his enjoyment of rich foods and scotch had thwarted any athletic attempts he may have had in his youth. He was much happier indulging in opulence that included gourmet food, beautiful centerfolds, and gambling at high-stakes poker games.

Social media channels hadn't existed when he first started, and he'd relied on magazine articles and fabricated stories of the extent of his wealth to create influence. When he discovered Twitter, he found his own mini megaphone with 140 characters to spread his gospel and amassed a large following. His opponent, a political lifer, was still using an outdated playbook that relied on television ads, smear campaigns, and handshaking to gather votes. The belief that the best candidate would win based on promises of what could be done for the American people was no longer enough. Engagement was the name of the game, and Coronet had learned early on that both good and bad reactions worked to his advantage. He could rile up a flurry of activity on his channel by pitting adversaries against each other. He just had to strike the match.

There was nothing he wouldn't say. Twitter favored him and did not enforce their usage standards for fear of angering his millions of followers. Besides, he knew the name of their game, too. It was all about money, and he generated a lucrative flow of ad revenue for the social giant by being divisive. It became a fine line of interpretation of what defined online bullying. He could do and say whatever he wanted as long as they were profitable. He didn't have the exact figures, but he was pretty sure that his channel contributed a hefty percentage of Twitter income, with eighty-nine million followers engaged with his content and the corresponding flow of advertisements.

■

Maxwell Hovick entered the Oval Office. The vice president was a nondescript man, selected by Dominic because of his willingness to step into a secondary role and not question the authority of the president. The middle-aged man filtered his life through a Christian lens and appeared faithful to his wife. He was a man who played by the rules, with the ordinances of God first and the rules of the country second. Max looked down at the paper in his hand. "I see that the campaign schedule has been set. Do you really want me to go to Georgia?"

"Yes. I'm going to Oklahoma while you're in Atlanta. We have a huge following there, and I think it's important for you to be seen in Georgia."

"There are rumors it will be more of a swing state come November. Your presence could make a big difference." Max knew he'd be blamed for a low turnout if Dom didn't get the results he wanted.

"There's nothing more to discuss." Dominic didn't share with Max that he had chosen Oklahoma because the arena was larger. He liked the cheers from the crowd around him and didn't want to waste his time at a smaller location. The second in command looked resigned. "As you wish. I'll do my best to promote your message to the citizens of Georgia."

"Don't lose sight of our cause. I am determined to win the next election. The future of our democracy is at stake."

Maxwell thought the president was being a little dramatic. After all, the country had survived a civil war and reunited, and the democracy was still intact. However, if there was one thing he knew after three years as the vice president of the Coronet administration, the president didn't do anything on a small scale. He had to be the center of attention. For now, Max was happy to stay on the sidelines.

CHAPTER 2

Kasey Kirby Kiel had an unfortunate name given to him by proud parents who had not realized their choice of the initials KKK for their son would cause him a world of aggravation. His family had a long history of Klan participation, but the tides had turned, and public opinion had shifted. The Klan still mobilized, but flaunting the affiliation could get one placed on a Hate Group list and closely monitored by the FBI. He'd switched the spelling to Casey with a C in college to make his life easier. Only those in the human resources department of *The National Times* newspaper knew the legal spelling of his name. He signed all his articles as Casey Kiel. No one gave it a second thought; his co-workers even called him CK on occasion, and he was fine with the designation.

He had grown up hearing about how superior he was to the Blacks who lived on the other side of town. He was told they were lazy, stupid, and only suitable for playing sports or menial tasks. His parents weren't happy when he received a full ride from a "Yankee" school. However, Columbia University was the top school for journalism, and for as long as he could remember, Casey wanted to be an investigative reporter. He liked solving puzzles, and words flowed easily for him. He'd panicked when he had arrived at school to learn that he'd been assigned a Black roommate. It was his first introduction to being called a racist when he complained to the housing office. He didn't like it. The department had refused to make a change, and he found himself sharing a room with Jamiel Jackson from Los Angeles. At first, he wondered how a Black person was smart enough to get into Columbia, but it didn't take long to learn that his roommate was brighter than anyone he knew.

As he immersed himself in his journalism studies, he learned the importance of being impartial and investigating all angles. It took a few months, but he slowly learned more about his roommate, and he started to question his parents' guidance and philosophy toward those who made up the "them" population. Recently, the "them" group, which had consisted of "those Blacks" when he was growing up, had expanded to "bad hombres" for brown-skinned people and "Muslims" for anyone who worshiped Allah or had a name they didn't understand. Casey tried to discuss his expanded worldview with his parents, but they didn't comprehend. They blamed Columbia for poisoning their son's mind and constantly tried to get him to transfer to a school in Georgia near their home. Since graduation, he'd only ventured home for Christmas, and even then, he tried to keep his visits to a minimum, using newspaper deadlines as a reason to leave. He loved his parents, but it was hard to see the world with their tunnel vision when he'd learned the world was so much bigger.

■

Erica looked at the donut light before her and made sure no shadows were cast across her face as she pressed the record button on her computer. She was ready to embody her online persona.

"Hi, y'all! Kiki here, and today is going to be a fun day! Look what I received in the mail." She held up a brown shipping box with a logo on the side that said Clever Cosmetics. "Now, if you've been following me for any amount of time, you already know how much I LOVE these products. By the way, be sure to subscribe to my channel. You can click here." She gestured into the air in the general direction of the lower corner of the video as she continued. "One lucky person is going to receive a Clever Cosmetics beauty bag by sharing this video. I'll put the deets below." She opened the box and extracted a variety of items.

"Be sure to start with a clean face. I'll put a link below to a great tutorial on how to have the best skin you can have, no matter your skin type, in just five minutes or less in the morning and again at night. No one wants wrinkles!" She paused and looked straight into the camera.

"As you can see, my face is freshly washed." She didn't share that she'd applied a little makeup to even her skin tone. She blended the product carefully and set a filter on her camera to ensure her skin looked natural and untouched. The freckles that plagued her throughout her life were not to be seen. Beauty was her brand, and she wasn't going to jeopardize her livelihood by being average. Her looks made her popular. Long, beautiful blond hair swept up in a bouncy ponytail helped convey her girl next-door image. She was fresh-faced and ready for the makeup application in her current video.

It took an hour to record the footage she'd need for the makeup tutorial, and she was pleased with how her face looked at the end of the video. She laid out the products on the tabletop and captured images of each item to allow her to cut between her face and the products. Clever Cosmetics would send her a free weekly package of products as long as she drove traffic to their site. With her specialized affiliate code embedded into the tracking URL, they could see the sales attributed to her channel, and she didn't have to bear the expense of products. So far, the arrangement has been working perfectly. She wondered who else she could contact for free stuff. Maybe a clothing company could make sure she had the latest styles. With her followers approaching 15,000, she was beginning to get what she requested.

She looked at her phone. Tony would be home soon. She hoped he would think she looked pretty. She hadn't planned on dating a plumber, and he hadn't shared with her what he did for a living on their first few dates. She knew he drove a new truck and was generous when they went out, and she thought he was cute, even though he was twelve years older than her twenty-eight years. It didn't hurt that he looked great naked. He also knew what he was doing in the bedroom, which was more than she could say about the men her age. She just hoped he'd quit smoking soon. Statistically, she was already going to outlive him. *Did he have to smoke, too?*

CHAPTER 3

Brad Taylor grew up in Placerville, northeast of Sacramento, which was commonly referred to as Hangtown. He was irritated with the City Council, which had voted to remove the noose from the city logo and instead focus on the history of the Gold Rush, with a person panning the water for fortune. Hangman's Tree was still a historic landmark, even though the tree had been chopped down decades ago as the city grew up around it. There was still a noose with a dummy named "George" hanging from a mock limb protruding from the Western facade building constructed over the tree stump. The effigy had depicted a Black man for years but had been replaced with a more innocuous-skinned figure in cowboy attire as the city faced cries of racism.

Brad didn't want to acknowledge the juxtaposition with the Farm Table Restaurant located next door. He saw Hangman's Tree as a tribute to the history of Hangtown, which was slowly being stripped away. Farm Table Restaurant was just a place to get an expensive burger and be served food that was way beyond his budget. It was another indication that the town he'd grown up in was changing in ways he didn't like.

He moved closer to San Francisco, and that's when he discovered Whites Restore.

Whites Restore had regular monthly in-person meetings in a church community room in Tracy, California. They'd told the administrators it was an AA meeting so that they could use the space for free. It also kept them under the radar of scrutiny from church officials. While most AA meetings were open to the public, they solved the problem of drop-ins by having someone guard the door.

"Are you a vet?" Nine out of ten times, the answer was "no," and the wannabe attendee would be told it was a restricted meeting for veterans only and denied entrance. Those who were veterans would be sized up for their potential interest in Whites Restore before being allowed to enter. If they were a person of color or questionable background, the secondary question about which branch of service they served in would adequately exclude them.

"Air Force."

"Sorry, we're all grunts here."

If the person answered Marines, the group were all squids or whatever would eliminate the potential attendee from joining them.

If the admitted potential recruit wasn't of like mind, they were weeded out quickly and reminded that all AA meetings were conducted with a code that allowed everyone anonymity. They didn't need to know it wasn't an AA meeting.

Whites Restore in Tracy was one of numerous chapters of the nationwide group, and they received directives from the elders elected to guide the group. Brad arrived early to the scheduled meeting to be sure he could contribute to the setup of chairs and be seen by the elders he desperately wanted to impress. He was thirty-three, and until he'd found Whites Restore, he'd been floundering, moving from one crappy job to the next. It was at the elder's urging that he join the Oakland Police Department. Several months ago, he'd been assigned to a beat position on the force. The elders guided him on what to look for while on duty.

The elder leading the Tracy gathering rose and started the meeting. "Please stand to repeat our pledge." The group obliged and repeated their mantra. "I pledge allegiance to Whites Restore and abide by the goal of restoring our great nation as outlined by our forefathers. I will act as a missionary for God to wash the filth from our shores. I am one of the chosen who has evolved in the eyes of God, and I am close to enlightenment and a place by God's side in Heaven. I will help cleanse those in need for their own elevation."

As the group returned to their seats, the elder started the meeting. "The national elders have acknowledged our branch and our efforts. Specifically, I want to commend Officer Brad Taylor. The national elders remind us that change happens quickly from within, and we should recruit many like-minded participants for positions in police forces around the United States and in the military. It is critical that we have a presence in organizations with might and power. Our mission is to reach those who see the truth of our purpose and are willing to step up to claim their power."

Brad felt a sense of pride at the acknowledgment of the vital role he was playing in Whites Restore. He'd found the group when he felt alone and isolated, without direction. He had been taken in and shown the way to make a difference. He was one of God's children, and his white skin confirmed he was evolving and elevated to do God's work. Blacks, Latinos, and Asians were mere animals who had reincarnated enough times that they were finally resembling human form and evolving toward the purity of Whites. It would still require many deaths and rebirths before they would be admitted at the gates of Heaven and embody their true White soul bodies. Brad was playing an essential role in their evolution.

The group explained that God would show them the way and guide them to the "Lessers" that needed their assistance. There was evolutionary work and learning that each person had to complete to transcend to their White greatness. God would show Whites Restore members the way when the time was right. They would receive guidance from the elders. Brad hoped that one day, he would take on the responsibilities of an elder. For now, he was excited to be shown and tutored in God's ways of purifying souls.

■

"There is a morally corrupt group of pedophiles that have infiltrated the Hollywood elite. They secretly steal children from orphanages and social services, abuse them sexually, and then sacrifice them in Satanic rituals. The internal Tribunal of the Higher World Court is focused on bringing justice for these horrific acts. I have firsthand knowledge of the atrocities that are being conducted. The children who are not tortured and killed for blood-drinking rituals are sold as sex slaves to the highest bidder. I have seen the classified files. A Rainstorm is coming, and these posts are the initial raindrops to keep you informed. I will share more tomorrow. Respect the word. You are being misled." — R.

The first post made the day before hadn't received much attention, with only a few likes and minimal shares. It was imperative that nothing identify the author of the posts. It was important how and where the information was shared; one's livelihood depended on it.

∎

Leon Levan logged onto the far-right message board he'd discovered a month earlier. Seeking commentators who shared his worldview led him to the BeWarned.com site. It became a daily ritual to read the posts that reinforced what he had long suspected: the government was corrupt, and officials eradicated the original one over a hundred years ago when the District of Columbia had been incorporated into the United States of America. The documents posted on the website showed that an incorporated version of the United States had replaced their democracy. Mismanagement and corruption had caused the corporation to default on its loan, and now the Pope and the King of England held the note. At first, he didn't believe it, but then he read additional documents posted by InTheKnowUSA, a pundit out of New York City. He read the documents online that first established the existence of the corporate entity and then the subsequent documents that showed the proceedings for declaring the default.

The BeWarned site was basic. It was possible to pin content to a personal dashboard so that individual posters could be followed easily. The site algorithm also served additional links based on reading history.

"Respect the word! You are being misled!" caught his eye and sparked his curiosity. The post was short and promised more information the next day. Leon pinned the post to his dashboard. It would be interesting to see what R was going to share tomorrow. He already knew it was going to be significant.

CHAPTER 4

Tony and Erica lay side by side in a tangle of bedsheets. A moment after completing their union, they both reached for their phones and focused on their social feeds. Tony scrolled through Facebook, and Erica turned to her Insta account. The first thing she checked was the number of followers. She was up five. "Babe! Five more!"

"Hmm?" Tony didn't look up from his screen. "What?"

"I have five more followers! And my next video is going to reach even more people. Hashtag becoming an influencer!" She tossed the sheet aside and stood up. "Where's my robe?" Tony had lured her to the bedroom as soon as he'd gotten home. She found the short, silky item on a hook on the back of the bathroom door, and as she wrapped it around her, she caught an image of her tousled hair in the mirror. *"Thank God, I already finished my tutorial."* Her lipstick left only a faint hue, and her mascara was smudged. She pulled a makeup remover cloth from a pouch, quickly removed the dark mark, and reapplied a fresh coat of eyeliner, mascara, and a swipe of gloss.

She felt beautiful when the first thing Tony wanted to do when he saw her was to have sex. They had a playful, albeit vanilla, love life. When she'd hinted at bringing some toys into the bedroom, he'd quickly assumed he wasn't enough, and she assured him that wasn't the case and didn't bring it up again. She kept her vibrator hidden in the bottom drawer in the bathroom and used it while watching kink porn on the internet when Tony was at work. She knew no matter what men thought, women were the ones with power.

■

Casey enjoyed the buzz of the newsroom around him. He had the luxury of coming and going without being tied to a desk; still, he found the camaraderie of the bullpen of writers energized him as he worked. Members of the group often collaborated on pieces and helped each other with fact verification. Together, they ensured the integrity of their reporting at *The National Times.* In turn, the staff had been awarded 132 Pulitzer Prizes since receiving their first one in 1908. Located in Georgetown near Dupont Circle in Washington, D.C., the paper was established as the premier reporting source of federal politics. Just out of Columbia, Casey had joined a smaller paper and got his feet wet with local politics in upstate New York. His original fantasies of solving cold cases and writing a weekly column as a beloved local contributor had quickly shifted as he discovered the intrigue of the political arena. He'd reported through three presidencies since joining *The Nat,* and he still marveled at the nuances of his daily stories with everything from politicians with mistresses, misappropriations of campaign contributions, and drug addictions as well as those legitimately seeking to improve the country made every day different.

Social media had changed reporting since his days at Columbia. It was frustrating to spend time digging for facts and then see algorithms on social platforms serve up falsehoods repeatedly. He saw it in his personal feeds as well. He'd purchased a stroller for his admin when the younger man was expecting his first child, and now Casey was being barraged with baby items daily. So much for privacy. At first, he embraced it as improved technology that gave him at least something relevant to view. Still, since he'd been assigned to monitor and report on falsehoods posted throughout social media platforms, he found himself questioning everything. *What represented the truth? How could you validate sources when a Google search served up numerous supporting documents that debunked the same information?*

He opened his laptop. He wasn't as interested in the mega social sites today. Facebook, Twitter, and Instagram could wait. Today, he was looking at the fringe platforms that were getting more attention and appeared to be the petri dish of alternative information. *How did one go about finding the fringe sites, the ones skating in the peripheral vision of the internet? This was going to be a fun project.*

■

Jamiel Jackson was stopped at a red light near downtown Charleston. He hadn't been to South Carolina before and rented a basic Toyota Corolla to navigate the streets. More than one time when he was growing up, he'd found himself stopped near his family home in Bel Air and quizzed about why he was in the exclusive neighborhood. He'd heard stories about the South and how Blacks were treated, and he wanted to blend in as best he could. His goal was to make it to his conference, give the keynote address on his research into pediatric nephrology, and return to the airport. He had a full roster of patients waiting for him back in Los Angeles, and he'd only agreed to attend this event because he could get the word out about the advances being made in his field.

He looked in the rearview mirror and watched a patrol car pull behind him. He was a board-certified doctor from an Ivy League institution, and he still felt his palms get clammy. The light turned green, and he looked both ways before easing his rental car into the intersection. Google Maps displayed the speed limit as 35 mph, and he kept his speed to 33. Not too fast and not too slow.

He drove two blocks, and the police car remained behind him, almost dangerously close. He didn't need to turn for another mile but opted to pull away from the police car. He signaled a right turn and maneuvered the vehicle to the side street. The squad car signaled and followed. Shortly after making the turn, the lights on the top of the official vehicle flashed, and a siren indicated that he was being pulled over.

Jamiel knew the drill. Turn on the car's interior light, lower the window, and place your hands on the steering wheel in clear view at positions ten and two. He looked into the rearview mirror again and saw two officers exiting the car. The driver was about fifty with a little paunch, and the other was in his mid-twenties. Both had sidearms, and the driver slid a baton into a loop on his belt as he approached.

"License and registration."

"My wallet is in my back pocket." Jamiel didn't want to make any moves that could be misunderstood.

"Then you better step out of the car so I can see you."

The doctor nodded and reached for the door handle. His movements were slow and deliberate as he released the latch and pushed the door open. He slid his legs to the pavement and stood up. He was several inches taller than both of the other men.

"It's in my back right pocket." He turned and lifted his suit coat to show that there was the customary bulge of a wallet, nothing more. Jamiel carefully reached in, pulled out the leather case, and turned slowly to face the man who had been driving the squad car. He flipped open the holder, extracted his license, and extended it to the officer, who took it and peered at it a long moment before speaking again. "California? You here to deal drugs?"

"No. I'm here for a conference." Internally, he recognized the irony in the question. In a way, Jamiel was there to promote drugs—the ones used to fight kidney disease. He knew the question was posed for illegal drugs. *Even if he was a drug dealer, who in their right mind would admit that to an officer of the law?*

"You sure I'm not going to find any drugs in the trunk of your car here?"

"No, sir."

"Run this license." The older officer handed the card to the younger one, who returned to the squad car. "I want you to sit on the hood of the police car as I take a look at this paperwork."

Jamiel moved to the front of the official vehicle and leaned against the hood. He could feel the heat from the engine, and he hoped it wouldn't mar his beige suit.

"Looks like you rented this car. You know a lot of criminals use rental cars to avoid tracing activity back to their own vehicle."

"I picked it up at the airport. I just flew in."

"From Cally-forn-I-A? Bunch of granola types out there, from what I hear. A lot of Mary-jew-anna. I bet you have a lot of drugs in this car."

"No, sir. Even if I did, how would I have gotten it onto the plane?"

"You think I'm stupid, boy?"

"No, sir." Jamiel wiped his palms on his suit pants and hoped he looked calm.

"I bet you met up with gang friends here, and they supplied you with drugs to sell."

The young officer exited the squad car and handed the senior officer the license. "No warrants, no arrests, not even a parking ticket."

"Could just mean that he hasn't been caught yet." The officer circled the rental car. "What's in this bag?" He pointed to the overnight satchel on the passenger seat.

Jamiel hated the thought of the older White cop rifling through his things. He had nothing to hide, and still, he felt powerless. Why was it on him to let this power-abusing thug of a police officer detain him and go through his possessions? It was because the two men used the rules from two different playbooks. A prominent, board-certified, highly respected doctor reduced to "Yes, Sir" and "No, Sir" because the consequences could be dire when interacting with a White cop. Too many Black men, women, and children had suffered at the hands of Whites throughout history.

Jamiel tried to glance at his watch subtly. He'd already been detained for twenty minutes. He'd given himself enough time to make it to the hotel to check in and find the conference coordinator. He would lose that buffer if the stop took longer than an hour.

The young officer approached Jamiel. "Why are you here?" He looked a little embarrassed by his older companion.

"I'm a doctor, and I'm speaking at a conference about kidney treatments."

"You? You're a doctor? Like a real doctor?"

"Yup, a real doctor."

"Hey, I've been having some trouble with acid reflux lately."

"Do you drink a lot of soda?"

"Soda? You mean Coke? Yeah, every day."

"You might want to cut back. The carbonation is probably giving you problems."

The young officer nodded. "That might be hard. We only eat at fast-food restaurants for lunch."

"You can try switching to iced tea."

"I'll try that. Thanks, Doc."

The older officer opened the car door. "I can search anything that looks suspicious within plain sight. I find this very suspect." He unzipped the overnight bag and pulled out Jamiel's computer, keynote lecture, and clothing. He found his toiletries bag and rummaged through the contents, looking disappointed in only finding a toothbrush, paste, razor, a travel-sized shaving cream, comb, and face soap. Not even any over-the-counter medications were inside the bag.

"Open the trunk."

Jamiel stood and walked over to the driver's side of the door. It took him a moment to find the lever that released the hatch. It frustrated him that he was powerless to stand up to the White officer. He knew that if he gave any resistance, his precious window of time would evaporate, and he risked being taken into the station. The two officers moved to the back of the car and opened the trunk. The older one was clearly disappointed to find that it was empty.

"Well, boy, you've done the right thing. You didn't obstruct the investigation of a police officer. I don't know what it's like in Cally-Forn-I-A, but here in Charleston, we have rules that need to be followed."

Jamiel realized he didn't even know why he'd been pulled over other than that his skin was black.

The younger officer filled in the blank. "We pulled you over because it looked like one of your back safety lights was out, but now that we've had a closer look, it appears that it was just an optical illusion from the sun."

The overweight officer handed Jamiel his license and car rental paperwork. "I still think there's a good chance you're here for no good."

"I'm flying back to California in the morning."

"That's fortunate. We don't need no drug dealers here. Take my advice, don't step out of line. You may not be as lucky the next time."

"Thank you." Jamiel's skin crawled at having to thank the ignorant prick. *Focus on the endgame*, he reminded himself. He slowly returned to the car, careful not to exert any sudden movements. He was about to start the engine when the officer added a parting comment. "You should be grateful that I'm a reasonable man. I could have taken you to the station to sort this out."

"Thank you." It was all he could think to say. In his mind, he had many other choice words, but he kept them to himself.

Welcome to Charleston.

CHAPTER 5

"You may have seen the news today that the actress Kara Presley died of breast cancer. This is not the whole story. She is one of the Hollywood elites found guilty during her Tribunal trial of wrongdoings against humanity and the democracy of the United States. She was a Satan worshiper and involved in numerous rituals where children were killed so their blood could be consumed by those in attendance.

They steal the children, their bodies, and their blood with the belief that it will make them stronger, but it does not protect them from the law. The High Court Tribunal found her to be guilty. She did not die of breast cancer. She was executed for her heinous crimes. She cooperated with the High Court, and they offered her the chance to have a death that saved her name in exchange for providing the names of others in her cartel. She agreed, which is why the false news narrative is reporting that she had cancer. I do not believe that it was fair to have offered her this deal. She should be exposed for who she was and how she died. That is why I am posting it here. She was a criminal of humanity. Respect the word. You are being misled. – R"

∎

The Dom stood at the podium facing the great nationalists of Phoenix. He paused a moment before speaking, taking in the excitement that filled the air around him. He was in his element. This is what he loved most about being the president of the United States.

"Good evening!" The crowd roared back their welcome.

"You give me hope for our country to shine once more! For too long, we have been lackluster at both home and abroad. My predecessors abused their power and let our country decline, more motivated by their interests than those of our great land."

Cheers filled the arena, and Dom continued, "We have seen the results of their incompetence. Jobs have been moved overseas. An influx of criminals has entered our country. Crime is rampant. The economy is fragile."

The president scanned the audience. "The great state of Arizona plays an important role in preserving American history and protecting our great democracy. You must vote for me in November."

The president paused, soaking in the cheers, clapping, and foot stomping. He spoke for an hour, and when he left the podium, he was confident that he'd carry the state of Arizona on election day. There was no reason to believe otherwise.

∎

Tony had a few minutes between jobs and reached for his phone to scroll through his Facebook feed. His friend, Jester, sent him a DM.

"Hey, I found a group you might be interested in. Meet for lunch?"

"Sure. 1:00 OK? I have a job that will likely go past twelve."

"Perfect. I'll meet you at Whataburger."

Several hours later, Tony pulled into the parking lot of the Whataburger on Southwest Freeway and scanned the line for his friend. The two met in high school before Jester became the bearded man with sleeves of tattoos covering both arms. He was a construction worker, and his mornings started early before the heat of the Houston sun made it difficult to work.

"Dude, grab that booth. I'll get us the usual."

Tony slid onto the plastic orange bench, securing their location as the lunch line snaked toward the door. The usual was triple meat, triple cheeseburgers with fries, and a Dr. Pepper to wash it down. There was no reason he had to let Erica know he was eating at the fast-food chain. He enjoyed connecting with Jester. No one even thought about calling him by his given name, Lester, except telemarketers and his mother. It wasn't long before Jester slid onto the bench opposite Tony and started divvying up the food. The familiar wavy orange W gracing the outside paper wrappers triggered feelings of comfort, and Tony didn't care if it wasn't the healthiest option for lunch. His arteries might harden, but at least he'd die a happy man. He peeled back the wrapper and took a big bite. Sauce oozed from under the bun, and he reached for a napkin.

"What is it about these burgers?"

Jester laughed. "I know, right?!" He opened several ketchup packets and squirted the red sauce onto the paper mat covering the plastic tray. He dipped several fries and coated them liberally before popping them into his mouth.

"Fuckin' looters. We're working on a remodel downtown. Last night, a group of protesters broke all the new windows we installed the day before." Jest took a bite from his burger and continued to talk while chewing his food. "No repercussions either. How is it that a group of Antifa or BLM thugs can storm downtown and wreck everything in their path and not get arrested? You know if we'd gone downtown and smashed windows, we'd be sittin' in a jail cell right now waitin' for a judge to determine our bail."

"What are we able to do?" Tony understood his friend's frustration; he'd been feeling it, too.

Jester pulled out his phone. "I found a private group on Facebook. I got an invitation from a friend of mine. Let me send it to you."

"What kind of group?"

"A group of like-minded people who want to mobilize to protect our community. Join. You'll see." Jester took a bite from his burger and wiped ketchup from his beard. "I'm tired of sitting idle while I see our city being destroyed. First, they take down the statue from Sam Houston Park, and now the police are letting looters set their own rules."

Tony acknowledged the irony of driving by the park the day before with the same frustration.

"Sounds interesting. I'll take a look."

CHAPTER 6

"The High Court Tribunal trials are continuing. Progress is being made to restore our great country to the democracy intended by our forefathers. The Constitution needs to be restored to the glory of 1776! For years, privileged and secret societies have been destroying and dismantling the core elements of our doctrine. They converted the democracy to a corporation, and the wealthy of the world are manipulating everything for their gain. Don't believe me? Do your own research. Respect the word. You are being misled. – R."

■

Tony propped himself on several pillows and settled in for the evening. Erica lay in bed beside him, intent on her phone. He'd been granted access to the private group Jest had shared with him at Whataburger. He scrolled through the list of postings made by the members. Many of them were animated gifs with patriotic messages and flags waving.

"Don't tread on me!"

"Sovereign citizens unite!"

"You can't disarm me."

"You'll have to pry my AR-15 from my cold, dead hands."

"We're coming after you" was overlaid on a picture of the Democratic Speaker of the House.

"Dang, what a shit show," he murmured under his breath. He had no interest in being part of this group.

"What, honey?" Erica didn't look up from her phone.

"Aah, nothin'. Just something that Jest sent me." He closed his browser window so Erica wouldn't see the images if she happened to look in his direction. He was relieved when he saw that she hadn't changed her focus.

"Did you post a new video today?" Tony knew how to distract her.

"Yes!" Erica was animated. "Let me see how many people have viewed it so far." She flicked her finger across the small glass screen, and it didn't take long for her to find what she was looking for. "542!"

Tony didn't know if that was good or not, but it sounded impressive to him.

"That's great, baby." He placed his phone on the charging pad on his bedside table and turned to face his girlfriend. "I'm proud of you."

"I know it's not that many." She answered his unasked question. "Every day, I get more followers."

Tony leaned over and kissed her. "I'll follow you anywhere."

"I need to get noticed by big brands to make a difference."

Tony kissed her again. He took her phone from her hand and placed it on her side table as he rolled towards her, his erection growing stronger.

"Is this big enough for you?"

"Tony! That's not what I mean!"

"Really? You don't want me to brand you?"

He put his hands between her legs and started making small circles with his fingers. He could feel her responding to his touch. He kissed her neck and moved to her nipples, taking one into his mouth and then moving to the next, playfully teasing her flesh with his tongue. He loved that she liked to sleep naked; there was no fabric to push aside.

"Tony! I, I..." Her voice tapered off as her arousal clouded her thoughts.

He positioned himself between her legs. He could feel her moist warmth. He smiled down at her, loving how she looked with tousled hair and passion-clouded eyes.

He repeated his question. "Is this big enough for you?"

"Yes, yes!"

"Do you want me to brand you?"

She reached for his hard cock and tried to guide him inside her, but he held back.

"Tell me how much you want this."

"Tony, don't be an asshole."

"Tell me!"

She moved underneath him again, opening her legs wider and welcoming his body. She clutched his butt and urged him towards her.

"If you were a good boyfriend, you'd fuck me when I want it."

"If you were a good girlfriend, you'd beg me for it."

"I don't need to beg for something that you want as much as me."

She had a point, and he thrust inside her, and they moved in a synchronized rhythm of a couple familiar with each other's bodies and desires.

He wasn't thinking about the Facebook group anymore. He wasn't thinking much at all as his body betrayed him, and he came inside her. *How had he been so lucky that they'd found each other?*

■

"The liberal radicals have embraced the power of the Hollywood elite that has been killing children and sacrificing their innocence, embracing the dark side of existence. It is time to banish them all to hell to pay restitution for their crimes. The High Tribunal is here to protect the children and your future. It distresses me to know that this activity has been allowed to fester for so long without outrage. Fortunately, it is possible to inform you now, and steps can be taken. Respect the word. You are being misled. – R"

■

Leon was excited. He found another post on the BeWarned site by R, clearly an insider within the government who knew firsthand that things reported by the traditional news were inaccurate. They fabricated stories to create their narrative in support of the powerful elite. He was sure that even the president of the United States, Dominic Coronet, knew that news channels that had once been respected and trustworthy had been bought by billionaires who were only interested in promoting their self-interests. The Rothschilds and the Rockefellers pulled the strings behind the scenes for too long, and a change was needed.

The Rainstorm is coming. Respect the word. You are being misled. It gave Leon hope to read the posts. For too long, he'd felt helpless and disempowered, a puppet in someone else's story. He believed older White men in the United States were being treated unfairly. Affirmative action had caused discrimination in the workforce, and he'd been forced out of his job six months ago. "Redundancies" is what he was told, but he knew otherwise. He'd been let go so some minority person could take his place. More and more brown-skinned people had moved into his neighborhood. He didn't even feel safe going downtown anymore. He lived in coal country in Pennsylvania. He heard a lot of Spanish when he went to the market. He didn't even live by the border. *Why were there so many of them here anyway? What had happened to his hometown?*

A wall was needed to stop the flow of illegal immigrants into the country Leon loved. It was going downhill with the influx of unsavory people sent by other countries that didn't want them. *Why keep criminals in jail at home when they could be deported to the United States to be someone else's problem? He was sure that the young men outside the market were part of a gang. What were they called? Crips and Bloods? They didn't wear bandannas, but maybe that was only something from TV, and they were still planning a vendetta against each other.* He bet they'd brought their turf war to Pennsylvania.

He read more of the comments under R's posts. People were starting to decipher and share more insights into what the posts might mean.

"This video explains more about the Rainstorm." A bit.ly link was embedded in the comments section. Leon clicked on it and found himself on a new site, Era News, with a tagline: *"We tell you the truth when others won't."* Before the video, an ad promoting six-month survival packs played. "Nationalists, don't be caught unprepared. Shortages are coming. Food is going to be the way you are going to be controlled. Don't let corporations force you to behave. Stock up now."

Leon hadn't even thought about that. Of course! Starve people to keep them in line. He'd already lost his job, and now, if there were food shortages, he'd be hungry too. He clicked through and ordered a six-month supply of dehydrated food packets for $1,595.

"We've partnered with military nutritionists to ensure you get maximum benefits from your food for longevity and health. You will need your intellect and strength when corporations try to control you."

Leon signed up for monthly payments of $134 to cover the cost using part of his unemployment payments. At least he wouldn't go hungry.

What was this Rainstorm he was hearing about? He looped back to BeWarned.com, clicked the bit.ly link again, and returned to the video page on Era News. He started the lead video and sat back. Images of the Liberty Bell, the signed parchment of the Declaration of Independence, and the Statue of Liberty filled the screen. The male voice-over started to tell the story.

"R is a nationalist. He is a government insider who has been sharing highly classified information to ensure that our democracy is restored to its former glory. For too long, pedophiles, Hollywood elite, sex traffickers, and morally corrupt people have been getting away with murder. The tribunals have started. The Rainstorm to disrupt this disgusting and disgraceful reign is brewing on the horizon. Dominic Coronet is the people's chosen leader to bring about a change in the old hierarchy. Restore America! Respect the word. You are being misled."

Leon watched as the video continued, determined to learn the truth.

CHAPTER 7

Casey rubbed his eyes. He'd been staring at his computer screen for hours, wading through a wide array of posts. There was a ton of information online, from the outrageous to the absurd: TikTok dance moves, cats being scared with cucumbers, and lots of video memes to emphasize any message a person wanted to send.

He was testing the social site algorithms to understand how information was shown as someone navigated from site to site. He already knew about retargeting with cookies and that the European Union had implemented GDPR rules that dictated that all site visitors know how their information was collected and used. However, it was still a black box to most Americans. Internet users worldwide clicked accept to get to the content they were trying to access without reading the terms of service. Others saw the acceptance alerts as a reason to move away from those sites and ironically exposed themselves to greater risk by sites that were not alerting users to how their information was being misused. He was pretty sure the cookies and tracking were still in place, just not called out by site owners who were not adhering to the privacy policies that had evolved significantly since the development of the internet. Many users were unaware of how their browsing data was being collected and disseminated.

Casey found a lot of information was hard to trace back to a credible source. With AI, video technology, and advanced editing software, it was possible to create videos that looked and sounded credible. He even found a video of an aged man claiming to be John F. Kennedy Jr., alive and well. While he hadn't actually seen JFK Jr.'s body in the casket, he was pretty sure the former president's son was dead and that he wasn't going to have a second coming similar to Christ. In the video, the man claimed to be staying under the radar and would come forward publicly when the time was right.

How is recording a video and posting it on the Internet for anyone to see staying under the radar?

On one hand, Casey couldn't believe he was being paid to browse the internet; on the other, he was struggling with the amount of minutiae online. There were firm believers: Kool-Aid-drinking conspiracy theorists who embraced a life that wasn't always as it seemed. *Was it hurting anyone to think that JFK Jr. was alive with a wife and three daughters "off the grid?"* That was the question. He wasn't a psychologist or a psychiatrist, for that matter, and he didn't feel equipped to assess the psychological response to being bombarded with all this content.

He reached for his cell phone. It was almost ten in the morning in California. He dialed his longtime friend and former roommate. Maybe Jamiel could give him a referral. No answer. He left a message and stood up to stretch. It was a good time to get coffee or at least step away from his desk and clear his mind.

■

Tony heard the ping of an alert and reached for his phone on the passenger seat of the white utility van covered with the "Ready, Set, Flow Plumbing" logo on the sides. It was a notification from the private Facebook group that Jester had mentioned called "Texas Freedom Fighters." He didn't know much about it and wondered how Jest had found it. He started to read the posts. It was a platform for saying everything he'd been thinking for months. "Why does everyone keep saying I'm privileged because I'm White? I've had to work for everything I've ever had. #NoTrustFund."

The car behind him leaned on the horn, and Tony looked up to see the light had turned from red to green. He tossed the phone back onto the passenger seat and pressed the accelerator. He was going to a residence in River Oaks, one of the most exclusive neighborhoods in Houston.

A few minutes later, he turned onto Inwood Drive, a tree-lined street parallel to the River Oaks Golf Club. He looked for the home listed on his work order. He parked in front of a stately brick home with a manicured lawn and pristinely trimmed hedges. A low brick wall covered with moss flanked the perimeter. He took the shallow steps in long strides as he made his way to the main entrance, carrying a small bag with plumbing basics. The van was equipped with a wide array of tools to handle any job.

He didn't get calls to this neighborhood often, but even rich people had plumbing issues. *I bet they think their shit don't stink like the rest of us.* He rang the bell, and a series of chimes could be heard echoing throughout the large interior. Tony stood, shifting his weight from one foot to the other, wondering how long he needed to wait before calling the number on the work order. He was paid as much to stand there as he was to be snaking a drain, so he figured he could wait a little longer. It took a full minute before anyone responded, and the door was opened by a Black woman wearing a service uniform and a yellow and white outfit, designating her as the maid.

"I'm Tony from Ready, Set, Flow Plumbing." It felt a little redundant, considering his work shirt had a patch with his name sewn over the left pocket, like many from the 1950s.

"Meet me by the carriage house." She gestured to his right before shutting the door. Tony turned back and followed the stone walkway toward the internal driveway. A covered drive-through area separated the main house from the garage, and he got a glimpse of a pool and another building in the back. Unsure if that was the carriage house, he waited by the side of the large residence. It didn't take long for the uniformed woman to appear.

"The issue is upstairs." She escorted him to the three-car garage. She unlocked the door leading to the apartment. The stairwell had carpeted wooden steps, and they climbed up together, Tony following behind the maid. "We had an Airbnb guest, and they complained the toilet wasn't flushing properly. They said it worked fine when they arrived, but it almost overflowed several times."

Tony depressed the handle and watched the water pool in the bowl, rising close to the top of the seat. Lifting the ceramic lid, he could see the chain and flapper were intact, and there was little residue or corrosion on the metal.

"No worries, I'll take care of it."

"Knock on the side door when you're done."

Tony returned to his vehicle and retrieved an industrial plunger and a coiled metal snake. It always amazed him how little people tried to fix their plumbing issues. He was pretty sure a few pumps of the plunger would fix the problem. He always found the sound of the clog clearing and the following glug of water to be satisfying.

He inserted the plunger and covered the bottom of the bowl. He moved the handle up and down, but no luck. Whatever it was, it wasn't budging, and he wasn't getting the rewarding sound of the water exiting the basin. He inserted the snake, and it got stuck pretty quickly. There was something solid that prevented it from going deeper into the pipes. He twisted the auger, looking for a way to break up the blockage or work past it. He inserted several more feet and continued to turn. He pulled it out and tried flushing again. The blockage was still there. He inserted the device several more times, twisting in hopes of dislodging the issue. The third time he removed the snake, he saw something yellow emerging into the bottom of the bowl.

He reached in and was able to extract a yellow rubber duck. Bathtime had apparently extended to a toilet swim for the toy. Toilet paper had gotten caught around the neck of the duck. He swished it around in the basin to clean the rubber. Flushing again to ensure the water flowed properly, he washed the duck with soap and water at the sink and dried it with a towel.

Not long after, the maid reappeared at the side door of the main residence. He held up the duck. "I'm assuming they had a child with them?"

"Yes, a toddler."

"Mystery solved."

After resolving the bill, Tony returned to the van and placed the duck on the dashboard with several other toys retrieved from other jobs. A G.I. Joe and SpongeBob

SquarePants also took maiden voyages down toilet pipes. He liked collecting the play toys to remind him his job wasn't completely disgusting.

◼

"Hey, Pam!" The Stanford sophomore looked up from her human anatomy textbook and waved to one of her classmates. Her empty lunch plate had been pushed aside so she could read. The portobello veggie burger at The Axe & Palm was good, and she could order ahead to optimize her study time.

"Hey, Asher." Pamela Jackson reached for her boba tea. "Want to join me for a few minutes?" The young Korean student slid onto the seat at the counter next to her and smiled. "Why did we decide to study pre-med? So much memorization!"

"It could be worse. We could be studying law."

The two laughed. Pam sipped her oolong tea and chewed several tapioca balls before swallowing. It was her daily addiction, and this was her second one of the day. She had a big test to prepare for and found little rewards for studying, like boba tea, were good incentives. She'd dodged the "freshman fifteen" by running three miles each morning.

"A group of us are going to Oakland to protest for Black Lives Matter. Want to join us?"

She wondered if he was asking because she was half Black, the daughter of a Black father and a White mother. She dismissed the thought. Asher was Korean, and she knew he'd faced discrimination, too. It was about standing up for the rights of all individuals.

She was grateful that Stanford was a melting pot of students from all over the United States and abroad. There was no room for highlighting race; instead, students focused on being the brightest and best in their classes. This was a place to excel academically and establish one's value and reputation.

She remembered the group interview when she'd applied to the elite college. She had been in a room off campus, and as the students introduced themselves and their high schools, it was a list of the privileged: Exeter, Choate, Emma Willard, Deerfield. When it came to her, she announced Marymount in Los Angeles, which was not a boarding school like the others but still a private, elite campus of all girls tucked near UCLA.

She'd learned that Asher had not attended an informational group interview and instead focused on setting his application apart from all the other overachievers with multiple extracurricular activities. Whatever he'd done had worked, and now the two sat side by side.

"We're meeting at the Caltrain station at nine, and we'll transfer to BART."

She was torn. Her father had taught her from an early age that there were Whites who were going to judge her by her skin tone. Some in the Black community would dislike that she was part White with a father who had "betrayed" his own race. Race issues were complex on both sides of the table.

She looked at her textbook. She still had twenty pages to review, and this was just the assignment for anatomy. She hadn't started her lab report for human biology.

"I don't know. I still have a lot of studying."

"Bring it with you. The train ride is at least forty-five minutes, and we'll have to transfer, too."

Pam paused and then nodded in agreement. "OK. It's important. I'll see you in the morning."

She took another sip of boba tea and wondered which one of the thick books was the lightest to carry tomorrow.

CHAPTER 8

Leon trusted R when he read his posts. He could tell there was truth in the information being shared. After all, no one would be able to have R's level of insight without having a security clearance high enough to open the files and access the content inside. R had also urged everyone reading his posts to do their research, and Leon knew what he'd found when he searched the internet. It was a matter of finding the correct search terms. "R" was too vague, and it was impossible to weed through the pages of returns that Google served up in milliseconds. Instead, he searched for Hollywood pedophiles, Rainstorm, 1776 Restoration, and additional terms. Quickly, he found a series of websites supporting R's claims.

He closed his computer and smiled. He'd done his research, and it confirmed he was on the right side of the truth. He did not understand that the Google algorithms determined which links he should see and were displayed based on his browsing history. He just knew that what he found supported what he'd read to date from R. There was no need to do more research; he'd found the information he needed. R was a prophet.

◼

The Dom rolled over in bed and plucked his phone from the mahogany bedside table in the presidential suite. 4:03 a.m. He had two hours before he would be required to rise and step into his role as the leader of the free world.

He scrolled through the news posts that had gone live since he'd last looked at his phone.

"Is Coronet the biggest con?" The headline jumped out from the sea of others. Of course, *The Heraldry Knightly*.

"Fucking idiots." It wasn't the first time the fringe paper had attacked his legitimacy. It didn't take long to scan the article. While most of it was baseless, there was one truthful paragraph that Dom had no interest in giving amplification.

He pressed the X icon on his phone, and Twitter filled his screen. He was amassing a more significant following each day. He smiled. He didn't follow many in return, content to have the focus be on his messages, his opinions. "Be careful who you hitch your wagon to," was his dictum. One picture, taken out of context, could enforce any number of attachments. It was better to control one's narrative.

"Time to shut down those assholes at *The Heraldry Knightly*." He knew better than to call out the article directly. That would empower the editors. Instead, he decided to attack on a more global level.

"Breaking… mainstream media is yet again proving they're puppets reporting falsehoods." Short and sweet. He pressed send. He wasn't the only person awake at such an early hour. He leaned back against the headboard and watched as followers started to reply.

"We love you, Mr. President!"

"F'ing False News!"

"CNN is corrupt. They're only promoting lies to #MakeTheMoguls."

The Dom liked the new hashtag that had surfaced lately. The Moguls were established money machines that were often tied to old-school money. Tellingly, the Coronet name was excluded, even though its corporate holdings surpassed those published for some "mogul" organizations. It appeared the distinction was self-made money versus family money amassed to the detriment of the middle class. It was ironic, considering that The Coronet Company was a legacy business that his father had started.

The Dom started typing. "They will stop at nothing to defame my name. Don't listen to the falsehoods. We will keep raining down on them until they are forced to report the truth!"

Two hours later, The Dom was feeling energized. It was going to be a good day. *I am the president of the fucking United States.* He would not tolerate any opposition.

■

"The Rockefellers and the Rothschilds are names you know! Their immense wealth is increasing while the majority of great nationalists struggle to put food on their table and a roof over their heads. The elites are stealing from you. They are preventing you from getting ahead. They do not believe the American Dream is for you! It is only meant to line their pockets. The High Court Tribunal is making its way through a long docket of cases. Don't help #MakeTheMoguls! The Rainstorm is coming. Follow the raindrops. They will show you the way. Respect the word. You are being misled. – R"

CHAPTER 9

Larry Stevens, the esteemed Democratic senator from Wisconsin, had always aspired to greatness. He'd been impressed at how easily he'd been able to win over voters in his thirty-plus years as a seasoned politician. Running for president of the United States was a completely different ballgame today than when he had entered the political arena decades earlier. Not only did he have to appeal to his constituents, he had to find a way to bridge the vast array of public opinion about what it meant to be POTUS. He was finding it difficult to straddle the line of moderation and liberalism when there was a growing divide in the United States. He was trying to find the speaking points that would make him appear like the right candidate for everyone, not just one silo of the Democratic Party.

He looked at the poll numbers from fivethirtyeight.com and realized that Dominic Coronet had done a great job of casting doubt on who Larry was as a leader. The seasoned politician had some not-so-kind choice words for the reality television star that occupied the Oval Office, but he didn't dare voice them out loud. He'd learned over the years that the walls had ears wherever he went, whether it was a live mic or an aide who overheard something worth a few bucks for sharing with the media. He'd made that rookie mistake in his youth and wasn't about to have that take him down as he ramped up his presidential candidacy.

He knew what Dom Coronet was going to throw at him. The president had a bully playbook without many nuances. Name-calling and deflection were the name of his game. Heaven forbid he would ever say anything about his plans for the next four years other than only he and he alone could save the country and preserve the edicts of their great land. Larry didn't share the same view, which prompted him to toss his hat in the ring for the primary along with seven other candidates. It had surprised him when his resume had worked to his advantage, and he'd secured the Democratic nomination after the others had fallen by the wayside for being too much or too little of what the people wanted in their next president.

Larry was confident that he could win the election. People were growing tired of the chaos that seemed a constant anchor to the Coronet administration. Many were ready to return to the established traditions of the presidential role and have the Oval Office occupied by a rational, reasonable, and politically conscientious veteran.

Larry turned on the television and rotated through various news channels, quickly scanning the on-screen banners for a pulse on the day's news. Some channels focused on foreign news; others stayed focused on domestic topics. Dominic Coronet was highlighted on many channels. Larry paused on CNN when he saw an image of himself.

"Can Larry Stevens beat The Dom in November?" The news anchor posed the question to a political strategist displayed on the screen from a remote location. "It's still too early to tell. Both men are under a microscope, and anything could undermine their campaigns. Remember how the FBI's release of information took down a prior candidate? However, assuming the status quo from now until the election, Stevens is definitely electable. He's got a solid track record and no skeletons in his closet. The Dom, on the other hand, seems to have many that no one cares about." The newscaster referenced the rumors of corruption and personal misconduct that swirled around the president. "Of course, we all know the stories floating around the internet. People are asking, 'What's in it for me?' The Dom seems able to talk directly to disgruntled voters."

Larry took note. He would discuss this with his core campaign team. He firmly believed that it was essential to know your adversary, and by God, he would use that information to his advantage.

When the segment ended, the channel switched to commercials, and he skipped to the next news show.

"Who is R, and should you be concerned about their identity?"

Larry paused. "What does that mean?" Curiosity kept him on the lesser-known news station.

The news reporter continued. "Is R a government insider sharing truths or just an internet troll manipulating people to feed their ego?"

The screen was split with two commentators, one an ardent R follower, whatever that meant, and another, based on the information box on the screen, was from the University of Pennsylvania Department of Sociology. The follower, dressed in a T-shirt with a large green R printed on the front, was getting bleeped as they replied. "What's with the pronoun bull—(bleep)? R is a nationalist and definitely a man. He knows of what he speaks."

The news reporter stayed surprisingly calm. "I appreciate that you've metamorphosed R into a male, but there's no indication in any posts that would indicate the writer's gender."

"There's no f'ing way that R is a WOMAN!"

"How do you know?"

Larry was impressed at how the show's anchor held his ground. He almost laughed as he saw the R supporter practically hyperventilate with a sputtering response. He finally blurted out, "There's no way a woman would have access to this information! Besides, I'm sure it's Dominic Coronet himself!"

"Professor, I'd like to hear from you. Could R be our very own president?"

"That's highly unlikely. He's got a country to run. While he would certainly have the security clearance to access highly classified information, it is unlikely that he would share it with a sprinkling of social commentary."

Larry had no idea who this mystery "R" person was and he paused before changing the channel to listen a little longer.

"The concern to me, and I'd go as far as to say, to the world, is that there is a large following amassing around an individual that to date has stayed hidden behind internet posts and a moniker."

"Are you considering this a conspiracy theory?" the anchor interjected.

"I prefer to avoid that term. That's a loaded statement to many and can cause people to get defensive about their beliefs or double down. I prefer to keep the conversation to the message resonating with the followers of R. Maybe the other panelist could share his thoughts on that."

"It's not a conspiracy theory! R tells us to do our research, and I did. I know what he says is true. The world is finally being rebalanced. The entitled elite who have strayed off the path of human decency are being held to their day of reckoning. The Rainstorm is coming!"

"We're out of time. I want to thank you both for joining us today. We'll have an update on the stock market after this commercial break."

As an advertisement filled the screen, Larry pressed the power button on the remote. The screen flickered before going dark. He felt a vibration on his wrist and looked down at his smartwatch. It was later than he realized. If he didn't leave soon, he would be late, and his mother had raised him with the belief, "If you want to be on time, be early." This had served him well throughout his career. He dismissed his initial thoughts of curiosity about R. He doubted that the story was anything more than clickbait and wasn't worth further consideration.

■

The news was beginning to highlight the oppression facing Blacks in America. Finally, they were covering the details about a Black person who had died at the hands of a White police officer. Pamela could no longer stand idle, waiting for justice from the White administration that conveniently looked the other way, writing off the actions as necessary in the line of duty. *How many people have lost their lives to injustice? Too many to name, too many to count.*

The body of a nineteen-year-old Black college freshman had been found hanging from a tree, and it had been deemed suicide. No Black person she knew of would ever opt to take their life with a rope. No one was talking about the lynching and how likely it was that it was at the hands of White men. *Why did a Black teen make them feel threatened?*

Her father had told her for as long as she could remember that she had to play by the rules. *Don't rock the boat; keep your head down and study hard. Your accomplishments will make you shine.*

Her father was a successful doctor and the son of a Hollywood promoter who had made millions promoting R&B bands in the fifties and migrating to the first rap albums to come out of Compton. Her grandfather also got a foothold in films and produced some of the most successful films in the 1970s.

Pam slid her anatomy textbook into her backpack and left her dorm room. She stepped aboard the Stanford shuttle that would get her to the Caltrain station at the edge of University Avenue in Palo Alto. The elite school and town attracted the best and the brightest from around the world, and many technological advances had been developed within a short radius of where she stood on the platform, waiting for the train to arrive from Mountain View. She scanned the area, looking for Asher and other students joining them for the demonstration. She saw the young man wave and step toward her, leaving a group of five other students.

"So glad you made it!" He gave her a quick one-armed hug.

"Me, too. I think it's important."

"I see you brought your books. We'll leave you alone to study."

The train hissed to a stop on the platform, and the group tagged their Clipper card passes as they boarded. The car had two levels, and as the group moved to the upper one, Pam opted to go lower to ensure she wouldn't be interrupted. Asher smiled and nodded, acknowledging her decision. She set the alarm on her phone for five minutes before the scheduled arrival time in Millbrae, where they would transfer to BART to make sure she didn't miss the stop. She allowed the stop announcements to fade into the background as she focused on the textbook in front of her, highlighter in hand.

She rejoined her group at the car doors, and the students transferred to the northbound train coming from the San Francisco Airport. The car was packed, and she resigned herself to leaving her textbook in her bag. She learned more about the others marching with her today. All attended Stanford in different areas of study. As they came aboveground at the 19th Street Oakland Station, Pam could feel the excitement in the air. They were marching along with the Black Lives Matter rally originating in Frank H. Ogawa Plaza downtown. Other protesters emerged from the BART station along with them, many holding signs and talking animatedly. Everyone looked empowered, but no one conveyed anger or hostility. The goal was to demonstrate peacefully and vocally to have their message heard.

CHAPTER 10

Tony opened the Texas Freedom Fighters page and scrolled through the posts. The content varied from comments to animated memes, conveying a central theme. There were sixty-seven members listed, and the group was still growing day by day.

"This is fucked up," one member posted. "Our history is being erased. The Confederate statues need to stay in place to remind us of our history, not be taken down to erase the past." Others on the thread chimed in. "We need to protect our history. We can't stand idle and watch our great city, state, and country go down the drain."

Tony read through the comments without making any personal posts. He agreed with the expressed sentiments and "Liked" several comments. As he scrolled through the messages, a meme flashed on a short loop, *"Patriot Power!"* with a man pumping his fist in the air. Tony watched it for a while as it repeated: *"Patriot Power, Patriot Power, Patriot Power."*

When had the country gone off the rails? Rosa Parks on the bus? Or was it before? Too many accommodations were made for Blacks. He wasn't getting affirmative action assistance when applying for work. It disadvantaged him that he was White. Others on the Ready, Set, Flow Plumbing team were Hispanic and Black. *How many White men hadn't been hired to meet the diversity quota for the agency? He guessed that number was two, the same number of Black men working on various plumbing company vans. Would his job be taken next?*

He read the information for a few minutes longer and closed his laptop. He would be late to work if he didn't get moving.

∎

It was two in the morning, and Dominic couldn't fall asleep. He didn't share a bedroom with his wife; she'd kicked him out years earlier. He'd just sent the exclusive call girl away. He had compensated her well to be discrete about sucking his cock. He wasn't looking for the girlfriend experience. He liked making her swallow his deposit, and she seemed to enjoy it, too. His wife had told him his spunk tasted terrible and had refused to give him blow jobs after he had held her head on his cock while he ejaculated. She'd gagged and spit it out. *"What the fuck, Dom?! You tryin' to choke me, you selfish asshole?" That was the nice thing about call girls. They loved sex; that's why they'd become prostitutes in the first place. They could get as much sex as they wanted and get paid, too.*

He didn't engage in intercourse. It was too risky. He'd taken precautions by getting a vasectomy, so children were not a worry. However, he knew gold-digging women well enough that one could claim some bastard child was his, and he'd either have to lie about sticking his dick in her or be exposed as cheating on his wife. *Blowjobs are perfect.* He got a physical release, got to play with some big boobs in his face, and no one could file a paternity suit against him. *No intercourse, no problems.* Some women required him to wear a condom before they would suck his cock, but he found it was just a matter of negotiation to remove that barrier. A few hundred dollars more was usually all it took for them to swallow. *It just goes to show money can buy you anything.*

He had no respect for those who didn't milk the system to their fullest advantage. He'd been using federal grants and bank funding to extend his real estate holdings for decades. Get lending on a vacant piece of commercial land, find a developer and build, withhold most of the funding until the job is complete, discretely funnel money to another project, and use bankruptcy to settle with the developer for pennies on the dollar while maintaining the asset. Corporate entities established for specific projects protected assets in other locations, and the shell game of moving money resulted in expedient growth, even if it meant the cash flow always had to come in or the foundation would collapse.

Borrowing from Peter to pay Paul served him well as long as "Peter" continued to give more money than "Paul" needed. He'd run for president on a lark, seeing an opportunity to sell his book, *Dealing the Deck to Win,* and funneling people into his convention centers, casinos, golf resorts, and hotels to make money. Campaign contributions became easy money, and he channeled millions to his properties for event fees. He made sure they paid the printed rate, even though everyone knew the print rate was the highest amount and rates were usually negotiated much lower for larger events. His constituents didn't seem to care, and some even applauded him for taking steps they saw as making him a successful businessman.

He opened the Twitter app. *"RESTORE America! Antifa and the Liberal Left EXTREMISTS have been eroding our great country for YEARS,"* Dom posted to his Twitter account. "Join me in Oklahoma for my next UNITE RALLY on Thursday. Come early. Doors open at 7 a.m. CROWDS!"

He was on a roll.

"Stop the ILLEGAL flow of UNDOCUMENTED PARASITES into our GREAT country."

"WE NEED A WALL to preserve our heritage."

Dom watched as his eighty-seven million followers started to respond and retweet. It energized him. He wouldn't return to bed now that he had tapped into his favorite social channel.

"Mexico WILL pay for the WALL. It is their responsibility to honor our border agreements! They have been lax for too long. My predecessor was WEAK and did not demand what is rightfully ours. Our great nation deserves to be protected from bad hombres."

He paused and typed again. "Our GREAT nation NEEDS to be protected. #BUILDTHEWALL."

Several hours later, Dom turned to the televisions in his private chamber. He had multiple screens that were tuned to a variety of news channels. Fox was his favorite and generally the station with the volume turned on. He also watched CNN, MSNBC, and PBS, as well as Good Morning America, Today, and Morning Joe. Knowing what the "false news" channels were saying about him gave him ammunition on his favorite stations that promoted his agenda. The world ran on keeping two sides fighting, and he saw an opportunity. Before he announced his run for president, he'd had just over three million followers on Twitter, and now he was about to reach ninety million. The presidency had expanded his influence far more than his reality television show had ever done. It had given him a stronger foothold and made him a household name.

Some people loved him, while others loathed him. He embraced both sides for the power they gave him. Keep the one side happy and keep poking the haters, and the rage escalated. There was power in that rage. He understood the benefit of playing both sides against one another. He was becoming godlike in the eyes of his followers. He could do no wrong. Money fixed his problems; he paid people to be quiet or highly vocal. Attorneys waving around statutes and precedents could muddy the waters anytime there was a gray area in his business ventures. Hush money fixed everything from strippers, call girls, or those who felt he'd overstepped the line.

It was just a matter of time before he pulled the levers to put the machine in motion. He had no interest in giving up the presidency after eight years, the current law for a presidential term length. He would change the 22nd Amendment, and the nationalists of America would let him. Any of his naysayers would be cast out like the pariahs there were. He looked out at the horizon as the sun started to rise. The sky was clear, and a soft hue of pink showed through the tree branches on the eastern lawn. He was invincible.

■

"Another Hollywood elite was executed today. Good riddance. It is time for this scum to be removed from the earth. This was the trial for the popular daytime talk show host, Ellie. Her full name was Eleanor Deacon. She, too, made a deal with the Tribunal. She repented for her sins and asked that her platform be used to correct the wrongdoings of her ways. Her show is extremely popular with many who do not know the truth. The Tribunal agreed to replace her with a lookalike to continue with the show and promote content. Now that you know the truth, you'll be able to see the differences in her appearance. The evidence is right in front of you. You'll also see the show return to promoting the true values of the United States. Respect the word. You are being misled." — R.

CHAPTER 11

Erica's followers just crossed over 17,000. She was becoming a micro-influencer and getting the attention of brands that recognized that she could bring them business by introducing their products to her followers. Last week, she'd promoted Clever Cosmetics and received a second box of products the day before. Today, a box arrived from a styling service. She could hardly wait to start recording to open up the box during the production. She'd paid for the box herself, but she was sure it was an investment that would pay off either with increased viewers or by attracting more sponsors.

She looked in the mirror and turned her face side to side, looking for any flaws in her makeup application. A line of foundation, splotch of powder, or unevenness of her lipstick recorded for all to see was not acceptable. She shrugged off her robe, which she wore backwards when applying makeup to protect her clothes underneath. She wore a pair of faux leather leggings and a thin-strapped black tank top with a built-in bra to easily slip into whatever items she received in the box without undressing on camera.

She was planning out the shots she would need. She had a customary backdrop behind her camera, which her followers were used to seeing: a credenza with a candle, several journals, and a vase of flowers that she changed regularly to show they were real even though they were just plastic and silk. It was easy to make different arrangements with the stalks from Michaels. Her favorite were the gerbera daisies with bright-colored leaves. Their simplicity did not detract from what she was doing in each video. She settled into her chair, turned on the diffusing donut-shaped light, and pressed record. She started with her customary opening.

"Hi, y'all! Kiki here, and today is a fun day! Look what I received in the mail." She held up the white shipping box with a blue logo branded with URStyleGuru. "I'm so excited because this is new to me, and we get to experience it together! By the way, be sure to subscribe to my channel." She was animated as she continued. "Plus, EVERYONE gets a discount code to receive 20% off your first URStyleGuru order. I'll put the deets below." She'd found a promo code online when she made her purchase, and while it didn't have the personalization that would have been part of a sponsored code, she knew that many on her channel wouldn't make the connection. They'd be thrilled about the discount and credit her for providing it.

She opened a pair of scissors, sliding one side of the cutting edge along the shipping tape before pulling the flaps open. "I spoke with a personal stylist, and you can, too. Let's see how well Emily did in selecting my first box."

Erica pulled out a tissue-wrapped item of clothing, oohed, and aahed her way through the contents. There were two tops, a skirt, a scarf, jeans, boots and a moto jacket. They mixed and matched well. She spent the next fifty minutes trying on the clothes in various combinations, parading before her camera while posing and commenting about how the clothes fit. She was fortunate to have a medium-tall build with legs longer than her torso. She found it easy to model the clothes. She wasn't tall enough to be a runway model, but her figure was perfect for video promotions in her living room.

She turned the video off and collapsed on her couch. It was tiring work to project excitement for nearly an hour of filming. Before she opened the box, she had also recorded screenshots of the URStyleGuru website to show her followers the process for signing up for their shipments. She was still wearing the skirt, striped top, faux leather moto jacket, and scarf but had kicked off the boots that were a bit too tight as soon as she'd stopped filming the long shot. She had kept them on and gushed about how perfect they were because she wasn't about to say anything negative about a potential future sponsor, but she had to wiggle her toes a bit to get the blood circulating.

She felt warm in her apartment and slid off the scarf and jacket. She still had several hours of editing before she could push the content live on her YouTube, TikTok, and Instagram accounts. She was getting traction. It wouldn't be long before she could quit her day job at a local salon and focus entirely on her followers. She loved the adoration and acceptance she'd found online. Customers in the salon were always so picky and self-absorbed. They usually sat in the chair and started spewing all their crap. She hadn't become a stylist to be anyone's therapist, but that's what happened at the beauty shop. She usually nodded and tried to remember enough details for the next visit to ask one or two questions, and her clients would start with their personal stories like it was the most engaging thing for Erica to hear. She'd learned early that if she were attentive, she'd end up with more significant tips and returning clientele. She still yearned for the day she wouldn't have to hear the minutiae of the tedious lives of Houston socialites. *Didn't they realize how lucky they were?*

The upscale salon catered to the well-heeled women of Houston who had lavish accounts, country club member-ships, and husbands who didn't closely monitor their spending. To Erica, they seemed to have extraordinary lives, and she hated hearing the women bitch. She dreamed of never cutting another person's hair again and getting away from all the toxic chemicals used to color, straighten, or curl hair. She wouldn't be chained to the salon forever. She was making the world a more beautiful place online, one product at a time.

■

Max sat across the desk from Dom in the Oval Office. "Have you heard about the person who goes by "R" on the internet?"

The Dom couldn't be bothered.

"I don't care about someone who can't use their full name."

"Mr. President, you might want to take a look."

"I have enough to keep me busy."

"Yes, I know. But this is different. He's declaring you a prophet." Max cringed internally at the idea. The idea of Dominic Coronet as a prophet went against his views of God and religion.

"A prophet? That's a new one."

"Here, take a look." Max handed over his tablet with the thread on the BeWarned site open in a browser window. "No one knows who R is; it's unclear who's posting. They only reveal that they have a high-level security clearance and are reporting from within the government.

Max watched as The Dom scanned the content. As vice president, he had access to a wide array of intel, but he wasn't aware of any secret "High Court Tribunal" conducting its own trials to eradicate the filth of the nation.

"Should we have Homeland Security or the FBI look into this?" Max looked at the stocky man before continuing. "I don't think there is any threat, but if what R says is true and there is, in fact, an insider, it might be worth trying to figure out who is breaching their clearance."

The Dom didn't look up as he flipped his finger across the screen, scrolling through the posts. "I don't think that's necessary; it doesn't look very threatening. How did you find it?"

Max didn't share that he'd received the post from a constituent in his home state asking if Max could get Dom to confirm his connection to R.

"I read a variety of posts every day to stay connected to the pulse of the country." There was a growing group of R followers, and Max was curious how much Dom knew of the posts. It was good to get confirmation from the president that he didn't know about the mysterious R. It was likely innocuous.

Max was also sure it wouldn't hurt to give the president something that could stroke his ego and free Max to find a way to resurrect his scrapped health care bill. He wasn't going to let the man in front of him deprive him of having a legacy. Max was a patient man. He would wait for The Dom to complete his two terms as president and then run for the position himself. As long as The Dom didn't do anything too crazy to tarnish his time in office, Max should be positioned well to carry on for their party. It seemed apparent that many in the United States had a tolerance for The Dom's antics. Max had thought several news stories reported during the campaign and his presidency would have taken the president down a notch or two, but they only reinforced his popularity with his party. The middle-of-the-road moderates were losing ground, and it was turning into a country of extremes on both sides. Max knew his health care bill could help bridge the two camps. First health care, and then he'd take on the next project to solidify his place on the future presidential ticket. He refused to go down in history as a milquetoast number two. He would make a difference in the world with the support of God and the country.

■

"The Rainstorm is coming, and here's another raindrop for you. I have been able to attend the High Court Tribunal trials, and the list of those accused is getting longer as more and more of the guilty are seeing the wrongs of their ways. The weak and morally corrupt always fall. One hundred thousand children were abducted last year, and a famous senator who infiltrated the political system has shown the court the extensive network for moving those children through a web of human trafficking. Billionaires have been buying the virginity of young girls. Others have been sacrificed in Satanic rituals. It is disgusting. The evil-doers are being stopped. Behind the scenes, our democracy is being restored. Our morality is being restored. Dominic Coronet is a strong leader. He has stepped into his role as president without indebtedness to the political machine. He knows what needs to be done to restore our great country. Respect the word. You are being misled. – R"

CHAPTER 12

Jamiel slid into his first-class seat on the Airbus A321, grateful he was leaving South Carolina without any additional altercations. He was pleased he'd had a successful keynote at the convention; however, he still felt a subtle rage simmering deep in his gut. He'd tried to shake the negative feelings from the day before and focus instead on the positives of his trip. Still, he kept mentally replaying the older police officer carelessly tossing the items from his overnight bag onto the car seat. *What gave him the right to touch his things? What gave him the right to use his badge to make Jamiel sit on the squad car as they ran his license and registration and detain him for no justifiable reason?*

Yesterday, he'd played by the rules and avoided an escalation that could have gotten him detained and even charged with some misdemeanor. Others in his situation who had opted to exert their civil rights hadn't always fared well: beaten, arrested, or worse, killed, all because they were Black. His college roommate Casey had told him once that he'd thought Jamiel had dodged a bullet by living in Los Angeles and not the South, but the reality was racism in the United States was prevalent everywhere. There was an unwritten code that many followed that elevated Whites in society and kept Blacks "in their place."

He settled into his wide seat and accepted the preflight drink offered to him by the flight attendant. The $1,200 ticket to fly from Charleston to Los Angeles erased his race. The airline personnel were well-versed in taking care of the people who could afford the highest-priced seats on the plane. He knew he was fortunate; his father had been successful, and that had opened doors to him that otherwise would have been challenging to get through, but he was still a Black man in a White world. A successful medical doctor was not immune to being pulled over by a Podunk police officer with a White supremacy bent. The younger officer had at least seemed to be more open. Hopefully, that was a sign of changing times. Jamiel couldn't help but wonder how long it would take for the older officer's views to rub off on the younger man. He knew that condoning bad behavior in people in a role of authority only worked to provide acceptance of the racist views he'd come up against his whole life.

Casey had called him the day before as he was about to start the keynote, and he'd pushed the call to voicemail. He'd been swept up afterward at a reception with questions and a conference coordinator who had made sure he'd been included in a speaker dinner and checked into his room quickly. A large pharmaceutical company picked up the expenses, and they would reimburse him for his ticket as well – another perk for being a respected doctor making advances in his field.

Jamiel had been able to board the plane in the first group, and the door to the jetway was still open, so he quickly sent Casey a text. *"On a plane heading back to LA. Will call you tomorrow."* He was surprised the two of them had maintained their friendship for so many years after graduation. He knew that Kasey with a K had asked for a different roommate when he'd first arrived at Columbia, and he'd thought the student from the "Deep South" wouldn't change, and yet Casey had shown his willingness to question the dogma of his upbringing. He still didn't fully understand the differences in their lives but saw his prior roommate as a successful, accomplished contributor to society. Jamiel suspected that Casey still had a somewhat skewed view toward Blacks. He liked to hope that, as a journalist, Casey could see how the vicious cycle was designed to keep Blacks in a subordinate position.

The flight attendant pulled the thick door of the plane inward and turned the handle to lock it into place for the flight. Jamiel switched his phone to airplane mode before he received a reply from his friend and settled in for the five-hour flight home.

■

Leon felt anger surging inside him as he read the latest post. *"Hollywood elite... pedophiles... tribunals..."* He'd been reading about the court proceedings for months. Today's message outlined something new. Apparently, an additional step had been taken when the District of Columbia had been established as the new capital as an appeasement to the North and the South due to its location. The incorporation document to insert Washington, D.C. as a region with "taxation without representation" was a switch in the nature of the government. The country was converted to a corporation, which was the true intention of the incorporation document. By changing the country to a corporation, those in power could utilize all the assets for personal gain. The country as a corporation could create profit for the owners.

He continued to scan the latest message from R and seethed as he read the content that showed him how much the elite in society were able to operate above the law. Not only were they getting away with murder and sex trafficking, they were profiting off the entire population. The social elite and the extreme liberals were at the core of the crimes. *What had happened to good old-fashioned morals?*

He could hardly make ends meet, and he felt helpless reading about people of privilege using their good standing in society to perform atrocities as well as strip the wealth from the country. Leon was trapped with nowhere to go. It gave him some comfort to know that the High Court Tribunal was making progress in their trials for crimes against humanity. He read again how a small group had hijacked the country for personal profit. Now, the Corporation of the United States was facing bankruptcy. The corporation was being disbanded to re-establish the government to ensure the country's assets wouldn't be mishandled again.

Leon took a deep breath. While R had been reporting the activities of the High Tribunal for months, it seemed as soon as one group of incorrigibles was executed, another swath of offenders was uncovered. It was about time justice was brought forth for the victims of these heinous crimes, and the guilty were finally being held accountable. With the most recent news of the conversion of the Corporation of the United States back to the intended structure of the U.S.A., the balance in the world was being restored. The United States was returning to the days of past glory. Those who were guilty of corruption were being held responsible. It was about time. For too long, people like Leon had paid the price of oppression while others danced through their lives, taking advantage of others.

He started typing. "R is a nationalist! He is the supporter of the true heroes in our great land. He has the knowledge to share about the wrongdoings that are finally being corrected after years of inaction. Without R, the truth would continue to be hidden. It is important work. Thank you, R!"

The rage he felt dissipated slightly as he made his post. He could take action and help spread the word. The Rainstorm was coming, and the "raindrops" from R were letting the world know that the crimes that had not been prosecuted for years would no longer be tolerated. Thankfully, the insider had found a way to share the information and protect his identity and, thereby, his access to insider information.

"Keep the truth flowing, R! It is great nationalists like you who are letting us know that changes are coming. The bad ways overlooked for so long are being corrected and eradicated. Those who have committed these Satanic ceremonies against GOD will be punished. Others who have been pilfering from the country will be accountable. Keep up the fight!"

He wondered what else he could do. R needed his support. He could help make a difference. He followed a link from one of the posts and found a video on YouTube. He'd watched many how-to and fix-it videos on the site but had generally steered clear of anything mundane. As he watched the man on the screen espousing the benefits of R's messages, he realized he could do the same thing. He wasn't sure how to make and post a video on the popular website, but he was sure there was a tutorial to guide him through the process. He typed a query into the search box, and the results filled the page. He clicked on the first video and started making notes.

The crackle of the two-way radio interrupted Brad's lunch of a burger and fries.

"Code 211 at Corner Liquor in Columbia Gardens. Available units, please respond."

Brad wiped his hands on a napkin. "Isn't that a block away?"

His partner for the day, a middle-aged man named John, nodded while he chewed and swallowed the bite he'd just taken of his cheeseburger.

"Let's go!" Both men picked up their cardboard boxes from In-N-Out and hurried to their patrol car.

Brad pressed the button on his two-way radio and relayed to dispatch that they were on their way as he slid into the driver seat. John took another bite of his food, and Brad tried not to show his irritation. *How could he keep eating?*

His partner, sensing his reaction, was quick to respond. "Chances are it'll all be done by the time we arrive."

Traffic was light, and Brad didn't turn on the siren. He didn't want to let the robber know they were almost there.

He saw the corner store and double-parked the car by the door. Both men exited the vehicle and extracted their pistols from holsters.

They hadn't entered the store yet but could see someone at the register.

Brad was sure he saw the flash of a gun and he cupped his weapon in both hands before stepping inside. He could feel the adrenaline surging through his body as he aimed his pistol at the thief in front of him.

"Drop your weapon!"

The young man, likely in his teens, didn't respond. He shook slightly, and Brad saw something metallic in his hand.

"Drop it!" Brad yelled again. The shopkeeper looked anxious, arms partially suspended in the air in an attempt to diffuse the situation.

"Aww, man, why did you call the cops?" The teen addressed the clerk. He swayed slightly before turning towards the two officers.

The clerk looked alarmed. "Wait! Don't shoot!"

Brad fired his weapon, watching as the bullet made contact and a small red dot started to grow. The confused man looked down at his chest before crumpling to the ground. Blood flowed from the wound and pooled on the floor. After a gasp or two, the young man's body went still, and it was evident he was dead.

It only took one shot, and Brad had helped a Lesser transcend closer to supremacy. He hadn't realized it could be so easy.

John stepped forward and knelt beside the limp body. "Oh shit."

The clerk was agitated. "That's what I was trying to tell you."

"What's wrong?" Brad was confused. *The robber had been stopped. Wasn't that why the clerk had called the police?*

"You missed the guy who robbed me. This is one of my regulars."

"What do you mean? He had a gun."

"No, no, he didn't."

Brad looked down at the hand that he thought had held a gun. It took a minute for him to register that the item was a silver-wrapped candy bar, not a weapon.

"Not cool, man, not cool." John stood and initiated a call with dispatch.

"Officer discharged weapon. Send backup."

Brad looked at the body on the ground. It didn't matter that the boy had been unarmed. He was a Lesser. The elders were correct. He was doing the work of God. He felt exhilarated. He could hardly wait to share the news at the next Whites Restore meeting. He just confirmed his life had meaning.

CHAPTER 13

Casey's guilty pleasure was reading declassified information to understand government mechanisms. It provided a glimpse into highly secretive content until it had incubated long enough or was no longer sensitive. Previously, an array of reports had been released about UFOs. While interesting, it wasn't particularly relevant to his investigative work on day-to-day government activities. This morning, he found a new report. He wasn't sure what it meant, but the Pentagon had just released 170 million dormant IPs to a small company in Louisiana named World Resources. The announcement of the vast IP transfer was made as part of the transparency reporting laws; information deemed "unclassified" was posted in the Pentagon activity logs that were made public. Since the data was considered unimportant, it wasn't monitored closely, yet the number stood out to Casey.

Millions of IP addresses. Casey knew the Department of Defense held a large amount of internet real estate. The IPs had a market value in the billions. How was that serving the best interest of American taxpayers? The posting did not share specifics about the transaction, and when Casey tried to find out more about the company in Louisiana, he found they didn't even have a public website. Checking Hoovers.com didn't yield much of a result either. The company was incorporated in Delaware. *Big surprise.* Many companies chose to incorporate in Delaware because of the business advantages. There had to be more to this story, and he was determined to find out. He took a sip of his now cold coffee and started to make Google queries.

There was a joke that spread around the office. "How do you hide? Be on the second page of Google results."

He looked for the company name again and scrolled through the first page of entries served up in less than a second. He ignored the three paid ads at the top of the page and the two at the bottom. The second page didn't have any ads. It was always interesting seeing what didn't rise high enough in the Google algorithm.

There were several variations on the company name; one was a designer in Minnesota, and another was a site under construction. He continued to probe. Still, nothing that appeared to be linked to World Resources. His job would have lost its appeal if it had been too easy to find anything. He felt energized by the dead end. It just meant he hadn't found the right path to unlock the information. He typed another query into the Google search bar and continued to read.

After an hour of sleuthing, Casey was finding more information. The release was related to a "security" project managed by the mysterious company. The Defense Department still owned the coveted IPs; however, Casey wasn't sure how the dormant IPs related to security. Numerous IP assets were handed over to a company without any front-facing identity. Leave it to the Defense Department to bury information in plain view. Maybe it was harmless, but Casey was too jaded and curious to leave the report unexplored.

More questions plagued him. *Why now? Why would these be released to an obscure company by the Coronet administration? Whatever project was underway, hidden in the shadows, wouldn't it be terminated if Larry Stevens were elected president?*

That was the intriguing part of presidential transitions between parties: Democrats and Republicans both had their own agendas. It wasn't uncommon for the new title holder to undo swaths of legislation when taking control of the most powerful post in the world. It served as a reminder to all that there was power to be wielded and a policy shift in play.

There was a good chance that whatever the reason for the release of IPs, the "security" project would likely get scrapped if Stevens won unless it was not significant enough to be on the radar of a new administration. The hairs on the back of Casey's neck prickled, indicating to him that wasn't the case.

■

Tony pushed through the doors to Whataburger and looked for Jest. It didn't take long to find him sitting with two other men he'd never met in one of the orange booths.

"Sorry, I'm late."

"No problem, dude. Grab your lunch and join us."

Fortunately, the lunch rush had already surged, and he could place his order quickly and return to the booth with his triple burger, fries, and Dr. Pepper.

"This is King." Jest pointed to a clean-cut, muscled man with yellowed, tobacco-stained teeth who appeared to be around fifty.

"King?"

"I know. Funny, right? King and Jester." Lester laughed. "And this is Ralph. They're new members of the Texas Freedom Fighters Facebook group."

"Nice to meet you." Tony slid into the booth next to Jest and looked at the men across from him. Ralph appeared to be in his late twenties, with dark brown hair and blue eyes that seemed to be recording everything around him. He was quiet and nodded a welcome as Tony sat down. King and Jest, on the other hand, were having a passionate conversation about the state of affairs in Texas.

"These Antifa and Black Lives Matter protests are threatening Texas."

"I know. Don't mess with Texas! They've got to be stopped from defacing and destroying our city. Did you hear about the wreckage in Portland?"

"Oregon? No, what happened?"

Tony felt like he was trying to catch up, entering a conversation in full swing.

"The city didn't take any action, and Antifa and BLM rioters looted the city and camped out downtown. It looks like a war zone. We can't have that in Houston."

During their lunch, Tony learned that Joe King was ex-military, and he talked about gathering other members of Texas Freedom Fighters to learn basic gun safety practices. "With the right preparation, we can defend our democracy. We can't let what happened in Portland happen here."

Tony watched as the other men nodded. He owned a hunting rifle and had spent many seasons hunting with his father and brother when he was growing up. Now that he lived in an urban part of the city and worked long hours, hunting was not an activity he pursued. Hearing the talk of the "kits," he felt a little self-conscious and ignorant around the other men. It sounded like all of them had some assortment of gear: handguns, bulletproof vests, night vision goggles, knives, helmets, and numerous rounds of ammunition. They talked a lot about their ARs or 15s, but Tony wasn't sure what exactly they were referring to other than it was some type of gun. He put it together that it was a particular weapon called an AR-15.

As the four slid out of the booth, leaving plastic trays littered with soiled paper with grease stains and smears of ketchup, the only remains from their lunch; King looked at Tony.

"Glad to have you on board. Jest speaks very highly of you. Says you're dependable and responsible. That's exactly what we need for Texas Freedom Fighters." Tony smiled and shook the older man's hand. It made him feel good to be recognized after the past forty-five minutes when he felt like a silent observer with little to add. "We need to protect our Texan history."

"Dang, Man, isn't that the truth! Damn, we need to protect the whole F'ing country, for that matter. There's a shit show brewing, and we can be prepared to respond."

"I'm going to use the men's room. Nice meeting you both. Jest, I'll call you later." Tony watched as the three made their way to the door, and then he reached for the plastic trays left on the table. He bussed the items quickly. He liked leaving their booth neat and clean for the next sit-down diners. He knew the staff at Whataburger made less than he did, and he wanted to help them in any way he could. It must be a thankless job. He looked around, and with the exception of the older manager, every employee looked young, likely students trying to make some pocket change. He'd never worked at a fast-food restaurant, and he thought about how crappy it must be as he moved toward the restroom before returning to his van.

The rubber duck on the dash made him smile. He'd soaped up the yellow critter well and didn't have the phobia of germs that many might have if they'd known where the duck had been swimming lately. There was nothing that hot, soapy water couldn't take care of in his line of work.

His next stop was at a retirement community. The elderly woman, Lettie, whose faucet was dripping, didn't realize how simple it was to remove the faucet cap and replace the washer inside. Chinese production had made plumbing products cheaper in recent years by using plastic washers, and they failed more frequently than the little metal, flat ring disk he inserted to replace the non-functioning item.

Tony had been to her home before, and he could tell she was lonely. She'd boiled water and made him a cup of tea while he'd been focused on the washer repair. He wrote up the invoice with the minimum call charge of sixty dollars and then wrote down a promo code to reduce the cost to $45. He didn't include the price of the washer; it could be absorbed in inventory. No one expected all the washers to be accounted for since they could easily be displaced in the van. He hated giving her the bill, but his dispatcher knew he'd responded to the call, and he had to document his visit.

"Lettie, are you sure there isn't a neighbor or someone who could help you with this? I hate having to charge you for such a simple fix." The older woman smiled. "Simple for you, sweetie. Don't worry about the money. Here, drink some tea with me."

Tony sat at the dining table. Brown oak chairs with carved, arched backs matched the farm-style table. A cross was hanging on the wall, and several silver-framed pictures were on the sideboard. *Was this what his future looked like? Elderly and alone with only memories to look at every day?*

Tony liked Erica a lot, and he loved her body and how she looked. Lately, their lives had been about sex and him listening to her about her increased number of followers and what free stuff she'd received in exchange for making videos about the products. She rarely asked about his day. He guessed he couldn't be surprised; plumbing wasn't an exciting career, and he didn't want to give her too many details about his work. He'd read once that the fish throwers in Pike Place Market in Seattle were often asked how they didn't smell like fish away from work; he faced the same questions about sewage as a plumber. He always showered when he got home, used an Old Spice aftershave, and ensured he smelled fresh after work. *People really could be stupid.*

He turned his attention back to Lettie and smiled. "Thank you for the tea. I appreciate it. I hope you enjoy the rest of your day." He stood and gathered his toolbox. The older woman looked sad as he headed to the door, and he suspected he'd be seeing her again soon to address some other plumbing item in her home.

■

"The secret societies who believe they can operate undetected within the political structure of the United States of America always screw up. They are victims of their egos and their weakest members. I learned today that the former first ladies of the United States were men dressed as women. The historic ritual is a tribute to William Shakespeare when the theater only allowed male thespians. No women were allowed.

Look closely, and you'll see that the prior president's 'wife,' Stephanie Bennett, has an Adam's apple that was surgically shaved down to be less noticeable. You can also tell by her shoulders and arms. Dominic Coronet's wife is the exception since the First Family are not long-term political incumbents. Respect the word. You are being misled. – R."

CHAPTER 14

Casey had been digging into the origins of the mysterious R, and the roads all led back to a hack of a website called BeWarned. He guessed he shouldn't think so disparagingly of the "news" site. However, considering that he still hadn't been able to validate anything with any substance, it was safe to say the site was a collection of fictional fantasies served up as clickbait to generate ad revenue. A fresh set of fantastical snippets would appear at the end of each article, and it was safe to say that the goal was to keep anyone clicking through the site for hours.

Who was he kidding? That was true for most websites on the internet with a revenue component. Engage and retain. Create a screentopia of either euphoria or discontent, and the engagement begins. He jumped slightly as his phone rang, pulling him away from his computer. He glanced at the device and saw his college roommate's name and picture on the screen.

"Hey, Jamiel. How are things?"

"Good. Missing Pammy. It's hard to believe she's already in college."

"Yeah, wasn't she in diapers last year?"

The two men laughed, and then Casey got serious.

"Can I get your perspective?"

"Sure, what's up?"

"I'm looking into the effects of social media on news and information accuracy. I'm finding some really wacky theories out there. Why do they get traction when they seem so far-fetched?"

He could hear Jamiel sigh on the other end of the line. "We're hard-wired to find patterns in life, anything that can be used to secure our safety and longevity."

"How does that work to toss out all critical thinking? It seems counterintuitive."

"Yes, but don't underestimate the importance of feeling in control. Fight, flight, and freeze are ingrained in us. Otherwise, the species would have died off millennia ago. If you feel empowered, you will engage. If you feel frightened, you will flee."

"What about freeze?"

"That's when your body is so overwhelmed it can't make another decision."

"Or you're playing dead when a bear is nearby?"

Jamiel laughed. "Yeah, because most of us come up against a bear in our daily lives, but you're not far off. It's a survival technique in certain situations."

"Still not sure how that ties into all the conspiracy theories I'm reading about."

"Let's put it this way. Think of something horrific you've observed in your life that you believe you have no control over."

"9/11."

"Great example. Senseless deaths."

"You asked for horrific. That's the event in my lifetime."

"So, the planes fly into the World Trade Center buildings, and you feel rudderless, out of control. The world is physically crashing down around you. Ash is in the air, thousands killed, and you're left wondering why. That's when your brain looks for something to give it sense. Up pop a variety of theories about the number of planes, burn rates, additional fuel, people who would normally have been on-site that missed that day, and other details that can be woven into an alternative narrative. Suddenly, things are slotting into place for people looking for something to have meaning. Of course, it was a bigger plot. Of course, there was someone behind the scenes pulling puppet strings. People want to believe it was more than a senseless attack."

"But it was a terrorist attack."

"Yes, but that doesn't offer any comfort or assurance to anyone. Terrorists can always strike again without warning. Conspiracy theories offer a sense of order and reason. This creates a false sense of security."

"Why false?"

"Because it's all an illusion. Everything is out of our control because we don't have a crystal ball for our future."

"So, patterns looking at the past to create calm for the future."

"Something like that. Don't underestimate the power of suggestion. There have been clinical trials where they've shown that it's hard to correct misconceptions when they create any sense of normalcy for the person who's clutching onto the information."

"So that's why JFK Jr. can be alive and well even though he died years ago?"

"Wait, what?"

"That's one of the theories circulating right now."

Casey could imagine his friend shaking his head.

"Wow, that's even wilder than I would have thought, but yes. JFK Jr. offers security, political normalness, and a return to simpler times before the towers were destroyed."

"That's crazy."

"Don't call it that. It's actually sane behavior, even if the beliefs are outrageous. It's our minds looking for patterns and order in the world."

"Dang. I just never thought it could be this misconstrued."

"People have different levels of needs to give them a sense of security. What you need is different from the person embracing the JFK Jr. story. Those different levels also create a divide because we all want to see each other as we see ourselves."

"Division if I call them crazy."

"Yup. They'll view you as misinformed and not enlightened."

"Sheep." Casey had been observing the increased use of the term to insult anyone who wasn't on board with their hypothesis.

Casey hung up after a few more minutes. Jamiel had given him a lot to think about. *If people were willing to clutch onto misinformation for a sense of security, didn't that present a real problem if an unscrupulous person or group was able to tap into that need?*

He opened his desk drawer and grabbed the jar of Tums. He chewed a tablet and tried to ignore the goosebumps and a sense of fear and anxiety that flashed through his body. He'd already seen how misinformation had swayed public opinion during the prior election. *What was going to be the arsenal used for the coming one?* The answer scared him and triggered his acid reflux.

■

Dominic looked out at the sea of supporters and inhaled deeply. He loved their adoration and wanted to take it all in. Signs with "Dominic Coronet is OUR president," "The Dom is Da Bomb," and "Dom 4 4 More" were being waved. He stood a minute longer as the thunderous applause and chants continued. He understood the value of making them wait for him to speak.

"Hello, Oklahoma City!"

Cheers erupted throughout the stadium.

"You are the backbone of our great country! You are the nationalists that understand the value of our agenda, the importance of keeping our borders secure from ILLEGALS trying to enter, and for making sure that other countries don't STEAL from us through unjust and unfair trade practices."

The audience stomped their feet, and the thunderous sound reverberated throughout the room.

"I am the ONLY president who has successfully dealt with these important issues. I am the ONLY president who will continue to fight for your rights."

Dom spoke for an hour and thirty-five minutes. He knew how to read the gathering and kept them whipped up with excitement. He left the podium with cheers, applause, and chants of "Four more years, four more years!" He was ushered backstage by his campaign manager, a harried man in his mid-forties, wearing a headset and carrying a clipboard. "You're always so inspiring," he gushed.

"Cut the crap. Why was the upper balcony empty? This place should have been filled to capacity with a group outside watching on big screens."

"I know, I know. We had a tremendous number of online sign-ups, so we expanded the venue to include those that wouldn't have been able to get in otherwise."

"Then tell me, what the fuck happened? What happened to my followers?"

"From what we can tell, you got trolled on TikTok."

"What do you mean, *TROLLED*?"

"A K-Pop group challenged all of their followers to reserve tickets."

"What the fuck is K-Pop? Is this a new Antifa group?"

The campaign manager tried not to laugh. He knew the president wouldn't see the humor in the situation.

"No, it's short for a Korean Pop Band."

"Korean?! What the hell?"

"Thousands of tickets were reserved by TikTokers who never planned to come. We didn't see the social posts, so we thought the reservations were legit."

"That is fraud! I want the Justice Department to look into this."

"It's not fraud, sir. Everyone will say they changed their mind about attending. It's their right to reserve tickets."

"Make sure this doesn't happen again! It is unacceptable."

"Yes, sir. I know, sir."

The Dom stepped inside the bullet-proofed vehicle that would take him to the runway where Air Force One was being prepared for his departure. The campaign manager started to step into the interior, but Dom stopped him. "Take another car." He turned to the driver. "Go. I'm done here."

The Dom settled into the soft leather seat and closed his eyes. He replayed the rally in his mind and basked in the reverie. He was going to win the election and have four more years. He'd make sure there were more years to follow after that. It shouldn't be hard to change term limits when his popularity was at an all-time high. He just had to pick the right time, and everything would fall into place. He'd leverage that he was a political outsider and making change from within. He'd convey that it would take more than eight years to undo the mess of the political lifers who held the office before him. His base would ensure he stayed president for as long as he liked. The thought erased the visual of empty seats from the recent rally.

He sent a message from his phone. "Oklahoma City has shown me that they are the people of this great country committed to preserving our democracy! A lot is at risk. Stay the course for four more years!" He had a much broader reach than just an arena. He had the attention of the world.

■

Larry felt tense as he scrolled through the channels on the television that his aide had rolled into his office. *What had happened to the days of simple newscasts with Walter Cronkite at the helm?* Americans had been happy and content to listen to the trustworthy man who reported every weeknight, and everyone accepted the information. Walter had been an authority. There was no reason to have doubts about the motives or the message. Today, the population was jaded and suspicious, and Dominic Coronet had taken the helm to keep them on edge.

Things had started to shift in the late seventies when news moved away from being a public service to an ad revenue generator for the three mainstay television stations. ABC, NBC, and CBS controlled the airwaves, with PBS taking a back seat. The first change came in the 1980s with the introduction of Fox News, and as cable expanded, content became a commodity that was demanded 24/7. Larry knew pining for days long gone would do him no good, but he still had faith in the American people that they could see through the hype and fanfare. He hoped that would be true when it came to Dom Coronet.

This morning, the president called into Fox News and babbled on and on. He wasn't making any sense as far as Larry could tell. Something about trade deficits that didn't ensure the country was getting fair treatment. *What an ignorant ass.*

Larry's cell phone rang, and he looked at the name on the screen. Sheila Lawson. His running mate had been carefully vetted to ensure that between the two of them, they catered to the broadest demographic of the Democratic Party. Twenty years his junior at 47, she brought a youthfulness and vibrancy to their ticket. It didn't hurt that she was assertive and tough. She had almost managed to transcend her gender. Larry knew when the leading reference in news reports wasn't her gender, Sheila would have truly broken the glass ceiling. For now, he was leveraging her mixed-race background to strengthen their chances of beating the incumbent. With a Latina mother and White father, she'd won the genetic lottery with fair skin and thick hair.

"Sheila."

"Hello, Larry. I don't know if you've seen the latest numbers. We're ahead in the polls by three points."

"I hadn't seen that yet. That's great news." With the election still six months ahead, it was premature to take the poll numbers seriously. The results could shift as quickly as the daily tides of the ocean. Washed up or washed out. Tomorrow, they could easily be down three points.

Larry didn't trust Dominic Coronet. He could hardly open his mouth or post on Twitter without making some defamatory remark about the two candidates. "Lazy Larry" or "Stupid Sheila" were commonly thrown out for his followers. Larry wondered why Coronet couldn't be more original, but he knew the answer. The attribute raised a question in voter's minds. Larry and Sheila decided early on in their campaign that they would stick to the facts and tell the American people their agenda for their time in office. Together, they believed they would win over the hearts and minds of more voters than the reality TV star who relied on chaos and disruption to lead the country.

They confirmed their agendas for the day. Sheila was flying to Georgia, and Larry was staying in D.C. They had a joint meeting with their campaign manager on Zoom in the early evening. They met regularly to ensure they kept their finger on the pulse of what mattered to voters. They had an election to win.

CHAPTER 15

"Our great leader, Dominic Coronet, entered the office of the president and took more than the oath on the Bible on the steps of the Capitol. He also took an oath to rid the world of the atrocities and wrongdoings of the Hollywood and industrial elites. This corruption extends to our courthouses, politicians, and corporate leaders. The Dom is here to restore our great history. He is outside the political infrastructure, and he did not groom a male 'wife' to honor the outdated practice of his predecessors. Melanie Coronet is all woman, aligned in restoring our great country to the dictates of 1776. Respect the word. You are being misled. – R."

■

Tony had two more jobs after his stop at Lettie's home. Afterward, he pulled his service van into the parking lot behind the office of the Ready, Set, Flow Plumbing company near tree-lined West Bellfort Avenue. It didn't take long to submit his work orders from the day and clock out with the dispatcher. He felt tired as he got behind the wheel of his F-250 truck and eased into traffic.

Driving down Bellfort Avenue, he saw a sign for National Guns and Armor. *How many times had he driven by gun shops without really seeing them?* They were common throughout Houston, and he suspected throughout the state. He flipped his turn signal on and waited in the middle of the landscaped boulevard for several cars to pass before making a left turn across several lanes of traffic into the gun shop parking lot. A weighted sign was outside indicating that there was also a shooting range on-site.

The building, a single-story nondescript cinder block construction, had a red, white, and blue overhang with the image of an eagle with shotguns crossed in its talons. A bell attached to the door jingled as he pushed the glass and metal frame inward to enter. He approached the display case counter and waited while the older gentleman behind the barrier finished ringing up the customer in front of him.

"Congratulations on your purchase. Our team is here to help with everything you need. We offer classes and can help service your cleanings, triggers, sights, barrels, and more!"

"I'd like to schedule time on the range for my wife."

"Absolutely." A few minutes later, the transaction was complete, and the appointment was scheduled. Tony stepped forward after the other man turned from the counter. "Um... I'm not sure what I'm looking for. An AR..." He couldn't remember the number from lunch.

"The 10, 15?" Seeing his confusion, the shop owner continued. "The AR-15 is very popular for home defense and hunting. Does that match your needs?"

"I think so." Tony peered into the case below him and saw a variety of handguns. A rack of shotguns spanned the wall behind the clerk. There were a series of compartments below the gun rack which housed boxes of ammunition. The clerk reached for a rifle, popped out the magazine, and placed it on the counter in front of Tony. It looked like a military weapon, nothing like the rifle he used for hunting.

"This is a great model, the Armalite Defender 15. It can be modified with whatever scope you'd like. It's a quick change to reload, and it functionally rivals more expensive models. We've found this to be the optimum choice to balance affordability and functionality."

"How much?"

"$750."

Tony wasn't sure about the purchase. It seemed so hardcore. It looked more like a gun designed to kill people versus animals in the wild. It was also a lot of money, although he suspected he could end up paying a lot more for other models.

King's words from lunch rang in his ears. "It's our responsibility to defend our great city and state." He knew Houston was changing around him. The Confederate statue had been removed, and there was general unrest brewing around him. He'd been hearing the frustration in the posts of the Texas Freedom Fighters Facebook group. He was worried that he'd wake up one day to find the city was no longer recognizable with an influx of liberals and Antifa.

"I'll think about it."

"Pick it up! See how it feels."

Tentatively, he reached out and touched the black metal. It wasn't that different than his hunting rifle. It was heavier than he expected but still relatively light. He tucked the stock to his shoulder, holding the gun parallel to the glass counter. He lowered it and placed it back on the case top.

"Nice."

"We have a carry now, cash later financing option, too."

"How does that work?"

"Easy. A quick credit check, and we'll set up automatic payments for you. Let me confirm the price." The man reached for a calculator and tapped out a few numbers.

"You can get this for as little as $45 a month."

Tony could manage that payment each month. One big payment would be harder to swallow.

His phone vibrated in his pocket. He was sure Erica was wondering where he was.

"I'll sleep on it."

"No problem. We're here every day." The shopkeeper put the rifle back on the rack. "Keep in mind we offer classes, and if you purchase from us, you'll get a lifetime membership to our shooting range."

"Sounds good. Thank you."

As Tony climbed back into his truck, he looked at his phone. Erica had sent him a photo of her in an outfit he hadn't seen before. She looked good. He sent a smiley face, taco, and eggplant emojis along with his ETA. The gun could wait.

■

Leon read the latest posts from R and smiled. He was teaching himself how to make videos on YouTube, deciphering the messages to spread the word. He didn't realize he was going to get a following so quickly. The videos weren't very polished; he still didn't understand how to edit the content, but he'd watched a variety of how-tos that showed him how he could record both his computer screen and his commentary simultaneously. He pulled up the BeWarned website and several others he'd found that documented the information being relayed by R. The content was out there for all to see. The High Court Tribunals were well underway, and he predicted that the court of law would reinstate the Constitution of the United States just before the next election. If there were any delay to the dissolution of the United States Corporation, the election would have to be held again. Leon clicked on a link within the supporting article, and it opened another site with more details on the process. As he read the material, he confirmed everything was on schedule, and the next election would restore the nation to its prior glory.

He hadn't voted for Dominic Coronet in the last election. He hadn't voted at all, convinced that it didn't matter in a government controlled by Super PACs and did nothing to benefit him directly. No one had done anything to save the coal miners, and his town had been decimated by unemployment and poverty. Now, he could see how The Dom was a savior fighting for the restitution of the United States. R shared enough that it was evident to Leon that The Dom was breaking through the barriers just by being elected. As a competent businessman, he brought profit principles to the government, which was long known for waste and corruption. The sham of a government, held up by a corporation and run by a secret group of elites, needed to be replaced with true Americans dedicated to the rights of the people. No more corporate greed funneling national assets to the coffers of the industrial rich. The Rockefellers and Rothschilds had stripped the country using the power of the corporation and run it into the ground while siphoning funds into their reserves.

Why wasn't mainstream media sharing this information? He already knew the answer. It was easy to see the mechanism of "real" news in the United States by following the money flow between the Hollywood elite and the industrial robbers. It only told the story they wanted you to know. The news was bought and paid for.

Well, they can't control the internet and the true nationalists reporting the truth. As far as Leon was concerned, R was a hero and should be applauded for shining a light on the hypocrisy of the current government. Dom Coronet entered the presidency from outside the political establishment and was not part of the corruption that plagued the government. He was leading the charge internally to restore the Constitution. *Back to 1776, baby!*

Today, Leon was relaying the new messages from R in his latest video. With the information he was transmitting for the world to hear, he was doing his part to restore peace and order to the land he loved. He was a true nationalist aligned with the mission of R. He was optimistic that the undesirables that had taken over his downtown would soon be deported back to the hellholes they came from. He wanted the streets to be cleared and safe to walk again. Several years ago, he'd added a second deadbolt to both his front and back doors, and recently, he'd added a third.

The world was being restored. Those guilty of crimes were finally being held accountable. One day soon, Leon hoped he could sleep again without the handgun under the pillow next to him.

It took several hours to finish the video. He felt a sense of pride as he released the content. His life had a purpose again.

■

"The Dom is restoring our judicial system. His Supreme Court Justice nominee, Boris Kerwin, is being sworn in tomorrow to the highest court in our country. The Dom is appointing those who know the laws of our country and the forefathers' intentions to federal positions. He is removing the weak arbitrators of our nation. It is time for our country to be restored. It is time for the Rainstorm to shower us with the power to resurrect our democracy before it is lost forever. Respect the word. You are being misled." — R.

CHAPTER 16

Casey laughed. He knew he shouldn't; he should remain impartial in a bi-partisan world. Secretly, he thought Dom Coronet was a pompous a-hole who had fabricated and exaggerated most of his past to paint a presidential picture. He'd seen too many reports of strippers, centerfold playmates, and beauty pageant contestants who had crossed paths with the married man. Somehow, he doubted that The Dom was in an open relationship. His wife, Melanie, was never found participating in extracurricular activities, and she didn't look pleased when news reports broke yet another story of the exploits of the man in office. Casey had also seen reports of misappropriated funds from his charity that had pushed the nonprofit organization to shutter its activities rather than face additional scrutiny.

Casey was laughing at the TikTokers who had reserved thousands of seats for the Oklahoma City rally and then were a no-show. Looks like The Dom wasn't immune to being ghosted and the butt of a good joke. It gave Casey hope that the younger generation was more aligned with human rights and less judgmental than the extreme radical right.

Casey looked at his computer screen. He'd been following a few fringe sites and reading the posts of an anonymous "R" for several months. Initially, he'd written them off as harmless when he saw the first ones that promised information but very little substance. Others still made outlandish claims that were hard to believe, yet R was getting traction. The comments and likes on the posts were increasing, and the posts kept appearing in Casey's orbit.

Casey shook his head. *What was it about the posts that were getting and keeping people's attention?* He would look further. There had to be a reason.

In addition to reviewing a wide variety of news, information streams, and internet trends, Casey also received newsletters and mailings from prominent political players in D.C., including the president's campaign emails.

"Breaking... Larry Stevens investigation needed!" was the latest email. Casey was intrigued by the emphasis placed on "breaking." Typically, it would be paired with the word "news," but Coronet's communications never used the complete phrase. It didn't surprise the reporter. The message reinforced the belief that The Dom was a government outsider who would shake things up. He was going to "break" the system.

As Casey continued to read the email, he was struck by the audacity of the message. It was full of misleading information, dubious claims, and an offer to make a "1000% impact" if one donated to the Coronet campaign. There was no reference to how that impact would be multiplied, and even the math showing the benefit didn't align with a 1000% improvement. *Why weren't politicians held to the same standards as corporate marketing campaigns?* There were strict guidelines for communicating with potential customers that limited puffery, product claims, and required offer disclosures. *It would be nice if politicians had to adhere to the same policies.*

Casey knew candidates wouldn't like the limitations. Also, readers didn't seem to mind the exaggerations and weren't complaining.

In the last two decades, the lines of entertainment and information had blurred with technological advances happening so quickly. The burgeoning of reality TV during the writers' strike also encouraged a curated view of the world. Influence came from many different people, with internet celebrities contributing to the ranks. It used to be a handful of Hollywood stars who shared the limelight. Now, anyone can find an audience and a following if they offer content compelling enough to get a like and tap on a subscribe button. These influencers could make a significant impact on public opinion. It made Casey's work a puzzle to decipher, and it wasn't always easy to identify trends and valid information. Some days, the hairs on the back of his neck would tingle. Sometimes, what he read caused a blend of laughter and astonishment. Today, his neck hairs were on full alert as he tried to shake the uneasiness he felt about the state of the country. He closed the lid of his laptop and stood up. A walk should help.

■

The president was a real prick. Maxwell Hovick had suspected as much before he accepted the role of vice president. He looked around his office and decided to take out his frustration on an unsuspecting couch accent pillow. He pummeled the filled fabric and picked it up to slap it against the arm of the sofa numerous times, trying to release his anger. He even said a few choice swear words, very much out of character for a man who lived by the laws of God. The Dom had reduced Max to his basest behavior.

The vice president had been working for months on a healthcare reform bill that would allow many citizens access to medical coverage they didn't currently have, and Dom had just tossed him under the bus. He'd made the public announcement on Twitter, of all places. Healthcare was important, but not as much as his fucking wall. *Asshole!* Dom was going to redirect funding allocated for the healthcare bill, Max's baby, and direct it to wall construction. It wasn't much of a wall, more like a series of dominoes that marked the border.

The part that irritated him so much was that the president cavalierly announced it on Twitter without even consulting him and without consideration of how it would make him look. Maxwell had been reduced to a lame-duck vice president who, at the end of his four-year term, would have little or nothing to point to as contributions in his role. Leave it to that arrogant, self-indulgent, narcissistic, repugnant man who occupied the Oval Office.

He should have known when he met Dominic Coronet for the first time. Maxwell knew he was being considered for the VP position on the ticket. He'd heard rumors about the morally bankrupt man before they'd met, but Dom had waved off the rumors in person. "You know how it is; any successful, wealthy WHITE man in our country is a target. Anyone who strives to undermine me finds that I don't take this lying down. Every woman who has accused me of wrongdoing has either dropped her case or been exposed as an opportunist. People always want to ride on your coattails if they think they'll get a free ride."

Max, lulled by the reasonableness of Dom's statements, wanted to believe him. The Dom had national recognition because of his successful reality TV show. Clearly, he was merely a victim of his success.

Maxwell had gone home and discussed the opportunity with his wife of thirty-six years, Nora, and they had both agreed if he was offered the chance to be vice president, he should take it. He didn't do much without consulting his wife. They had the same core values and beliefs. They answered to God first, with their country second. Max, to honor his wife and his commitment to God, was never alone with other women, just like his wife was never alone with any other men. Even still, he was anxious that he might make a mistake. He noticed the young staffers at the White House, and there were always beautiful women at the rallies. *Would he be too weak and become a sinner?* It was a sin to covet another man's wife, and he was sure that extended to coveting any woman who wasn't Nora.

They were best friends and confidants. They still shared a bed but had stopped having regular sex as his political career progressed. They were both virgins on their wedding night, and their sex life had never been exciting. While intercourse was pleasant between the two, it never had a sense of urgency and desire. Both of them seemed content to stop their sexual encounters after their two children were born. Their boys were now grown men, both married with their own families. The coming-of-age conversation about sex had been uncomfortable and awkward, and Max had been relieved when they didn't question him much. It was better for them to discover information elsewhere.

Maxwell, exhausted after assaulting the office couch, collapsed onto one of the cushions, the pillow still clutched in his hand. He was grateful that he was alone and no one had witnessed his outburst. He'd let his emotions control him. He would find a way to contribute to his country. He would find a way to make a difference. He just hoped Dominic wouldn't interfere again.

It was a beautiful day in D.C. Casey had been staring at his computer screen too long. He had been trying to interpret the clues he was uncovering, and he'd stepped away from his desk, walking for almost an hour trying to piece together the information he'd been reading. The president had been in rare form on Twitter in the early morning, and he still marveled at the man's choice to conduct official business across the social platform. Gone were the days of procedure and protocol defined by generations of prior politicians. The Dom wasn't a politician and didn't understand how the government worked. He managed his presidency the same way he tackled his reality TV show: tease, bully, and entertain. Everyone liked to show up for a catfight, and Dom pitted both sides against each other by tossing Twitter grenades into his social feed almost daily. Casey assumed the older man liked the chaos. The Dom wasn't a leader; he was an instigator.

Without a destination in mind, Casey wandered to the National Mall and walked the large expanse stretching from the Capitol Building to the Lincoln Memorial. It was interesting to think about being this close to the president and yet so far away politically. Finding a way to report without a partisan bias had been easier when both sides of the table could hear what the others had to say. Somewhere along the way, there had become a deep divide with a line only crossed by perceived traitors from each party. One side yelled foul play, and the other screamed too much government. Either way, he saw a collision on the horizon. It scared him to think of the role misinformation could play in the country's future. He'd been following a trend that was emerging online. He had first noticed the anonymous poster who signed entries with the letter R weeks ago, and it was disturbing to see the posts getting mainstream attention. Casey had tracked the first posts to a site called BeWarned, and even the ominous nature of the URL added a menacing quality to the messages.

How is this getting traction? From what he'd read, there was a lot of boasting and proclamations of position within the government, with R preaching from an online pulpit to anyone who would listen. What made this particularly unusual was the influence of others online that helped disperse R's information, adding their interpretations and a sprinkling of other conspiracy theories circulating on the web for years. From what Casey could piece together, the posts had evolved to spread "raindrops" of information leading up to the "Rainstorm" about to shower down on those abusing the system.

During the morning, he'd been watching videos posted by PoliticalPunditPA, whose bio indicated he was Leon Levan from Pennsylvania. There wasn't much information about Leon before he'd started his channel. He didn't appear to be on Twitter or Instagram, and his Facebook page was sparse. A Spokeo search returned three Leon Levans in Pennsylvania. He was either a 62-year-old man from Sunbury in Northumberland County, a 23-year student in Easton, outside of Philadelphia, or a 47-year-old gay man in Pittsburgh. Casey's money was on Sunbury based on the image of the man in the videos.

The disturbing information that had propelled Casey to leave his desk for a walk was the talk of the coming Rainstorm. Linked to a "High Court Tribunal" that was prosecuting those who had committed crimes against humanity, Casey spent hours trying to find anything of credible substance. He was beginning to believe you could tell people the sky was green and the grass was blue as long as you showed a supporting image. *What had happened to critical thinking?* In an age of technology where videos and photos could easily be doctored or fabricated, it was easy to provide "proof."

Casey was becoming disillusioned with the recent discovery of a man claiming to be John F. Kennedy, Jr. waiting in the wings to reemerge into public life. *When had the country gone ape-shit crazy?* He'd covered the story in 1999, and he was confident the son of the thirty-fifth president was still dead. It shows how much people wanted the fairy tale from the family deemed American royalty.

His cell phone vibrated in his pocket, and an image of his college roommate showed on the screen as he pulled it from his pocket.

"Hey, Jamiel, how are you?" A confirmed bachelor, Casey enjoyed hearing about Jamiel's wife and family as the call started with a brief update.

Casey smiled. "I still can't believe little Pammy is attending Stanford."

"Imagine how I feel." Jamiel's laugh had a hint of sadness. "Time marches on, my friend."

"Everything OK with you?"

"Yeah, sure. Just super busy. Treating patients. You know, the usual."

Jamiel didn't share the incident with the police officers in Charleston with Casey. He hadn't told anyone, including his wife, and he'd learned to push his rage down and focus on the things he could control. He'd always be more intelligent and wealthier than the two police officers. The thought made him feel petty and egotistical. *How does one find a way to accept and love those who direct hate at others?* It was a process he still struggled with. He focused on the conversation with his former roommate. The other man asked, "Can you refer me to a psychiatrist or psychologist? I'm trying to get insights into why people get sucked down the rabbit hole with conspiracy theories."

"Sure, Casey. It's not my specialty, but I can make a few inquiries. Can I get you a name in a day or two?"

"That's great. I appreciate your help."

After a few more minutes and a quick update on their day-to-day lives, Casey said goodbye and returned his phone to his coat pocket.

As he walked along the wall commemorating the Americans who had fallen during the Vietnam War, he tried to get a sense of the loss. There were so many names, each with a family that experienced tragedy with a member ripped from the fabric of their existence. *To what end?*

The Rainstorm is coming. Casey looked up at the cloudless blue sky and hoped the feeling in the pit of his stomach wasn't a premonition of things to come. Would people throw away the democracy offering "liberty and justice for all?" The postings of R and the pundits spreading his gospel kept referencing a return to 1776. If you ignored that 1776 was when the Declaration of Independence was written, and the U.S. Constitution followed years later, maybe the statement by R had some credibility. However, Casey thought the Constitution document was flawed by not recognizing women and Blacks as contributing members of society, so he was unclear how returning to the original pillars set forth by the forefathers was better for the country. Over the two centuries since the inception of the United States, the doctrines evolved for a reason. However, romanticism around "returning to 1776" didn't take into account what that would mean for the country.

He reminded himself that the Civil War had created a fissure in the country, yet the republic had survived. Was the Rainstorm about to start a crack that would break it apart for good?

Casey had an underlying uneasy feeling that he couldn't shake.

How do you create a revolution? Create discontent and sell the notion that a new leader can restore prior glory. Casey could see how R was setting the stage.

CHAPTER 17

"Corporations want to control you. They will not stop until they have microchipped everyone in the world. This microchip will be used to force behavior. You will no longer be free. You will become a slave to whatever whims they desire. Do not lose your sovereign freedoms. The Rainstorm is coming. There will be a day when we have to fight to maintain our freedoms and to restore the government to the will of The People. For too long, the wealthy and elite have been above the law. The High Court Tribunal is laying the foundation by removing the filth from society. Dominic Coronet is our savior. He is the one with the power and the knowledge to restore our democracy. Respect the word. You are being misled. – R."

■

"Misguided sheep!" The Dom was in rare form. "The liberals are willing to stay idle and let ILLEGALS enter our country. Bad hombres who are here to steal from you! They will steal your JOBS, your CARS, and ALL your valuables." The crowd in the Houston arena booed. "I am here to SAVE our country. No one has done more to protect our land than me." Cheers erupted around the room. The Dom loved the adoration and the attention. He leaned forward toward the microphone.

"You know Mexico is paying to deport these criminals to the United States. They want this to be our problem and not to take responsibility for the filth within their borders." The audience started to chant, "BUILD THE WALL... BUILD THE WALL... BUILD THE WALL..."

"Instead of using that money to deport illegals, they should be working with us to fortify the borders, so together we can stop this ILLEGAL and MASSIVE influx of criminals flowing from crap countries." The audience responded with approval.

The Dom liked the alliteration. He made a mental note. He'd use that phrase again, especially since it was received with thunderous applause and stamping feet.

"A STORM is coming! Have no fear! CHANGE is on the horizon!" The Dom knew his strength was his ability to rile up the audience and build them into a frenzy. His weakness was staying too long to soak up the energy in the room. He felt like a god, looking at the packed stadium and hearing the cheers of support.

He spoke for another thirty minutes and stepped away from the podium after an hour and twenty-two minutes. His campaign manager met him at the bottom of the platform. Dom was pleased with the attendance. "Well, at least you fixed that problem from Oklahoma. Let's ban that app. What's it called? Tic Tac? We need to shut that down."

"TikTok, sir." The campaign manager kept the rest of his thoughts to himself. Telling the president that his executive power only extended so far and that he had no grounds for silencing the social platform would just launch a spew of rage in his direction. The younger man was secretly obsessed with several TikTokers who mimicked the president's speech. One woman, in particular, had gathered quite a following.

He braced himself as he broached the sensitive topic with The Dom. "We've been conducting polls after each rally, and you're showing strong numbers with your base." He started with the good news. "However, there are portions of the country that you carried solidly during the last election where we are seeing a decline in support."

"What are you telling me?"

"We might want to schedule in-person visits to the most at-risk areas." The manager waited for the president to rage and was surprised when The Dom agreed. "Schedule it. I enjoy connecting with my followers."

The campaign manager sighed silently as he realized the president was still basking in the adoration of the attendees. He made a mental note to engage when The Dom was distracted and boosted by a rally.

■

Tony and Jester sat in Tony's F-250 in a line of cars, all trying to inch their way to the Toyota Center exit in the Central Business District in downtown Houston. They tossed the two signs they'd been given when they arrived into the bed of the truck. One was red with "Save Democracy," and the other was blue that read "Keep America Safe." Both men were animated and excited.

"He's awesome, man! I can't believe The Dom came to Houston. Thanks for inviting me." Tony moved his truck two feet forward and hit the brake again. Jester smacked the dashboard. "Dang, it! It was even better than I expected. He really understands what's at stake, what's threatening our country."

"I saw a few people wearing shirts with the letter R. Any idea what that means?"

"Nope, but I'm sure a quick Google search will tell us."

Jest reached into his jacket pocket for his phone and typed, "What is R?" He scrolled through the results. "Says it's a conspiracy theory."

"How do they know that?"

"Not sure, still reading."

The two men were silent as Jest scanned the online information. "Says R first started posting on BeWarned."

"That's a reputable site. I don't go there often, but I've found good information in the past."

Tony finally made it to the light that fed traffic onto the road, flanking the stadium, and he accelerated to make it through the intersection as the light turned yellow. "Whew, just made it!" The two men settled in as Tony maneuvered toward I-45 South to take them to Southeast Houston.

"Says here that there is a tribunal court and that The Dom is leading the charge to correct the wrongdoings of a corrupt secret society."

"That sounds about right after seeing him tonight. I didn't expect him to be so charismatic, but I guess that makes sense. He commands attention."

"Yes. This is exactly what we need right now. Our history is being threatened. I knew he was the right person to lead our country."

"He is delivering on his promise to clear the muck from government."

"Do you have time to grab a beer?" Tony looked at the clock mounted on his dash. The rally had gone longer than he anticipated.

"Sorry, man, gotta get home. Erica is expecting me."

"You're a lucky man, my friend. How'd you end up with a beauty like her? I'd bang her."

Tony looked away. He didn't want to talk about Erica with Jester. His friend made everything sexual, and he didn't like to share the details of his bedroom activities.

"I don't understand women. I guess you look ok. Got a few wrinkles and some gray hair." Jest reached over and tousled Tony's hair. "She got Daddy issues? Is that why she dates you?"

"Come on, Jest, cut it out." Tony swatted at the other man's hand.

"You know I'm just envious, dude. I haven't had sex since that bitch Tina moved out. Just jerkin' off to OnlyFans." Jester didn't mention his recent go-to fantasy had been imagining every which way he could fuck his friend's girlfriend. She was pretty, petite but not too small, and always smelled nice. He was a crappy friend fantasizing about the blond woman. He usually pulled up one of her YouTube videos and touched himself while he watched her modeling clothes or putting on makeup. Tina hadn't worn makeup, and he didn't generally like the taste of lipstick, but with Erica, it was different. She looked like a princess. He wanted to be happy for Tony, but that didn't mean he would stop thinking about banging his girlfriend.

■

"Sex trafficking out of Tickle Your Fancy Day Spa has been shut down! This massage parlor in Atlanta, Georgia, was a public-facing business. The High Court Tribunal, using information from the trials, successfully stopped the flow of young girls through this establishment. They were being routed throughout the United States and Asian countries using the Underground Railroad. There are still many other businesses operating to distribute virgins to disgusting men who will defile their virtue and force them into sex acts with many men. This is not what God intended. We must restore faith in humanity and protect them from this evil influence. You will not find this information in the mainstream media. Do your own research if you don't believe. Respect the word. You are being misled. – R."

∎

The election was several months away, and polls showed that the president was running neck and neck with the liberal candidate. The Dom didn't know why he wasn't sweeping the numbers. He'd lowered taxes since he'd taken office, and immigration was a hot topic at his rallies that always held his followers in a frenzy.

His campaign team continued to tell him, "You've got to find a way to appeal to the moderates. Immigration is important to communities that have seen an influx of refugees and a reduction in jobs. However, it's probably not the topic that will get Jane Does in Kansas to the polls on election day." Coronet's campaign manager tried to delicately nudge the president to expand his political agenda to cast a wider net, but the president was adamant.

"The wall is how we're going to win. Those commie liberals have blocked us from getting the funding we need to fortify our borders. This is unacceptable." The campaign manager sighed. The Dom had fixated on this topic and thought it had more of a superpower than it did. The coal miners in

Pennsylvania were asking how they were going to put food on their tables, corporations were pressuring for trade bills, and the Middle East was pushing for more defense deals. The Dom thought he could run the country like a scripted reality TV show. Fortunately, many qualified people were pulling levers behind the scenes to ensure the day-to-day machine kept running.

"Crime is the ticket! Crime impacts everyone!" The president gestured wildly to make his point.

When the stocky man was in a rage, the campaign manager knew it was better to stay silent or say very little.

"Yes, the wall is important." He said nothing about the decline in crime rates over the past decades. The Dom was stuck in a time warp from the 1980s when crime had reached a fevered peak.

"Let's take it head-on at the upcoming rallies. Here's a tentative schedule to review." The campaign manager was learning tactics from the president. He diverted the paunchy president's attention to get the rally assignments made if he could make the man in front of him believe it would benefit his cause.

"We've scheduled Hershey, Orlando, Des Moines..." He continued reading the list, "Nashville, Milwaukee..."

It didn't take long for Dominic to nod approval and choose the venues he'd attend and which he'd leave for the vice president.

"Make sure Maxy-Laxy gets the word out. He's on this ticket, too."

The campaign manager noticed the nickname for the vice president, designed to diminish the manhood of the politician with more acumen than The Dom. Anyone just had to turn on any reality TV show to know that name-calling was the way to create drama, and The Dom used the ploy often. Weakness and name-play were all manipulative techniques. Dominic Coronet was redefining what it even meant to be presidential. What surprised the manager was that most of the country didn't seem to care. Entertainment and divisiveness, which his followers gobbled up, fueled the election battle. Others took a more apathetic approach, showing little interest in the governmental machine. Those expressing a leftist view had their agenda and ideals to promote. Regardless, it seemed that important policies and procedures during previous elections were taking a back seat.

What was happening to the country? How did he feel about being a part of the political manipulation? "It's a paycheck, it's a paycheck," was the campaign manager's internal monologue, alternated with "Retire in style, retire in style." He could sell his soul a little longer if it meant umbrella drinks on a beach somewhere after this next election.

CHAPTER 18

Erica lay in bed, looking up at the ceiling. She could hear Tony's measured breathing, indicating he'd fallen sound asleep next to her. He'd asked her to attend a presidential rally to see Dominic Coronet earlier in the day, but she thought the president was repugnant. The way he viewed women made her uneasy. She didn't know if the accusations of his sexual predatory behavior were true or not. Still, whenever she saw him slip into her social feeds, she quickly diverted her attention elsewhere. Fortunately, it didn't happen often, with her online focus on clothes, makeup, and lifestyle hacks.

She quietly slipped from the bed, her naked body protesting the loss of the covers. She pulled on her robe and tiptoed from the room. She opened her laptop and replayed the video clips she'd recorded for her next post. She hadn't received boxes from Clever Cosmetics or URStyleGuru this week, so she'd been left to fill the Kickin' with Kiki schedule with a request from one of her followers. Many times, the suggestions were from people truly wanting more information, but recently, she'd been getting many requests from trolls trying to get her to do things that could make her look appalling. There was always a risk of not being responsive to followers, but she'd learned the hard way that if she responded to everything, she could end up without control of her narrative. The internet was a seductive place. The excitement of increasing viewership and subscribers subsided like a drug that wore off. Only another round of likes could boost one's feelings of self-worth.

Erica was a beautiful and clever girl, but her self-doubt kicked in during her vulnerable early morning hours. There were others she saw as prettier, smarter, and more creative. *How could she compete for attention without reducing herself to the absurd and comical?* After two years of producing content, she was starting to get laser-focused on her intentions, and she chastised herself for being pulled into an internet rat hole by a follower. She dragged the video clips to her recycle bin and pondered how to start over. She didn't have much time, promising new clips every Thursday. It could be a grueling schedule, and she'd learned always to have several ideas in progress, but this week, her attention had been elsewhere.

She'd received a call from one of her mother's neighbors who said she'd left her apartment door open and wandered off. Her mother was almost seventy. Erica was the only child of Peter and Dorothy Evans. Her parents had been in their forties when she was born. She'd been their "miracle" child, conceived after years of failed attempts to start a family and as her mother had been approaching menopause. Her father had passed away two years ago, and she was having to finally admit to herself what she'd been trying to ignore for a year; her mother was slipping into a haze of dementia or Alzheimer's. All she knew was she hadn't been the same after losing her spouse of forty years.

Erica had lost valuable production time as she drove to her mother's neighborhood in north Houston and maneuvered through the network of streets looking for her mother. She finally found her, walking near the Kroger grocery store. Parking her car, she approached her mother.

"Hey, Mom." The older woman, with faded beauty and sadness in her eyes, sparked to life when she saw her daughter.

"Erica, you didn't tell me you were coming."

"What are you doing here?"

Her mother looked around. Confusion washed over her face. "I... I... I don't know. Where am I?"

It pained Erica to see her mother like this. The vibrant, loving mother who'd been overly protective of her as a child was a shell of the woman she used to be. At first, she'd thought it was related to grief over losing her husband, but her mother's condition was getting worse, not better, after time to process the loss.

"I love you, sweetie."

"I love you, too, Mom. Should we get you home?" The roles of mother and daughter were reversed, and Erica lovingly guided her mother into the passenger seat of her Toyota Corolla.

In the early morning hours, Erica was trying to make sense of her jumbled emotions. Tony had put two rally posters on their dining room table when he got home, and she wondered how important it was to him to embrace the political path he started on by attending the event. They didn't talk politics. Their days were filled with sex, play, food, and socializing. She wasn't a big fan of Jester; he leered at her when they were in the same room. She didn't mention it to Tony because he didn't seem to notice, and she knew they'd been friends since high school. There were battles not worth fighting if she wanted to preserve her relationship with her boyfriend.

She hadn't told him much about her mother. Fortunately, the few times they'd been to her home for dinner, her mother's condition wasn't obvious. She liked Tony and kept encouraging her daughter to think about "settling down; don't wait to have children so you can enjoy them for as long as you can." Erica hadn't felt the baby clock ticking yet, and she hadn't discussed children with Tony. It seemed too soon in their relationship.

She wasn't ready to share her mother's uneven behavior with Tony. They'd only been dating for ten months, and she didn't want to scare him away. *Would he think she was going to get Alzheimer's and leave her before it became an issue?* She didn't know why she thought Tony would bolt. Maybe it was because he was forty and had never been married. None of his prior relationships had lasted more than three years. Her father had been a devoted and caring husband until the day he died of a massive heart attack, so her family history didn't give her a reason for her distrust; so why was she so hesitant with Tony?

She opened up a blank document and started to type. *What did she want for her channel? Her life? What were her goals? How could she get there?* There had to be more to life than this. She started making a list and hoped something on it would give her a sense of direction.

∎

"Do not despair! The Tribunals are taking longer than expected because of how far-reaching the crimes are against our great country. Do not let this delay discourage you. All nationalists will have their voices heard. The court must be fair and impartial in conducting the trials to rid our nation of this filth. The courts recognize that while extensive evidence supports these crimes against humanity, there still needs to be equality in court conduct and process. It is possible that some of these criminals, facing their crimes, have accused innocents as retaliation. It is exciting to see the world being restored! The edicts of 1776 will return! The Constitution of the United States will be restored. Those who have been undermining and destroying our democracy are the ones about to be destroyed. Respect the word. You are being misled. – R."

■

"Are you sure there isn't another doctor I can talk to?" Jamiel was consulting a patient with a kidney disease. "I mean, they say you should always get a second opinion."

"Of course." He opened a drawer in the exam room and extracted a paper from a page divider within the drawer. "Here's a list of clinics and medical doctors in the area specializing in nephrology." When he saw the confused look, he added, "They focus on kidney health."

The patient took the paper, and Jamiel stood up to leave the room. "Be sure to confirm they accept your insurance, or you could be looking at a hefty bill."

The medical system in the United States needed fixing, but that wasn't Jamiel's problem. He was trying to cure people, not the system.

"If you'd like to continue your treatments here, you can schedule at the reception desk."

It was hard to know if the request for a second opinion was because he was a Black doctor or if the patient was genuinely interested in hearing another medical professional's guidance on treating his condition. Jamiel tried not to take it personally, yet subtle comments and queries had followed him his whole life. It wasn't hard to develop an internal dialogue about it being because he was Black. Too many times, it was at the root of queries. He wasn't paranoid; some older patients had flat-out stated that they wanted to talk to a White doctor. Younger patients were more subtle, but race views were passed down from generation to generation. *How was it going to stop?* He'd gotten criticism from his own family when he brought home a White woman, the woman who ultimately became his wife. He hadn't thought about pursuing a relationship with anyone. He'd fallen for the inquisitive documentarian with a love of Belgian waffles and the Macy's Day Parade. She just happened to be White.

He looked at his roster. One more person to see at his office. He would stop by the hospital on his way home to check on several patients who'd taken a turn for the worse and required more monitored care. He could prescribe the best medicine available but couldn't control how closely his patients would follow his advice. Patients with diabetes and high blood pressure who didn't take steps to control either one were usually the ones needing escalated care. During medical school, he'd seen patients who continued to smoke even after they'd undergone disfiguring surgeries to combat cancer. He guessed sugar was no different, with an allure that overpowered the logic of eating healthy. He'd watched enough patients to know it was difficult to shake addictions.

It didn't take long to visit his hospitalized patients, and he was grateful they were in stabilized condition. He even signed off on the release of one for the following morning.

He removed his white lab coat and draped it on the passenger seat of the car before slipping behind the wheel of his 8-Series convertible BMW. It was a coat that defined him and let the world know his place at the hospital, but at the end of the day, he was ready to be husband and father, Jamiel. As a doctor, he was always on call for his patients, but he defined boundaries the best he could.

He left the top up on the car and pulled out of the Cedars-Sinai parking garage onto South Robertson, and within a few turns, he was on Sunset Boulevard, making his way home to Pacific Palisades.

CHAPTER 19

The Dom was in the middle of a Twitter tirade, stoking the fires of his re-election campaign. "The false news is lying to you!" He'd been sending this type of message even before running for his first election. It was extremely useful to establish his own narrative.

"Critical race theory is flawed and should not be taught in our schools. It undermines our democracy." He flipped to his favorite topic. "Our southern borders are fortified with the new wall, and my program is unprecedentedly successful!

"If we do not protect our rights, liberals will destroy everything." The Dom recognized the importance of creating fear. It paralyzed people and got them focused on one thing. He smiled as he read through his tweets.

"Don't let the Radical Left take our democracy."

"We must fight the forces of evil ready to steal our sovereign rights!"

He chose his words with intention. He didn't care which message his followers focused on; all were designed to rile up a sense of urgency and fear that only he could address. He was determined to keep his place in the White House for years to come.

It was another sleepless night. He'd gotten up to relieve himself. When returning from the bathroom, his phone had been within easy reach and distracted him from falling asleep again. He watched as people liked his comments. He smiled when he saw followers attacking each other verbally over remarks made. Anyone who made any negative comments directly to The Dom was immediately removed. It was censorship at its finest. The Dom got to control the dialogue, and he rewarded those who were his most adamant supporters with a limited number of reposts. He also enjoyed launching what he liked to think of as "Twitter grenades" and sit back and watch the aftermath. It was a win-win all around. He built a mass following of people who either loved or detested him. He dug the trenches deeper and sat back to watch the show.

He didn't care what the polls said. He was going to win re-election. Never underestimate the power of celebrity. His opponent was a lifer politician who knew how the government worked and how to turn the wheels of administrative output, but he lacked the ability to make it sexy. *Blah, blah, infrastructure. Blah, blah, debt ceiling. Nothing sexy about that.* However, Dom knew how to rile up an audience, and many channels were willing to play along.

"That stupid dumb fuck Larry Stevens is asleep at the wheel. There's no way he's going to win. No energy."

The Dom switched on the bank of televisions in his private office and watched the news feeds with interest. If he got bored, he could call Fox News and have a live microphone at his disposal. They say the president is the Leader of the Free World. They had it wrong; he was the leader of the airwaves. He got to dictate the narrative, and he would squash anyone who disagreed with his statements. He was where he was supposed to be, adored by millions and the power of the U.S. presidency at his fingertips. It wasn't his fault that all his predecessors hadn't wielded their power more effectively. They tried to adhere to a set of standards put in place two hundred years ago. The internet, computers, and instant news weren't even in existence when the country was founded. With the advances in technology came algorithms and ad sales. The big money was being made in the background, with discontent fueling the fire. He just had to strike the proverbial match to set the kindling ablaze. He wasn't moving out of the White House any time soon. He'd have four more years and ensure he would have more after that as well.

His eyes darted from screen to screen, reading news banners. He smiled. He was being discussed on eight of the ten shows, and the other two were on commercials. It was going to be a good day.

■

Tony pulled into the gun shop parking lot when he saw no other parked cars. It looked like he could have the clerk's full attention and ask about putting together a kit. He didn't want a slew of other gun owners overhearing his conversation. He didn't mind if the store employee knew how little he understood about the setup; he guided customers through purchases every day. It was the gun-carrying and proud-of-it Texans he didn't want to be privy to his questions.

The bell on the door jingled as he entered, and the smell of wood and metal greeted his senses. There was a lure to the shop, and he could understand the appeal of exploring various options for gun ownership. It was empowering to think about how a gun could be used to hunt wild game and protect one's property. It was taking a stand for the things one believed in: defending one's home and country as well as providing sustenance for oneself and one's family.

"Welcome back!" The same man from before was behind the counter. "As I recall, you were looking at this." He reached for the AR-15 on the rack behind him and placed it on the counter. Tony had only been in the store about fifteen minutes during his last visit over two weeks ago, and it impressed him that the man remembered.

"Yeah, that's the one." Tony touched the stock of the weapon. "Do you know what a kit is?" As soon as he asked the question, he mentally kicked himself. Of course, the owner would know.

The clerk was unfazed by the question and smiled. "There are lots of options for putting together a kit." *Nice.* The clerk didn't make him feel stupid, just inquisitive. "What are you thinking about?"

"I'm not sure. Some friends and I are going to do some training."

"Target practice? Something else?"

Tony wasn't sure what to share. He was still new to the group that identified as a militia, and something inside him made him hesitant to share details with Erica.

"Proper gun handling, defense training, stuff like that."

"Smart move. Too many people buy guns and don't take the steps to understand them. It's more than aiming at a paper target."

Tony let out a sigh of relief. He felt a sense of trust for the seasoned clerk and didn't question his recommendations.

"Generally, a kit consists of a variety of items. The basics are a rifle, handgun, knife, and vest. From there, you can add any number of things: holster, headgear, including night vision goggles, more body armor, sights for your rifle…actually, there are lots of modifications for your rifle."

Tony nodded and mentally tried to picture the items being mentioned. The man behind the counter started collecting various items and placing them on the countertop alongside the AR-15. It didn't take long to cover the glass top and obstruct the view of the items below.

"Don't let this overwhelm you. You can always start with a phased approach. Plus, we offer payment plans."

The Texas Freedom Fighters group had been discussing fortifying themselves to protect the history of Houston and their state, along with the country, if threatened. Tony loved Texas. It had been his home for his entire life, and he'd been raised to be proud of his five-generation-long heritage. His family had been in Texas since before the Civil War and fought hard to conserve the Confederacy.

"How much for all of this?" He watched the clerk check tags and enter prices into a hand-held calculator.

"You'll also want some ammunition. I suggest you start with 1000 rounds. None of this does you any good if you can't fire your weapons."

The older man finished entering the last number and held out the calculator. The price displayed was more than three month's salary. "We also have that payment plan if you want. We call it 'carry now, pay later.'"

Tony hoped his surprise at the number on the calculator hadn't shown on his face. "That's more than I can do right now."

"No problem." The clerk paused. "How about if I take care of the sales tax for you? I can give you interest-free payments for a year." He tapped on the calculator and held it out again with a reduced number. "This is the monthly payment amount."

Tony pondered for a moment. They were scheduled for training in two weeks, and he wanted time to get comfortable with the items before attending. Showing up with new, fresh, out-of-the-box items wasn't exactly how he wanted to establish his place in Texas Freedom Fighters.

"I can make that work. I'll take it." Tony felt a rush of excitement.

"Great choice. You're going to be really happy. Let me get the paperwork started."

An hour later, Tony emerged from the store carrying a large canvas duffel bag with the store emblem emblazoned on the side. The assistant had thrown in the bag for free to consolidate everything for easy carrying. Tony was grateful for the bag, even if it did broadcast the contents. He put it inside the cab, hesitant to leave it in the bed of the truck. As he drove home, he could smell a mix of the metal, oil, and plastic of the contents beside him. Generally, he hated shopping, but this was different. This was empowering. This gave him a sense of purpose.

He drove the remaining distance to his home. Tony pulled the canvas duffel out of his vehicle and entered the apartment he shared with Erica. He wasn't sure what he wanted to tell her about his purchase. They weren't married, and it was his money. They kept their finances separate, and he didn't know how much money she had other than she was starting to develop a following online, which apparently could make someone money. He didn't understand much about what she did as a side hustle from her salon job, but she always looked great and made time for him, so he was happy.

He tucked the dark bag into the back of the closet, under the portion of the rod that contained his clothes. Erica's side of the closet was stuffed full, and she rarely slid the door on his side open. When they first moved in together, they'd had an epic fight when she'd cleaned out space for her things and thrown out his favorite red plaid shirt. She didn't know that he'd worn it the last time he'd gone hunting with his father before the older man died of lung cancer. She unwittingly tossed the item that connected him to his father when he wore the shirt. She climbed into the dumpster behind their complex and opened the various bags until she found the missing shirt. He hugged her when he saw her splattered with spaghetti and smelling like rancid food but holding the coveted item. They'd showered together, sex repairing the damage of their fight, and from that point on, she didn't throw out anything of his without asking first.

He would find a way to tell her about the contents of the duffel bag soon. He wasn't confident in what to say because he wasn't exactly sure what it meant to be part of Texas Freedom Fighters yet. One thing was for sure: he knew he was taking the right steps to preserve his and his family's history. He was sure she'd understand why that was important to him.

■

Leon devoured the latest post from R. He began seeing himself as a disciple of R, spreading the gospel. His life hadn't had much meaning before he found the postings, and now he felt reborn. R was a nationalist fighting evil from within the corrupt government, which needed to be restored to the prior vision of the Founding Fathers.

He'd expanded on R's posts, and when the information shared was not very detailed, Leon interpreted the messages with information he'd read in other comments. He was putting the puzzle pieces together. Leon was the chosen one; he was there to spread the word. Restoring democracy was on his watch. R had confirmed that The Dom was a prophet of the highest level, and Leon was determined to be one of his most devoted supporters. No one could tell him otherwise, and his growing group of followers reinforced the critical role he was taking in the dissemination of information. For too long, false narratives were circulated by the government, which wanted to control the masses. He was done with being one of the sheep following mindlessly.

He pressed record and started his assessment. "You are being misled! Respect the word of R. He knows of what he speaks. There are still many among us who have not learned of the atrocities being conducted in the underbelly of our nation. The High Court Tribunal is reversing these wrongs. Educate your neighbors, your friends, and your co-workers. As more people awaken to understand the threat to our country and democracy, they will join with us to preserve and protect our given rights outlined in the Constitution of the United States. Big government and corporations have eroded our rights, and we need to reset the wrongdoings and restore the nation to the pure form of democracy as proclaimed in 1776. The Rainstorm is coming. We will no longer stay idle as our greatness is diminished to a flickering light that can be blown out with one tiny whisper."

R had been silent for almost a week, but more raindrops had been posted earlier in the day. Leon felt giddy when he saw the words. He had been like a heroin addict going into withdrawal with R's silence.

"If you are a follower, you do not stand alone. You are like so many other Americans: the clerk in the store who made your coffee this morning, a librarian, your neighbor sitting next to you in church, your eye doctor, and so many more that cannot be identified by their appearance. Until you disclose your allegiance to R, you look like all the other sheep, being herded by controllers who do not have your interests at heart. People may call you crazy because they do not understand. They have not been awakened to the wrongdoings YET! The exploiters who manipulate and rule the world, who have been untouchable until now, need to experience retribution for their crimes against you. With R's nationalism and selflessness to spread these raindrops, the time is now to learn about these atrocities. These monsters among us can no longer abuse children without facing their day of reckoning. You know that the secret dwellers of the Deep State are about to be exposed. Dominic Coronet is bringing justice and restoring our great nation. He is the only one able to break through the chains of government to destroy the system from within. He is here to protect you from a damned and plundered society. You know that there will always be a confrontation of good and evil that cannot be avoided as evil is once again relegated to return to the depths of Hell, and good will triumph in the end. You know the Rainstorm is coming to wash away sins and evil. Nationalism is about to be restored. You will know your allies and the others who unwittingly support the elite with their ignorance. It is time to be prepared and to fight for our sovereignty. Believe in the power you possess. Believe in the word of R."

Leon stopped the recording and replayed the visual. It was perfect. He published the post and smiled. He had performed his duty. He had delivered on his purpose in life.

CHAPTER 20

There was no need to involve Maxwell Hovick. The less he knew, the better. The Dom had summoned several key players to help secure his win in November. He had found a former CIA operative and a former FBI agent, both looking for ways to assist the president. "The Cleaners," as he boastfully referred to them, were to clear the path to victory. The Dom transferred a sizable sum to an account, giving them a wide berth to complete their objectives.

"Find anything you can to discredit Larry Stevens. He can't be as squeaky clean as he claims to be. I'm sure he's got some skeleton in his closet. A mistress or two, a gambling addiction, a drug or alcohol problem. Find it!" The implication didn't need to be added: *If you can't find anything, make something up.*

The Dom knew that his campaign could benefit from any rumor made about Stevens, and as long as it couldn't be traced back to the president or his team, it would cast doubts in the voters' minds. Even if it were ultimately revealed as false or inaccurate, the damage would be done. They could keep the Stevens campaign spinning on defense mode for the months before the election. The name of the game was to discredit the other candidate in any way that would bolster the Coronet ticket.

The former FBI employee was updating The Dom. The president couldn't remember the man's name and wasn't motivated to ask. If anyone fucked up, he'd be able to swear under oath that he didn't even know his name.

"We've infiltrated the Stevens campaign headquarters with an informant who has direct access to the senator. We're tracking his whereabouts and plans. We're doing everything possible to ensure he's perceived as unreliable."

"I don't need the details. Just keep the doubts circulating in the press. There's no reason Stevens should pose a threat in November. We're going to win this election!"

"Of course, sir. There is nothing that gives us concern."

"Good, good. That's what I want to hear."

The CIA retiree chimed in, "We've bugged key locations, as well as tapped into Stevens's phone."

The Dom knew these actions abused his power as the president, but he didn't care. The end justified the means. Anything they could learn to undermine Stevens and ensure he held onto the presidential office was acceptable. No one was going to deprive him of more time in the White House.

∎

Casey read through his article one more time, looking for any typos or enhancements. He'd written parts in a fevered pitch, trying to capture everything clearly and accurately. Other sections had taken time as he cross-referenced and fact-checked his statements. Internet posts did not adhere to the same rigors of validation as his work. It distressed him that anyone could post content without any basis of truth and that content could seep insidiously around the depths of the World Wide Web. The irony wasn't lost on him that he and his peers were the ones coming under attack as writing a false narrative and being manipulated by an imaginary puppeteer.

He knew nothing was perfect. *The National Times* depended on advertising, just like the internet sites providing clickbait for prolonged user engagement. The paper at least appeared, in his observation, to operate with the intent to be ethical and fair.

Where is the line for morality? At what point was a post entertainment, and at what point was it a dangerous manipulation to make money? Casey wasn't sure he had an answer. Instead, he focused on what he could do: write articles showing how conspiracy theories were propagating at a fast incubation rate and how they were having a negative impact on families across the nation.

It amazed him how the stories got intertwined, and certain factions believed elements of some theories but not parts of others. At the core of all of them was an authoritative narrative that gave people a sense of security even as it espoused the demise of the world as he knew it.

He'd been observing a growing rift with people doubling down on their stances online. He'd found numerous instances of friendships being severed and family members not talking to each other anymore. There was lots of name-calling and destruction, with one group emerging as the most rabid: the followers of R. Casey had found the original posts, but to date, the identity of R remained a mystery, even with a plethora of predictions made online. This was a story to watch closely, even if it did make him incredibly anxious about the future state of the United States of America.

Pam, Asher, and a few other Stanford students departed the 19th Avenue BART station and quickly became engulfed in a sea of Black Lives Matter protesters near Frank Ogawa Plaza. It didn't take long to feel the excitement and urgency in the chants echoing throughout the large crowd. Large Black Lives Matter flags were ruffling in the wind, along with various signs. "Stop Lynching Black People," "I just wanna make it home!" and "Equal Rights for All" were some placards around them.

"Look who's here!" a woman next to Pam said out loud. "This feels different."

"What do you mean?" Pam wasn't sure who had the clout that the woman referenced.

"Girl, look aroun' ya." EVER'BODY here. Asians, Latinos, and even White people have all come out. That's a sign of change!"

Pam was thankful she'd taken the time from her studies. She could sense this was history in the making. She dreamed of a day when both sides of her heritage accepted her in a broad sense.

Someone with a megaphone started a call and response. "Whose lives matter?"

"Black Lives Matter!" roared the crowd.

The chant continued for several blocks and faded as people slowly trudged toward the square. Pam had never been in a gathering this large. People around her were smiling and conferring with each other in solidarity. There was a positive sense that their presence was being acknowledged, and the injustices from the past were being aired publicly.

KRON 4 News had their van parked nearby, highlighting how the protest had sparked the attention of traditional media outlets.

Pam's textbook remained unopened in her backpack. The naivete that she would have been able to study had disappeared as soon as the group had boarded the northbound Caltrain car, filled with others from the South Bay making a pilgrimage to the East Bay. The hum on board was palpable and exciting. She'd made a decision that her studies could wait.

∎

Brad Taylor had been assigned to the Black Lives Matter protest. He was paired with a dumb shit named Andrew. When he'd subtly hinted at the mandates of Whites Restore, Andrew had not responded. Clearly, he was a lost soul. As a proud member of Whites Restore, Brad wanted to be vocal and spread their goals. However, the elders had advised that he keep his affiliation on the down low. The elders had recommended that he join the police force, and he'd committed to getting his badge. "Keep your friends close and your enemies closer" was their mantra. "You can promote our agenda from within; you will find your like brethren and restore our place in history when the time is right."

Brad and Andrew were dressed in riot gear, and so far, the protesters were marching peacefully. It was a mixed group with mostly Blacks, but as Brad saw it, a bunch of White traitors had joined them as well. Didn't they see how they were being hurt by the rights the protesters demanded? There was no win in the end for Whites if they gave everything to the filth invading their cities.

Brad and Andrew were assigned to stand alongside the march, and it irritated him that the other officer smiled and responded to the protesters who yelled out their thanks. He looked around for anything that could provide him a way to help Lessers transcend. He'd felt empowered the day he shot the man at the store, and he wanted to continue with the cleansings.

"Thanks for being here, man! Being able to express ourselves is an American right!"

Brad wasn't sure how this helped promote the mission of Whites Restore. They'd been standing on the sidewalk for almost two hours, and the sea of people didn't appear to end anytime soon. He felt agitated, with lots of pent-up emotions he couldn't display. *This was bullshit. Why hadn't they been ordered to disperse the mob?*

One of the protesters slipped in front of the two officers and fell to the ground hard, losing her grip on her water bottle. Andrew had moved forward to help the young woman, and Brad watched the water bottle roll toward his foot. Andrew's back was to him, and he saw an opportunity. "You! You there, down on the ground." When the puzzled group around him didn't respond, he yelled even louder. "NOW! DOWN on the ground." He clutched his weapon and stepped forward. A group of protesters sank to the ground while the sea of others continued their movement forward. *Would one of them be armed?*

"What are you doing?" Andrew had turned, and Brad continued, adrenaline fueling his actions.

"Someone threw a water bottle at me." He turned to the group on the ground.

"Who threw this?"

The group looked at each other, perplexed, and didn't respond.

"Face this wall, now!"

The group, unsure how to navigate from a seated position, slowly stood and went to the wall. Brad touched his communicator and summoned a van. "I have detained several protesters who were instigating a riot."

"Man, this is uncool. They didn't do anything wrong," Andrew pleaded.

"You didn't see it; they were creating public unrest."

Brad began to bind the hands of those in the group with zip ties, read them their rights, and pushed them down to the sidewalk again. He warned several of the White protesters and allowed them to rejoin the gathering. As misguided as they were, they were still moving toward enlightenment. Their skin color showed him they were almost ready to transcend, whether they knew it or not.

He looked down at the seven Blacks and one Asian remaining, and he knew he'd done the right thing to restore greatness. While he hadn't helped anyone transcend, at least these people would pay the price of undermining democracy. They had to remember their place in the world.

CHAPTER 21

"What the hell, Tony?! You just ruined my shot."

Erica was frustrated. Her latest video wasn't flowing easily, and she'd already counted eight cuts that would be needed to splice together a working version of her opening. The reality was that Tony walking behind her hadn't ruined anything, just given her another reason to start over. Some days were like this when nothing seemed to go right. She was on a posting schedule and didn't have the luxury of time. She was due at the Snip N Sip Salon in forty minutes but still didn't have much usable content.

She stopped the recording, took a deep breath, and let it out slowly. She looked at Tony, his expression apologetic. "Sorry. I shouldn't have yelled at you. I'm just anxious about this video."

"Why? You make them every week. You're a natural."

Erica smiled at the compliment. "I don't know why I'm so nervous. It's just I'm really close to 20,000 followers, and I'm trying to get more sponsorships."

"Don't worry. If there's one thing I know, you're amazing."

Tony guessed he wasn't a very good boyfriend. He rarely watched her videos, but she always looked good when he came home, which he rationalized as watching her. *Why did he have to view a recording when he had the live, in-person version to talk with daily?*

Tony was happy to have the day off from crawling under homes and smelling like crap by the end of the day. He was fresh out of the shower and looking forward to some time alone.

"You goin' to the salon today?"

Erica nodded. "Yes, I thought I could squeeze this in before my shift, but I guess it'll be better if I try again when I get home." She stood from her makeshift studio and turned off the light diffuser. "Can't hurt to go in early. I told my manager I'd help her stock the hair color shipment that arrived yesterday." She picked up her purse and dug out her car keys. "See you tonight." She gave him a quick peck of a kiss and left their apartment.

Tony looked out the window and watched Erica leave before heading to their bedroom. He felt a little guilty that he was hiding this from Erica. He would tell her soon.

He pulled the heavy canvas duffel from the closet and unpacked the items onto the bed. The AR-15 was unassembled to fit in the bag, and he placed the pieces on top of the striped bedspread. Next, he pulled out a Glock handgun and leg holster, camouflage shirt, and pants individually wrapped in plastic, which he tore off before adding them to the pile. They felt stiff, and they smelled like new clothes. It probably wouldn't hurt to toss them in the washing machine to remove the creases that broadcast the items were brand new. Next out of the duffel was a protection vest with a tag dangling from the armpit. He'd also added a sight for the AR-15, knowing how useful the one on his hunting rifle had been when lining up a shot.

Speaking with Jest and King at their last lunch at Whataburger, he learned Texas Freedom Fighters intended to respond, not incite. He appreciated that approach. If he did find himself in a response mode, the sight would be helpful.

He'd also learned that King's first name was Joe. Joe King; joking. *What parent thought to do that to their child?* Along with Lester the Jester, they were a motley crew, considering Ralph also had a double meaning to his name. Tony was thankful his name didn't conjure anything beyond Anthony or a high-roller.

He fished out the boxes of ammo and the spare cartridge for the handgun. He wasn't sure what to do next. The guns were new and didn't need cleaning. He could smell the metal and gun oil used to ensure the components didn't rust or lock up during use. There was something comforting about the smell. He picked up the handgun. He'd never fired one before, and the store clerk had given him a coupon for a free hour with an instructor at the shop's on-site range. He aimed it at the closet door, using his left hand to cradle the butt as he'd seen in many action films. "You comin' at me?" he said, mimicking the line from a movie he'd seen recently. He added his own thoughts, "You can't steal my history." His reflection in the mirrored closet door looked confident and in control.

Tony was excited, looking at everything laid out on the bedspread. The smell of gun metal, new clothes, along with the boxes containing ammunition gave him a sense of security. He could control his destiny, his future. When the statue had been removed from Sam Houston Park, he'd felt helpless. Being part of something bigger, something of substance, could help correct the wrongs being inflicted against Texan history. He liked that he was taking steps to preserve his heritage.

■

"American nationalists! The High Court Tribunal is progressing in restoring our great democracy, but they need your help! There will be a time when you'll need to stand up for your rights and your freedom. You will need to identify who is a true nationalist and who has sold their souls to the Devil. Satan worshipers have rejected God and instead embraced a life of debauchery. Until now, they have been able to commit heinous crimes without retribution. They have raped and killed helpless children, stripped them of their innocence, and destroyed their futures. It is time for these egregious scumbags to pay the piper. The destruction of the faction committing crimes against humanity is looming! Trust the process and know you can help restore our great civilization! Follow the anointed one! POTUS is leading the charge. Nothing can stop the momentum. The tipping point is upon us. If you don't believe me, do your own research. Investigate the truth beyond the false news narrative that pollutes our airwaves. Take off your blindfold and see the world as it is! Only you can ensure that corruption is coming to an end. Respect the word. You are being missed. – R."

■

Larry Stevens tried to recall the aide who accused him of groping her in a hallway. He was pretty sure he would have remembered something like that. He wondered how much money she was offered to fabricate the story. He sighed as he realized he was jaded after years in politics. Money made the world go round, and the aide's accusations must have been funded. He hadn't been inappropriate. He knew the consequences and had seen many men before him fall from grace.

Larry consulted his campaign manager. "How do we address this? The election is in two months."

"I'm conducting a quick poll to get a pulse check on the information. If enough voters don't seem to care, we don't respond. If it's creating a risk to your election, we'll craft a message to address it."

"Keep me posted. These are the critical weeks, and I don't trust the other side. If there's one thing I've learned during the Dominic Coronet presidency, it's that any actions previously considered political decorum got tossed out the window. I don't want to make the same mistake the prior Democrat running for office made by believing that morality and respect would beat out bravado and bluster."

Even as he voiced it out loud, he recognized he was old school, a dog unable to learn new tricks. He still had faith in the American public that they would see the value in procedure and structure. He had an extensive social media team in place to craft his messages across a variety of social platforms, and he blamed the demise of the political structure on snippets and sound bites. The American people seemed to have lost any sense of an attention span and ability for critical thinking. Even as he thought it, he knew he wasn't being fair. The system was inherently broken by lobbyists, manipulations, promises, and packaging of agendas to push through legislation. He missed the days when members from both parties would argue their agendas on the House floor and eat lunch together while on break. Partisanship and compromise had become bad words. Each side dug a line in the sand, with anyone who crossed that line viciously persecuted verbally and at the ballot box.

He saw his run for the presidency as his last chance to save the country from reality TV stunts and shallow promises. The Dom didn't seem to care that there were a variety of internal and external threats looming on the horizon that could destroy their democracy: an aging population, cheap labor abroad, climate change, and a massive debt that had hit a tipping point. For a party that espoused financial responsibility, the Republicans certainly had done a lot to run it into the ground, growing the deficit to a number with so many zeros at the end that it was hard to fathom.

He would remain optimistic that the American people had grown tired of the chaos of the last four years and were looking for the political arena to return to a more neutral state. He knew that's what he longed for, and he knew he wasn't alone. Yet he wasn't ready to count his win yet. Emotional responses could be blown out of proportion and could derail any campaign. That's why this last-minute accusation from an aide about something that happened over a decade ago shouldn't and couldn't be taken lightly. He just wished he knew who was encouraging her to take aim now to dislodge his campaign.

He poured himself a neat whiskey and sunk into his leather chair. He could see himself winning the election. He closed his eyes and pictured the news outlets reporting the final results. He'd been using the law of attraction and manifesting techniques daily for months. He could feel his win. It was just a matter of days before all would be revealed.

CHAPTER 22

"I can't eat another bite." Erica pushed the pizza box away to avoid the temptation of another slice. She didn't eat much in front of Tony. She hid her binge eating from him. She wasn't as bad as she used to be. Previously, she'd forced herself to vomit the excessiveness of her indulgences, a trick she'd learned from a former roommate. She hated the vileness of vomit in her mouth, erasing the flavors of the food she'd just eaten, and she switched to laxatives as a way to move the food through her system quickly.

Tony was flipping through his Facebook feed. "Jester invited me to join a private group."

Erica didn't like Jest, and she wasn't sure what group he would be a part of, considering, in her experience, he didn't seem to do much other than watch sports. Maybe it was a fantasy football bracket.

"You know how much I hate seeing Texas history being erased."

She'd heard Tony reference this before when Confederate statues were being removed from parks around Houston, and she nodded in affirmation.

"I found a group that is dedicated to preserving our history."

"Like creating an archive?"

"No, to keep the statues in their place and to preserve our history."

Erica wasn't sure why the statues needed to stay. They just looked like a lot of archaic metal to her. *Wouldn't it be nicer if there was a fountain or a garden instead?*

"How ya gonna do that?"

"We're going to assist the police to keep order and peace whenever there is social unrest."

"What do you mean?"

"I mean, we're going to be trained on how to support the police and, if needed, our troops. Like the National Guard."

"Trained how?"

Tony took a deep breath. He didn't want to hide his purchases any longer.

"We're part of a militia."

"Tony, are you crazy? You could get shot."

"No, no, sweetie. The goal is to protect, not to fight."

"But guns mean things could escalate out of control."

"No, they mean things will remain in control. We're only showing up to defend. We won't fire our weapons unless fired upon."

"Do you hear that? Fired upon?! I don't want you to get hurt." His heart warmed, grateful for the affirmation that he meant something to her. "Don't worry. We're attending military training this weekend."

"Military training? Did you join the military?"

Tony laughed. "No, not at all. Several ex-Army personnel are part of the group, and they will show us how to preserve and protect."

"I don't know, Tony. This makes me nervous."

He decided he wouldn't show her everything at once. Maybe the handgun was a place to start. If she saw the tactical gear, she might be frightened. He knew he would be safe with the correct gear and training. She'd be on board when she learned that, too.

◼

"It is time to take stock of your possessions and learn how to protect yourself when the Rainstorm comes. There is talk about the dollar being restored to the gold standard, and that standard is being redefined and enhanced by modern technology. The currency will have a different value after the High Tribunal has reestablished our Democracy. Buy NatCoin currency now to be prepared. Don't be caught waiting for your dollars to convert after the Rainstorm. Cryptocurrency will protect your assets and keep food on your table. Those who do not heed this advice will find themselves waiting for the uninformed masses of sheep stampeding to convert their funds. As with any transition of value, there will be a time of adjustment. This can be as smooth and effective as possible with more nationalists taking steps now. Protect your assets! Be prepared. Respect the word. You are being misled! – R."

◼

The sun was beginning to rise as Jamiel opened the garage door and backed his car out of his driveway near Sunset Boulevard in Pacific Palisades. He waited for the perimeter gate to slide open, and soon, navigated to the famous street that spanned the length of Los Angeles from downtown to the ocean. At various locations, he could see glimpses of the

Pacific Ocean, and he expressed internal gratitude that he was fortunate to live in the exclusive neighborhood that Whoopi Goldberg, Chris Rock, and Sugar Ray Leonard called home. He wasn't the only Black person, but he didn't have the same recognition they did. He was successful but not a known figure in the community, and several times, a police car had followed him as he turned onto his residential street. Even driving a BMW that cost six figures didn't make him immune to scrutiny. Many assumed it was stolen.

Leaving early, he could make it to Cedars-Sinai in about twenty minutes, a commute that would double in time the later he left. His first stop was the well-known research hospital to check on patients admitted for more extensive care.

He had a full schedule and opted to head south toward Malibu to connect with the freeway that would take him to the La Cienega Boulevard exit instead of meandering through the twists and turns of Sunset Boulevard. He could drive the famous stretch through Beverly Hills on his way home.

His cell phone rang, and it startled him. He was not expecting calls so early. His wife had still been sleeping when he'd left, and he'd spoken with the attending doctor on call that morning before he left the house. Nothing during that call had concerned him about his patients. Glancing at the dash, he was pleased to see Pammy's name and pressed the answer button on his steering column.

"Hey, Sweetie. How's my girl?"

"Oh, Dad, I'm sorry to bother you. I've been arrested."

"Arrested!? What do you mean? How?"

"I went to Oakland yesterday with friends to protest at a rally. We were detained for a while, and then they arrested me for disturbing the peace and inciting a riot."

Jamiel couldn't believe the accusations. His daughter was a bookworm, not a rebel. "Where are you now?"

"The Oakland Police Department. Dad, I'm scared. I got separated from my classmates and I don't know where they are. They weren't in the same cell as me."

"I'm on my way, Pammy. Hold tight."

Jamiel was grateful he hadn't passed the 405 South freeway connection, and within several miles, he was altering his route and driving towards LAX. First, he called the hospital and arranged to have someone else check on his patients. He decided to let his wife continue to sleep. There was no need to alarm her until he had more information. Getting the next flight to Oakland was his first priority after ensuring his patients were getting the care they needed.

Fifteen minutes later, he pulled into the short-term parking lot of the international airport. He located the airline with a flight on the departures board and headed to the ticket counter. It didn't matter how much the ticket would cost for a flight that left in forty-five minutes. He could afford it.

■

"The Rainstorm is coming. Here are the raindrops I can share today. The High Court Tribunals are concluding their trials, and the faction of elites that have been abusing the system are paying the price. Executions, the final and ultimate punishment for their wrongdoings, are underway. In order to preserve peace and order, there are temporary 'lookalikes' who are assuming the roles of the guilty disgraced until their transgressions become public knowledge. These are the true nationalists, stepping into positions as the horrific evil who have fallen with disgrace. Look at the attached photos. You can see how the lookalike is close enough to fool most people, but anyone who sees these images side by side can see the subtle differences. It won't be long before peace and order are restored to our great land. Evil will fall, and greatness will be before us. Dominic Coronet is leading the charge. Respect the word! You are being misled. – R."

■

Leon was thrilled. Dom Coronet was being broadcast, signing an executive order to allocate funds to build the wall along the southern perimeter of the country. During his proclamation, he had made a reference to R.

"I respect my word. I made a promise to the nationalists of this great country, and today, with the signing of this executive order, I have upheld that promise." Leon watched as The Dom scrawled his loopy signature across the bottom of the leather-encased sheet of paper and held up the document to a flurry of flashes as the media representatives captured the story for their broadcasts.

Was The Dom also the prophet R? Originally, Leon hadn't given a thought to the identity of R, happy to accept the high-level security clearance as a reason to stay anonymous and enough credibility to support the statements being posted. He'd been posting hundreds of videos breaking down the communications, and he was seeing how The Dom could be in the position with the highest security intel. It wouldn't surprise him.

Leon typed his query into the Google search box: *"Is R Dominic Coronet?"*

Clearly, he wasn't the only person making that assessment when Google auto-completed his question with predictive text. Leon clicked through the results and started reading. *"Dominic Reginald Coronet is R! He's using his middle initial to be discrete and to show those who follow his lead will see the truth of his identity."*

Leon couldn't believe he hadn't made that connection before. *Of course! R is The Dom!* Leon didn't need to read further. He'd done his research and knew in his heart that The Dom was the prophet R. The BeWarned site that hosted the first posts of R was chosen for the ability to remain truly anonymous. R, working from within the establishment, had to secure his identity to safeguard his position and ability to share information. He would undermine his presidency if anyone determined his identity. Leon knew why The Dom was being secretive. He remembered the first promise he'd read months earlier: "I guarantee you that what I tell you is the truth. You know this information is accurate. If you have doubts, do your own investigation. You will find that what I share is gospel. Respect the word. You are being misled. – R."

Taking his lead from R, Leon had hopped from one site to the next, most of them supporting the claims posted by R. There were some detractors in the mix. Still, mostly it appeared to be the false media trying to discredit R's posts as conspiracy theories and lies. Leon turned his back on the traditional news sites he'd relied on for years. He'd always liked Bobby Krenshaw on CNN, and yet it was becoming clear he hadn't been enlightened. He was operating using deceitful information. The false news was being manipulated by the faction, which was committing horrible crimes that Leon tried not to imagine. The thought of children being tortured and used for atrocious blood-drinking rituals was horrific.

Leon returned his attention to the television. As The Dom lowered the insignia-stamped folder and addressed the cameras before him, Leon watched intently, convinced that the president was talking directly to him. He knew that The Dom understood him and was sending him information through the broadcast.

"Changes are coming. We have allowed the liberal elite privilege for too long. Be prepared to fight for what is rightfully yours. Today is another step in restoring our great democracy by securing our country from illegal immigrants, criminals, and the filth who are trying to penetrate our borders. If they think they can enter our country, they are wrong. A storm is coming."

Leon scribbled the president's words on a piece of paper and scanned for raindrops; any hints of messages from R.

"Storm... penetrate... elite..."

Leon knew what it meant. The Dom was working from within the government to dismantle corruption, and he'd practically proclaimed he was R. His research, along with the messages from The Dom, showed it was clear that all of them were on a mission for God. Leon saw the importance of spreading the word. He relied on the webcam built into his laptop for his videos — nothing fancy, no special lighting. He didn't realize it unknowingly provided him with credibility by viewers who were turned off by anything too slick, something they attributed to the false narrative and the wealthy who could afford fancier equipment.

"Nationalists! Dominic Coronet just signed an executive order and has proclaimed what we already know; the liberal elite are raping and destroying children's lives for Satanic rituals. Changes are coming. We will need to fight to protect and preserve our great land. I am convinced The Dom is R. He said so himself today, acknowledging the need to 'respect the word.' Do your own research and join me. Be prepared to show your allegiance to our president and to fight for our sovereign rights. You are being misled no more."

He didn't edit the video, and it didn't take long to post the proclamation. Standing up, Leon started pacing the room. There had to be something more that he could do. He spent five to six hours daily combing through raindrops, looking for insights and confirmation. His research led him down a variety of paths, and each had a series of details that needed to be shared with the world.

Leon did not understand that algorithms served up additional sources to review every day and were designed to keep his attention on pages with a flow of paid advertisements. Leon formulated a more detailed and birds-eye view of the proselytizing of R each day without knowing the information that flowed in was based on his usage of the internet browser.

"God has brought me down this path. I know I am appointed. I am a disciple of R." Leon updated the tagline to his YouTube channel. He could feel it in his bones. Positive things were on the horizon. There was a way for the United States to be restored to its former glory. He took pride in knowing that he was one of the first followers of R and that he would be rewarded.

CHAPTER 23

"Holy shit, you've got to be kidding me?!" Casey read the news banner that popped up on his phone and clicked through to the extended article. "A suspect has been taken into custody after he stormed into Tickle Your Fancy Day Spa with an AR-15 rifle, proclaiming that he was there to release children from oppression that were being sold into sex slavery. The assault came as quite a surprise to a bridesmaid party that had reserved the entire spa for a day of relaxation and pampering before the wedding to be held tomorrow."

Casey wondered if that wedding would happen after the events of the day and continued reading. "The intruder, a man who appears to be in his late 50s, kept insisting that he was there to free the children. After terrorizing the staff at the spa and throwing open doors to each treatment and stock room, he finally admitted that maybe his information wasn't accurate. Internet rumors spread the belief that Tickle Your Fancy is a code for pedophiles to purchase young boys and girls for sex. It must have surprised the gunman only to find bridesmaids and mimosas. There wasn't even a male stripper on-site."

Casey smiled. It was easy to look for the levity of the situation, but his smile quickly faded. *How had this rumor even gotten traction?* Casey wondered about the psychology behind believing information found on the internet that pushed the boundaries of credibility. *Wouldn't law enforcement have shut down a sex ring if there were any substance to the rumors?* He'd already read about people making claims that John F. Kennedy, Jr. was alive and well, even though his plane had crashed near Martha's Vineyard decades ago. When asked about it, the response was that Junior was "laying low until he was ready to join as the running mate with Dom Coronet." Casey shook his head. "Don't tell Maxwell Hovick." The last time Casey had checked, Max was not only the vice president but the current running mate on the ticket with The Dom for the election weeks away. So why would the believers cling to such an absurd idea?

Casey decided to reach out to one of the believers posting on Twitter. In a few moments, @4MoreYears responded to his DM. "I saw JFK Jr. on a YouTube video. He said he'll be back in the public arena soon, but he's staying under the radar for now."

Casey typed his reply: "How can recording a YouTube video that anyone, including yourself, can watch, be considered 'under the radar?'"

The R devotee responded with a pat answer. "Do your research."

Casey stopped trying to make sense of it. He WAS doing his research. It seemed too convenient to resort to the handy phrase when something couldn't be explained. Casey had been looking into the messages of R for several months, and he was observing a growing, almost cult-like following. *Where was the critical thinking? Where was reason in the equation?* From everything he'd observed so far, anyone could be converted to the "church" of R. The scary part was there was no way to tell who you were engaging with. More ardent followers wore some type of R attire, whether it was a vinyl letter emblazoned across their T-shirts or a single letter pin on a lapel, and were starting to go public. Others, he was learning, remained quiet and behind the scenes. There were too many altercations with friends and loved ones who were still unenlightened.

Every day, he opened his work email to find a reader pleading for information on how to restore a friendship with someone "lost" to the prophecies of R. *Maybe R stands for rabbit hole?* He made light of the situation because, at his core, it terrified him. He could see the growing adoration and blind following of a group that encompassed both young and old, wealthy and poor, professionals and blue-collar individuals. To date, he hadn't identified any single stand-alone data point that would hone in on the appeal. Something resonated with people across the country, and he was determined to find out why.

■

"My daughter was arrested yesterday at a rally."

"Name?"

"Pamela Jackson."

"The charges against her have not been filed yet."

"What charges?"

"Says here that she was brought in for trying to instigate a riot."

"My daughter is a student at Stanford. That doesn't sound like her."

"Parents never really know their children, do they?"

"I know my daughter, and that's not who she is."

"Don't underestimate the mob mentality of a group."

"Can I see her?"

"For now, she's in a holding cell. The charges will need to be filed or dismissed by the end of the day. That will determine if you need to post bail or if she'll be released."

"Is there anyone I can talk to about the charges?"

"You'll be able to consult an attorney if charges are filed. For now, it's a matter of waiting to see what happens next."

The heavy Black clerk looked at Jamiel and softened slightly. She leaned in and lowered her voice. "Look, most of the time, kids are brought in to cool off. Since she has no priors, there's a good chance this won't be filed." She looked down at the paperwork and leaned closer to the counter, so her whisper could be heard.

"It looks like someone threw a water bottle, but no one can link it to anyone specific, so my money is on dismissal but I didn't tell you nothin,' hear?"

Jamiel nodded and stepped away from the plexiglass partitioned desk. He stepped outside and pulled out his cellphone. It didn't take long before Casey answered.

"Hey, what do you know about the arrests made at a protest?"

"I didn't think you had time to protest with that caseload of yours?"

"Not me. Pammy."

"Oh shit, dude. I'm sorry."

"A group of Stanford students came to Oakland yesterday to protest in a Black Lives Matter rally, and she was arrested."

"What are the charges?"

"Nothing's been filed yet."

"OK, that's good. Normally, if there were going to be filed, it would have happened fairly quickly. The fact that it's the next day is a good indicator they'll be dropped." Casey paused. "Of course, this is hypothetical. All jurisdictions have their own modus operandi, but generally, they must be charged within 48 hours or released."

"This could hurt her chances of getting into med school."

"Don't think about that right now. Focus on the fact that there's been nothing filed yet. It's a waiting game." Casey didn't share that the arrest could potentially create a record for Pam whether she was charged or not. They would cross that road later.

■

Pam sat in the jail cell and stewed at her predicament. They'd taken her backpack and, with it, her textbook and phone. She'd been granted her customary one call and had contacted her father. It comforted her that he knew where she was and was on his way. *He'd be able to help her, wouldn't he?*

She tried to concentrate. Closing her eyes, she worked her way around a mental image of the human body. Starting with the upper extremities, she ticked off the names. "Scapula, Clavicle, Humerus..." There wasn't anything funny about her situation. "Radius, Ulna, Scaphoid... Lunate, Triquetrum, Pisiform..." As she mentally worked her way around the body image in her mind, she counted on her fingers to ensure she remembered all thirty-two. "Hamate, Capitate, Trapezoid..." She certainly felt trapped, and it was hard to concentrate. She wondered how this would impact her current enrollment at Stanford and her future med school applications. Surely, Stanford wouldn't punish her for attending a protest; she'd only been walking with the other attendees. She still wasn't sure why she, along with the others around her, had been forced to the ground and ultimately arrested. Asher had been detained with her, but she noticed that several others, all White, had been allowed to rejoin the marching group. Seven had been arrested, all Black except for Asher, an Asian man.

They had been placed in different cells, and Pamela shared her confinement with a variety of other women, several of whom had been arrested with her. "Yo,' girl. Did yo' notice how whack this is? No surprise to me that us Black girls ended up here. Catch and release if you're White; arrest and detain if you're Black!"

Pamela nodded, afraid not to acknowledge the woman but not in the mood to engage in a conversation, either.

"Funny thing, tho... yo' a light-skinned girl. I bet ya have a lotta White in ya, but it just goes to show that no matter what, if there's just one drop of Black in ya, ya Black in the mind of these mofo's. No escaping that reality, mixed girl."

Pamela was used to not fitting in on either side of her extended family. Her father's family was upset that he didn't marry a Black woman, and her mother's family was upset that she didn't match to her full potential, whatever that meant. Her father was an Ivy League medical doctor. *Who did they expect their daughter to marry for more status?* She loved her grandparents. She pushed the feelings down, not wanting to see the shadows of racism within her family.

Over the years, the marriage was accepted when they attended in-person functions. However, Pam was pretty sure that comments were still made behind their backs. Her cousin had even shared once that there was a bet on when her parents would divorce. Somehow, her mother and father seemed immune to the chit-chat, and they'd focused on their immediate family and adored their daughter. Her father was proud of her accomplishments, and she thought he secretly was thrilled his daughter had chosen to follow in his foot-steps. *How was he going to react to her arrest?* Being tossed into a jail cell and not tucked away safely in her Stanford campus dorm room or library, she'd let him down. A lump filled her throat as she fought to keep the tears away. She'd seen too many television shows. She was afraid to appear vulnerable around the other women sharing her cell.

She sent a silent message to her father. "*Please get me out of here, and I promise I'll do better.*"

She released a deep sigh and started to mentally tick off the 206 bones in the human body. "Metacarpal 1, Proximal Phalange 1, Distal Phalange 1…" Anything to keep her mind occupied.

"Yo, mixed girl."

Pam tried to ignore the woman, but without her textbook or phone to look occupied, she came off as rude or hard of hearing. She knew the nickname was directed at her. She looked at the dark-skinned woman, dressed in cutoff jean shorts, a Hella Oakland T-shirt, and a pair of wannabe Chuck Taylor Converse shoes, and tried to smile.

"So, is yo' daddy White? Is that how you got that pretty light skin o' yo's?

"No." She kept her answer simple in hopes of ending the conversation. It didn't work.

"Yo' mama went lookin' for a well-hung Black man to make her sing in the bedroom? Let me guess, yo' was an accident? Bet no White woman ever plans on having a mix-race baby."

Considering how many rounds of IVF her parents had gone through before she was conceived, she knew she wasn't an accident, but there was no way she was going to share any information with the nosey girl.

"Yeah, some'n like that." She dropped the syllable, trying to mimic the talking style of her cellmate, not wanting to draw any more attention to herself. She was in a no-win situation. If she spoke "too White," she was a sellout to the brotherhood; if she spoke "too Black," she could alienate those in her White community. Pam had spent her whole life trying to fit in and played a balancing act; not too full of herself but not too dismissive, either. She had to work for what she had, but she'd noticed that was true for all her classmates, regardless of their skin tone. You didn't get into Stanford by not applying yourself. It didn't stop many people she knew from judging her for her choices. She hoped medical school would provide the only microscope she'd have to endure, but unless there was a major cultural shift in the United States, she knew where she lived. When she'd arrived at the protest, she'd felt optimistic. Sitting in a jail cell after doing nothing except be Black, she was feeling a wave of rage wash over her. So many years, she'd pushed down the comments she'd endured from both sides of her family, classmates, teachers, and now her cellmate. *Why did this have to be her narrative every day? Why couldn't she live her life like any other person? Scratch that, why couldn't she live her life like a White person?* The anger was welling up inside, and she tried to tamp it down.

She'd already endured being fingerprinted, photographed, and placed in a jail cell. She tried to shrink into the corner and avoid detection.

∎

"Mr. Jackson?" The desk clerk beckoned Jamiel from the chairs in the entranceway. "Your daughter is Pamela?" He nodded. "She's being charged with Penal Code sections 404, 409 and 415."

"What does that mean?" The numbers blurred in his head and, without context, meant nothing.

"She's being charged with riot and unlawful assembly, failure to disperse, and disturbing the peace."

"That's not my daughter." The clerk continued without acknowledging his statement. "Her arraignment will be tomorrow. You can post bail on her behalf, or she can stay detained until the hearing in the morning."

"How do I post bail?"

"Here's a list of bail bonds companies. We don't make any recommendations. You are responsible for investigating your options and the fees associated with these services." Jamiel took the list printed on both sides on a sheet of blue paper. "Do I need to post a bond, or can I pay you directly?"

The clerk looked at him and then at her computer. "Says here that the bail is set for $10,000. You got $10K layin' around? Generally, a bail bond company will charge you 10% to post the bail on your behalf. You won't get that back, but it's much easier than coughing up ten grand."

"What if I pay the full ten?"

"Assuming your daughter attends her arraignment and future hearings, you'll get it all back."

"Who do I pay?"

The desk deputy looked at him skeptically. "How you got that kinda money?"

"Credit card." Jamiel didn't want to waste any time. He was used to the judgments about his financial status. He wore a nice shirt and dress slacks but nothing indicating that he was a doctor. Even in the 21st century, there were those who were shocked to find out he was a medical doctor as if a Black man couldn't make something of himself.

"Well, you don't pay me. You need to pay the county clerk."

Two hours later, he received a payment confirmation from the clerk's office.

"Now what?" Jamiel wasn't sure where to go next.

"Now you wait. We'll send over the authorization for release. It will take some time for them to process the defendant." He never thought he'd hear his daughter referred to as a defendant ever in his life.

"Where is that?"

"Back at the police station."

He felt tired as he made his way back to the previous building. It was nearing three in the afternoon—he realized he'd missed his morning breakfast, and lunchtime had come and gone hours ago. His day wasn't at all how he'd planned. He could wait a little longer to eat. He was sure Pammy would be hungry, too, when she was released.

CHAPTER 24

Brad pulled on a T-shirt with a green letter R contained in a square outline. He had been following a pundit named OurTruths based in Pennsylvania. The YouTube videos were detailed, painting the story of horrific deeds that were being contained through the work of R and like-minded nationalists. It spoke to him and the other members of Whites Restore. He felt his eyes had been opened to the behind-the-scenes mechanisms that manipulated the world around him. For too long, the powerful elite had been atrocious in the way they chose to live their lives and to worship the Devil.

Brad was God-fearing, and he knew that the almighty power of God overcame darkness with loyal followers like him. Satan would continue to rise in an attempt to gain power, but the Devil would remain relegated to the depths of Hell. Weak-minded men and women were susceptible to the lure of evil, but Brad was strong, and he knew that White Americans were God's chosen children. Anyone who wasn't White wasn't pure. Their skin was a sign of God's ranking. He knew people were destined to repeat their lives to evolve to greatness. With loyal dedication and focus, a person's skin would become lighter with each reincarnation. Only when you achieved pure whiteness could you transcend from the learning lives to an eternity in Heaven. Killing anyone of color was a gift to help them achieve purity and ascension into Heaven. The teachings of Whites Restore outlined the process in their handouts. Brad was able to gauge the level of his enlightenment by comparing the color of his arm to the swatches of color in the literature. He was close to ascension. He needed to remain on earth to fulfill his destiny by aiding darker souls to evolve to their higher selves. He was destined to help the inferior filth of the world to evolve. He was a messiah and embraced his commitment to the pledge he'd made when he'd joined Whites Restore.

It frustrated him that there were Whites who did not value their evolution and were throwing it away by sacrificing children. It was no longer as simple as cleansing society for White purity. It was essential to know if those who did not value the color of their skin needed cleansing as well.

R spoke of the importance of knowing your alliance. The Rainstorm was coming, and it would be imperative to uphold the gospel of R.

Brad buttoned his uniform shirt over the R T-shirt and tucked both into his duty pants before pulling on socks and shoes. He zipped up a black Columbia windbreaker to hide his uniform and picked up his duty belt. He lived about thirty minutes from the Oakland Police Station, and he didn't feel comfortable being in his car without backup if someone were to identify him as a cop on his way to attend roll call.

He wasn't ready to show his affiliation with R yet. The elders had advised him to stay under the radar at the police department until they received the sign that the storm had arrived. He felt a wave of excitement. The next election in a few weeks would be the Day of Proclamation. Dom Coronet was going to be elected and communicate to the world the power that he wielded over the pedophiles and Hollywood elites who believed they were above the law.

The Day of Proclamation would also be when the world would see the results of the High Court Tribunals. In the meantime, it was his moral responsibility to assist with personal cleansing and the promotion of all towards heavenly ascension.

■

"Pamela Kiesha Jackson!" The police officer called out her name, and she jumped to her feet.

"That's me!"

"Bail has been posted. Come with me."

There were lots of forms to sign, and she read through them carefully to make sure she knew what she was signing. It was all administrative, explaining her rights, her hearing date, the terms of bail, and confirmation of the return of her personal belongings. As she reviewed the items in her backpack, she realized her phone had died; the battery depleted while she was detained. Without her phone, she wasn't sure how to find the closest BART station. She hadn't thought about bringing her phone charger for a rally she planned to attend for an afternoon.

Finally, she was given permission to walk out of the holding area, and as she pushed through the doors leading to the building exit, she saw her father and started to cry. She'd never been so happy and relieved to see him. All the emotions she'd been pushing down bubbled to the surface, and she wiped the tears from her face with her hand.

"It's okay, Pammy. I got you." Jamiel hugged his daughter, and the two stood for a moment while Pam regained control.

"I'm sorry, Dad."

"Don't be. I'm sure you didn't do anything wrong. This will all be resolved soon."

"I still don't know what happened."

"Hungry? Let's get some food. That will help you feel better, and you can tell me what happened."

The two walked to the exterior door, and Jamiel pointed to the rental car parked five stalls from the entrance. They found a restaurant, slid into a booth, and accepted the laminated menus offered by the bored hostess.

"We're known for our mac and cheese. Your server will be with you shortly."

"That sounds like the perfect comfort food." Pam usually avoided high carbs, but as her stomach growled, she made an exception.

"Are you alright?" Jamiel was concerned about what his daughter had been through in the past eighteen hours.

"Dad, I swear I don't know why we were singled out. We were walking along peacefully, and then a police officer yelled at us to sit on the ground."

"Was anyone else in your group arrested?"

"Part of the group was released back into the rally. Asher and I were in a group with others around us that were arrested but that we don't know."

"Asher?"

"He's in my anatomy class. I wonder if he's been released yet."

"Does he have anyone to post bail?"

"You had to post bail?"

"Don't worry about it, Pammy. I'll get the money back after you've attended your arraignment and other hearings."

"I don't know about Asher. He's Korean and here on a student visa." Suddenly, her worries seem insignificant. Asher had a lot more to lose than her.

"Dad, my phone needs to be charged, and I have no way to reach him. How do we find out if he's okay?"

Jamiel pulled his phone from his pocket.

"What's Asher's last name?"

"Choi."

After a quick Google search, Jamiel dialed the county clerk's office of Alameda County. "I'm trying to find out if bail has been posted for Asher Choi." They waited for a few minutes while the call was transferred. After another query, Jamiel nodded.

"Yes. Thank you. I appreciate your help."

He hung up the phone and placed it on the tabletop.

"There's no bail set."

"That doesn't make sense. We were taken to the police station in the same van. I know he was detained. Why wasn't bail set?"

"According to the county clerk, no charges were filed for Asher."

"But..." Pam's voice tapered off as she processed the information. "I don't understand. Why was I charged, and he wasn't?"

"Great question, Pammy. Great question."

Internally, Jamiel vowed to find out why.

■

Tony wore his new camouflage pants with a black T-shirt and carried the duffel with the other items he'd purchased to his truck. He was meeting Jester, King, and Ralph at the shooting range. He was looking forward to using the pistol. It had a firm feeling in his hand. At first, it had felt heavy, but as he'd pushed the cartridge into the handle, it had felt solid, and he felt protected.

He navigated to the gun shop where he'd purchased his equipment and saw that King and Jester were talking animatedly in the parking lot. They paid range fees and signed a waiver that outlined the range rules. Tony's membership was free because of his purchase; the two other men paid a nominal fee.

The clerk who sold him the handgun gave him some pointers on how to hold his arms forward, creating a triangle with his arms and body. He grasped the gun and cradled it in both hands. Closing his left eye, he aligned his shot to the center of the circular bullseye at the further length of the range. He emptied his cartridge and pulled the paper target toward him. He was disappointed he'd hit the target way outside the intended location. After three rounds, both King and Jest were being supportive, which almost made him feel worse.

"What eye are you using to sight the target?" King genuinely seemed interested in helping him.

"I'm closing my left eye. Is that what you mean?

"Yes. We all have a dominant eye. Try aiming with the right eye closed instead. Tony wasn't sure how favoring one eye over the other would help, but he didn't want to be ridiculed by anyone for being a lousy shot. He pinched his right eye closed. It felt strange and not as comfortable as when he closed his left eye, but he looked down the length of the gun barrel toward the target, lined up the center circle, and pulled the trigger. After emptying the chamber once more, he pulled the target towards him. To his surprise, there were holes in the target hovering around the center. It was the closest he'd come to being inside the smallest circle.

"That's what I'm talkin' about!" King held up his hand, encouraging Tony to slap his palm. "Once you figure out your dominant eye, you'll find you can actually hit shit."

Jest was hitting the target regularly, and seemed like a natural before Tony learned that he'd been practicing with King for the past several weekends. "A bunch of us from Texas Freedom Fighters are talking with an ex-military member. He's agreed to walk us through training. Nothing like Navy Seal or Marine shit, just the basics; how to load and aim, what to do when confronted, and even some info on medical care. Wanna join us?"

Tony nodded. Knowing he had a dominant eye and seeing how it improved his skills, he felt comfortable agreeing to join the larger group.

"Great! I'll DM you the details. It's next Saturday."

"What time?"

"Morning. Not sure when just yet."

"That works. I promised Erica we'd go out in the afternoon."

"Man, you sound pussy whipped." Jest didn't like it when Tony chose Erica over their time together.

"You're just jealous."

"Let's shoot!" Jest changed the subject. They went through a few more rounds before leaving for Whataburger.

Tony purchased several more boxes of the bullets before they left. He wanted to be prepared for the following week. He tried not to think about the money he was spending. It was expensive fighting for Texan history.

CHAPTER 25

Max lay next to his wife, looking up at the ceiling. It was early in the morning, and her rhythmic breathing indicated she was still fast asleep. He envied her ability to slumber with ease. He'd been awake for over an hour, and only now that the first rays of light were creeping around the heavy drapes covering their bedroom windows did he debate about nudging her awake. They had an understanding in their marriage that they would work in tandem with each other. No decisions were made without the other one, and they accepted the consequences of their choices together. There was no room for blaming the other for a situation. They shared the same vision for their future and supported each other in that quest as outlined by their faith in God and Country.

He had hoped to talk with her the night before, but a last-minute rant by The Dom had pulled his inner circle into the Oval Office to listen to the portly man ramble through a myriad of topics. The border wall was his favorite topic, and he returned to it over and over again like a broken record. Congress had denied his latest funding request, and Dominic was beside himself trying to get what he wanted.

"I promised a wall to my followers, and, God Dammit, I'm going to deliver the biggest and best wall!"

Max was frustrated and angry. The indulgent, petulant man-child had already stripped his health care funding and was now looking for other workarounds to get the construction companies money to get started.

"I need to show that immigration into our country is being halted and that the Undesirables are being kept out of our great land. The election is almost here. The wall should have been completed by now."

Maxwell still wasn't sure who the Undesirables were. He hadn't seen any data that validated The Dom's claims of increased violence and crime from illegal immigrants. He doubted the president's claims that countries were intentionally exporting their worst criminals to keep them out of the jail systems at home. He doubted anyone coming into the country illegally would draw attention to themselves. Instead, he suspected they stayed well below the radar and performed jobs no native-born Americans would want to do. Personally, he was grateful for the farm labor that came across the border to pick crops to keep the costs low at the supermarket. Max and his wife were the lucky ones. Max and his wife were tithing more than ten percent of their earnings to the church and had been able to send both of their children to private colleges. They could afford to pay for their groceries, but he knew many in the country had to make difficult choices on whether or not they should eat or pay for their medication. It was expensive to live in this country with any level of comfort.

"Nora, you awake?" Maxwell gently touched his wife's shoulder. No response. He debated about waiting a little longer but nudged her again, hopeful she would respond. "I need to talk with you."

Nora rolled over and pushed sleep from her body.

"What's wrong, honey?"

"Nothing, nothing's wrong." He pushed down his worries and anxiety that had been preventing him from sleeping. It wasn't fair to pull her out of sleep to ease his discomfort. Nora knew her husband well and propped herself up on the pillows.

"What's going on, Max?"

"I'm worried about Dominic."

"In what way?"

"He's been particularly derailed lately. He doesn't stay focused, and it's almost impossible to talk with him."

"We knew he was a narcissist before you accepted the role of his vice president."

"Yes, but this is worse than personal indulgences. He seems unwilling or unable to understand how our government works."

"Isn't that the appeal? That he can 'fix' what's broken by not being a career politician?"

"Yes, that's what we thought, but he doesn't seem happy with anything unless he's tearing it apart."

"What do you mean, dear?"

"He changes his mind constantly."

"He's a man used to sound bites."

Max appreciated his wife's insights. "Do you think that's all this is?"

"Yes, he's like a pit bull that's sunk his teeth in and won't let go. You've seen him at rallies. How many times has he gone off script to get a reaction from the audience?"

"You're right, Nora. I'm probably making a bigger deal out of this than I need to. It's just frightening to think of him navigating the tasks of his office without respect and reverence for the laws of the land."

"He strikes me as a lot of bluster and not a lot of might. He's all about the show with very little substance. I'd be more concerned if I thought he had any understanding of the power at his disposal."

Max pondered it for a moment. "Good point, Nora. He can posture as much as he wants, but it doesn't mean he's going to destroy our country."

"The country has survived much worse than Dominic Coronet, and it will continue to thrive now and when he's no longer in office."

"I had hoped that we would have been able to promote our agenda more easily by agreeing to be on his ticket."

"You have power at your disposal, too, dear. Don't forget that the vice president role can allow you to step into the role of president one day. It's just a matter of time. As long as Dominic Coronet remains popular with his following and the economy holds up, you'll be able to run to be his replacement after four more years. It will pass quickly, and even Dominic Coronet will recognize that the term limit for his presidency will require him to step aside. He's got to endorse you. It's important that he believes that we're on board with all of his craziness. In time, we can promote our agenda, but for now, we have to stay focused on the long game, not the individual play-by-play."

Maxwell laughed. Of the two of them, Nora was the pragmatic one. She could easily see the benefits of staying on the sideline, and she'd built her instincts around knowing when it would be time to propel her husband's aspirations to obtain their goal.

"Let's try to sleep a little more, dear. You'll give yourself an ulcer if you keep stressing over the things you can't control. Just remember, Dominic Coronet is just a mouthpiece for his ego megaphone. If he isn't yelling loudly to promote himself, that's when I'd get nervous. He's harmless even if he is unpredictable."

Maxwell spooned his wife, and her breathing quickly became rhythmic again. He wished he could be as confident as Nora. She had good instincts, and he suspected she was right again this time, too. She hadn't been in the Oval Office to hear firsthand the crazy comments coming out of The Dom's mouth. The president was beginning to understand the power at his disposal and was broadening his horizons beyond the showmanship of selling the reality star persona he'd created. What scared Maxwell the most was that The Dom was beginning to see himself as invincible and unstoppable, regardless of how far away from democracy his objectives were.

He continued to stare at the bedroom wall and tried to reduce his anxiety. He could only hope Nora was right.

■

"Attention," the ex-military officer yelled at the group before him. Solicited by the Texas Freedom Fighters to provide training, the man in his late fifties had maintained his short, military buzz cut.

Tony didn't know what rank he'd held in the Army. The imposing man demanded respect from the group. About thirty members of Texas Freedom Fighters had joined the expert, whose name Tony couldn't remember. The curt command to commence training stopped the various conversations that rippled through the group, and they looked at the man before them.

"It is critical that you understand how to respond in any situation out in the field. How you respond could make the difference between life and death as well as between peace and chaos. The goal of Texas Freedom Fighters is to preserve our great history. Militias have been a large part of this history. YOU are part of this history. Remember, it is not our place to PROVOKE and incite action. Our role is to respond as needed to PROTECT and maintain our land and history."

"Hear, hear," could be heard scattered among the group.

"It is critical to remain in control at all times. We do not incite violence but instead protect our land and our history. You will always enter any given situation with a buddy. This buddy is your defender; together, you have strength. Alone, you can be isolated and put into danger. DO NOT find yourself cornered without the ability to move. This is when things can and will go sideways."

Tony stood next to Jester, King, and Ralph. The four looked at each other and silently paired off. Tony stood with his high school friend and the other two men paired together.

"Everyone here should be comfortable pairing with anyone in the organization. Your buddy is your protection, not your best friend. If you have paired with someone you came with, raise your hand. Now, look around you and move to be with someone you don't know."

"Sorry, Jest, gotta move."

"Today, we're going to go over the basics of your weapons. You are not carrying a gun or a rifle. You are holding your weapon. A weapon is used to protect yourself. Do not lose sight of the distinction."

During the next forty-five minutes, they learned how to disassemble their weapons, as well as load, clean, and properly hold them for optimal use.

Tony and his partner didn't talk much at first. Tony didn't learn much about the other man except that he'd driven thirty miles from outside Houston to be there, and he was very familiar with the weaponry in front of them.

"Yeah, I'm also part of another group closer to my home near Austin."

"You came all this way?"

"You bet. This guy is really well-known in the circles. I wouldn't have missed his training, even if today is a little basic."

"Circles?"

The bearded, tattooed man wearing a blue plaid shirt and jeans extracted a vape pen from his pocket and inhaled. As he let out the vapor, he answered. "Each militia consists of a group, or circle, of members. We all share the same doctrine for our membership."

"Everyone?"

"Well, that's the idea. Of course, there are always the ones who are there because they like the idea of being part of a military response team. They don't care the reason."

"I see."

"I look at it this way. I'm learning how to fortify myself and my home, and I will defend my property as best as I know how. This is bigger than that. This is about defending democracy and protecting our history. I'm not going to let people take away my heritage without a fight."

Tony nodded. It was comforting to know he wasn't alone. He'd learned a lot about handling his new weaponry and how to use it safely without accidentally shooting himself in the process.

"You should come to Austin sometime. You can meet some of the other guys."

"That's an idea. I'm here with several friends. Maybe we can all make the drive." Tony was curious about the other group. *Was it like his training partner described? Were they all of like mind to the Texas Freedom Fighters?* Before they discussed it, he hadn't given it any thought that they were just one of many other militia groups around the United States.

"Our group responded to an Antifa threat. It was awesome. We were there in force, holding a line, and a bunch of white Sprinter vans showed up. We saw them assess the situation, and they drove off. We were able to stop a riot from happening and destroying our downtown."

"Antifa?"

"Bunch o' liberal mutherfuckers... anarchists trying to destroy the world. It all starts as a 'peaceful protest,' but Antifa sees a chance to infiltrate and destroy. We're making sure that don't happen here in Texas."

Tony felt a sense of pride. He'd felt rudderless before he'd found TFF. Knowing they were banded together with a common cause was comforting. Additional groups, like the one near Austin, were showing up to help maintain their democracy. Maybe the world wasn't going to go to hell as quickly as he'd thought.

After the training, Tony introduced his partner, Jim, to his friends.

"Ya'll should come over next weekend. We have a doctor showing us some medical basics. We've been able to help people who've gotten hurt at protests."

"Hurt how?"

"So many ways. People throw stuff. Other times, the police fire rubber bullets and release tear gas to disperse the gathering. We can help anyone who has a problem. Everything from dehydration to an injury."

It was inspiring to learn more about the various training options. They connected on social media, and soon, the group was texting details for the following weekend. Jim also invited them to a Discord channel. Tony was surprised by the level of engagement. The Texas Freedom Fighters Facebook group was just the tip of the iceberg.

Looking at the time on his phone, Tony realized he'd been away longer than expected. He'd promised Erica they would go to Olive Garden and a movie that night. Maybe she'd want to come with him next weekend, and they could get barbecue at The Salt Lick in Austin before returning to Houston. He wanted her to know more about his growing affiliation. He knew she didn't fully understand why it was so important to him, but he was sure that she would support him once she learned that it was a more significant movement than just him.

He waved goodbye to the group of men and made his way to his silver truck. Sliding behind the wheel, his mind was made up. He'd go to Austin next weekend and bring Erica with him. He'd be sure to find something for her to do while he was at the training session, and they could explore the city that liked to designate itself as weird. Austin was less than three hours away, and he marveled at the differences between the two cities. Austin focused on keeping it weird, while Houston took pride in the Johnson Space Center that controlled many NASA missions. It hadn't occurred to him that Austin would have any sort of militia, being a liberal island contained in a broader sea of conservatives, but he knew that the city had a lot of like-minded people, too. It was still part of the great state of Texas.

He was fifteen minutes away from his apartment. He had a lot of pent-up energy. He hoped Erica was home; sex was a great outlet.

■

"The puppeteers behind the scenes are finding that the strings they've been able to pull for so long are being severed. They are losing their hold and power over this great nation. Dominic Coronet is our savior and leader, restoring our nation to greatness. We are the chosen ones. The Dom's predecessors gave away our place in the world power. Fortunately, he is here to restore what those in the previous government sold to the highest bidders. No longer will the nation be ruled by Corporate America but for the people and by the people. You will be called upon soon to take a stand for your greatness. However, be aware and be warned: There are those among us who will not want to have these changes. They are the enemies of the state. They are the ones who will need to fall when the Rainstorm comes. You may know them as your butcher, the mother next door, or your dentist. If they have not made an allegiance to the truths outlined here, as well as to Dominic Coronet, they will not be able to remove their blinders and see the truth. The truth is what will prevail in the end. Everyone has a choice to make, and choosing which path to take will determine their fate. This is the time for strength. This is a time for resolve. You know the truth. Do your own research, and you'll find what I say is true. Respect the word; you are being misled! – R."

CHAPTER 26

Erica wasn't sure who Tony was these days. The man she'd fallen in love with had been attentive and caring, and they'd had many nights getting to know each other. Lately, ever since he'd discovered the Texas Freedom Fighters Facebook group, he'd been almost rabid about the changes happening in Houston. She didn't understand. *What did it matter if there was a statue in the park or not?* The presence of the Spirit of Confederacy bronze didn't change history or reinforce it in either way, as far as she could tell. Maybe she was missing something. *Wasn't it just a hunk of metal?*

She was doing laundry and slid open the door to Tony's side of the closet, looking for dirty clothes to complete a load. She found a canvas duffel bag on the floor. The gun shop logo on the side of the bag gave her a sense of what the bag might contain. He was still at work, on a shift for another four hours. She pulled on the straps. As she dragged it to the floor outside the closet, she found it was heavier than anticipated. She unzipped it and was dismayed to see a variety of gun parts, a vest, goggles, a handgun, and numerous boxes of ammunition.

She was used to the gun culture of Texas, but she'd thought Tony was different. He only had a hunting rifle, and he hadn't touched that during the nine months they'd been dating. *What was he doing with all these things now?* There were still tags on some of the clothing, and the bag smelled new with a hint of metal and fabric.

"Jester." She muttered the name under her breath. This must be his doing. She'd never liked Tony's high school friend, and she knew better than to criticize the bearded, tattooed friend if she had any hopes of a long-term relationship with Tony. The two men had known each other since high school, and she hadn't even known Tony for a year yet. Her eyes welled with tears. *How could she have misjudged him? Was he really a man stockpiling ammunition and guns, or was he the man who made her coffee each morning before he left for work and laughed with her in the evening while watching movies on the couch?* She was having a hard time reconciling the two sides of his personality.

She wiped away her tears and sighed. Time would tell her more about him. In the meantime, she didn't want him to think she was spying on him and his activities. She hoped he would share more with her soon. She would be sure to listen to him so she could decipher who he was. She wasn't ready to leave, and yet, if the duffel was any indication, she realized she may not be able to stay either.

Erica pushed the items back into the bag and zipped it closed. She returned the black bag to the same spot in the closet and hoped she'd left everything as she'd found it. He'd never have to know that she'd discovered the contents inside the duffel before he was ready to share that information with her. She knew she had to retain his trust if she wanted to preserve their relationship. It was an innocent discovery while searching for dirty clothes; she instinctively knew he would see it as an invasion of his privacy.

■

Leon had amassed over 300,000 followers without slick production values and by promoting his truth. His videos were basic, and he spoke with the passion and insights of a prophet guided by his teacher. He was proud of the work he was doing to spread the word. R's messages were disseminated to thousands of people, and his following was growing.

Someone asked him recently in the comments section of one of his videos if R was a woman. Leon had been caught off guard. *R a woman? Impossible! There was no way a woman would be in a position with this level of insider knowledge. R had to be a man.* Leon was pretty sure that R was a lot like himself, an older White man who was witnessing the demise of their nation. *Yes, there was no way that R was anything but a White man of power.* He had shown that over and over again each time he posted. The messages spoke to Leon in a way that only a fellow White man could resonate with him. He was confident it was Dominic Coronet himself. Leon had to stop reading the comments in his video feeds. There would always be people who were ornery just for the sake of being disagreeable. They would pay the price. The Rainstorm was coming, and from what Leon was piecing together, if you weren't aligned with R and his insights, you ignored him at your peril.

He was getting ready to record the following video. Leon had spent the past two hours researching the latest R post and found a site that confirmed what he'd already suspected. A new monetary system was being put into place. He pressed record.

"The incorporation of the United States of America is about to be dissolved. As one of the outcomes of that disbandment, a new currency will replace the American dollar. Without the gold standard in place and with a currency tainted by bankruptcy, the reestablishment of the forefathers' intentions of 1776, a new currency, known as NatCoin, will become the true currency of the United States. It is now possible to convert your dollars to NatCoin through a cryptocurrency site converter. Do not be alarmed if the value fluctuates. That is expected as the currency conversion is occurring. The high demand for a currency that is the recognized pillar of the United States monetary system will show its true value in the months ahead. The time is now. Do not wait to convert your U.S. dollars to NatCoin, or you may find that you end up with fewer dollars than you started with. Only those privy to the behind-the-scenes insights will know when to show allegiance to R and stand up to the evil factions trying to destroy the democracy. We will not take this lightly. Fight for your rights, or you may find you have nothing."

Leon had seen hints of the new currency for weeks, and only recently had it been identified. He wasn't sure how to acquire NatCoin at first, but a quick Google search walked him through the process of creating a virtual wallet to exchange funds and open up an account with an online currency broker.

On the site, he bypassed the privacy and terms of service links and accepted the disclaimers. He knew reading the documents didn't make any sense. If he wanted to purchase NatCoin, this was his only option.

He looked at his phone screen and typed the security code displayed on the sign-in screen on his laptop. Verifying his identity and opening the account didn't take long. NatCoin was listed; he would get two for every dollar he invested. He'd been warned that if he waited too long to convert his U.S. dollars, he'd find the cost for conversion would be prohibitive or worse, that the dollar no longer had any value that could be leveraged into NatCoin. R had warned that the Restoration would render the current currency obsolete as soon as the Rainstorm was underway. R had provided a timeline for the High Court Tribunal to be concluded. Leon had mapped out the raindrops from the postings, deducing the Restoration would occur after the coming election and before the newly elected president of the United States was sworn into office in January.

He calculated his rent and living expenses for the next three months and kept that portion in his savings account. He initiated the transfer of the bulk of his savings to his new crypto account. Once the transfer was confirmed in approximately three days, he'd be able to make his purchase of NatCoin. Hopefully, the exchange rate would still be favorable.

■

"The Great Revival is upon us! The president is removing the criminal element to pass legislation that will reestablish our great land. Follow the money, and you will know the offenders. They think they can buy their way out of guilt. They are wrong. What has worked in the past works no more. Respect the word. You are being misled. – R."

CHAPTER 27

It alarmed Casey to see the growing shift in sentiment toward R, the anonymous person posting content on the BeWarned website that was being broadcast more widely through YouTube and various other social channels. At Jamiel's recommendation, Casey scheduled an interview with Dr. Robert Denton, a leading psychologist at Johns Hopkins. Several months ago, R had only been reaching a small and rabid group of followers, but in a short period of time, his messages were speaking to a more mainstream audience. The raindrops, as the clues were called, were being dissected and discussed by R followers. The reporter hoped the doctor could shed light on the movement's growth.

It distressed him to see the changes in news reporting. *The National Times* was a reputable paper with over a century of accurate reporting. Yet, many were calling *The Nat Times* a manipulated entity serving the powerful faction of evil. Casey didn't feel like a puppet to this so-called elite. If anything, he was dictated to by the advertisers. The corporations paying for ad placements were the ones that called the shots, not some nefarious puppeteer of the faction.

He had approached his editor to discuss his concerns, but his warning had been disregarded.

"Casey, there's always someone taking shots at us. The liberals think we're too tough on them; the far right calls us sellouts. Our responsibility is to report fairly and equitably. History will determine the outcome."

There was so much manipulation of content online and social algorithms serving up content that Casey wasn't so sure the old rules were valid anymore. *How do you stop the social machine when anyone with a computer and a social profile can say whatever they wanted?*

He'd been watching various sites, and one thing was emerging as a constant. When content was deemed incorrect and pulled down by a hosting service, it insidiously morphed onto other platforms with an extensive array of redirects to reinforce the content.

"Do your own research" was a rallying cry of R. Yet, in Casey's observation, the sites were intertwined with an attempt to appear independent from each other. The messages and cross-links were designed to create a curated trail of information.

Dr. Denton filled in the blanks. "If someone were to see a post only once, it is easy to question the content. However, if someone were to see the same thing many times, it gives the content a sense of credibility."

"So, what you're saying is that the narrative can be false, but if it's seen enough times, it takes on an aura of acceptance?"

"Exactly. Also, as a species, we pay attention to things that are negative because that helps us survive."

"What do you mean?"

"It's tied to our basest instincts. When we were nomadic and fighting for our lives daily, remembering that a tiger was dangerous could save you."

"But we don't run into tigers in our daily lives now."

"That's correct, but the hard coding is still there."

"But that doesn't explain why this content is so popular."

"It's easy to be drawn to the negative for a variety of reasons. Survival hard coding is one aspect, but there's also a sense of comfort."

"Misery likes company?"

"In some ways, yes. However, I would argue that it's bigger than that. Another aspect to consider is that someone is tapping into human nature for a reason."

"Tell me more."

"You need to ask yourself who is benefiting by publishing this content."

"Follow the money?" Casey was putting together the pieces. Investigative Reporting 101: money was usually at the root of every story.

"If you can. With so many sites popping up with unknown ownership, it's almost impossible to know who is benefiting by someone believing any particular story." The doctor paused before continuing.

"There's more to the manipulation than money. While that is motivating as a basic revenue model, you have to ask the question about what entity benefits."

Casey felt the hairs on his neck. It was a sign that he was onto something important.

"Entity?"

"Yes, it could be anyone or anything, really. What foreign power benefits by undermining the U.S.?"

"Russia?"

"That's the familiar threat. It could be China; it could be Poland. It could be anyone who enjoys undermining any established system or manipulating people for satisfaction. If

I had to wager, I'd say that more than just one group is looking to benefit by a broad spread of any particular narrative."

The two men spoke for another ten minutes before Casey hung up the phone. On one hand, he felt validated that his instincts had been correct, and yet, on the other, he felt terrified. *How could you track something when you didn't know how far-reaching it was?*

■

"Be prepared for the return of the gold standard. For too long, your paper money hasn't been valued against anything of substance. It is time the preciousness of gold-backed our currency. Do not delay; purchase NatCoin online; it's the only gold-backed crypto. This new currency will replace the paper dollars, which are nothing more than an illusion. Respect the word. You are being misled." — R.

Leon smiled as he read the posts about the United States Dollar being a shell game managed by the Federal Reserve, which wasn't even a bank. With interest rates rising, it was evident that the elite powers were doing everything they could to keep people like Leon strapped and struggling. They were raping the country and hoarding the wealth generated by their transgressions.

The Rainstorm was coming, and Leon knew all the wrongs would be made right again. "Liberty and justice for all" would be the mantra that would support everyone by restoring the country to the constitutional rights that had been outlined when the United States declared its independence.

Leon logged into his new NatCoin account. The transfer initiated a few days ago went through, and he was pleased to see that the exchange rate had stayed constant. He opened a new browser tab and logged into his checking account. He couldn't believe the balance. He'd set his YouTube videos to allow ad interruptions several times during his recordings, which had paid off. He knew he'd been amassing a following of like-minded individuals who regularly tuned in to hear his interpretations of the R posts. The raindrops left by R were cryptic to many. Leon had established himself as an expert, and people were tuning in to hear his assessments. He didn't realize that getting the word out would be so lucrative.

He had already converted several thousand dollars to NatCoin and planned to transfer even more. He wouldn't be caught holding onto worthless paper when the monetary system was restored to the gold standard.

He clicked through to the order page. He debated about how much more of the cryptocurrency he should purchase. The Rainstorm was coming, and with it, there was new money to leverage. He wasn't going to starve. He wouldn't have anything stand in his way to shop and put food on his table. The survival meals he'd already purchased were tucked away in his garage, ready for consumption when the food supply would be cut off. Still, NatCoin ensured he could buy anything he needed while the monetary system shifted to the new order currency. Leon felt terrible for anyone who wasn't paying attention like he was. Those who weren't prepared would be caught up in red tape that could prevent them from having access to their money. Leon wasn't going to accept the risk.

■

Dom read the latest post by R. He liked the notion of being a modern-day prophet, and the popularity of the posts showed that others embraced him in that role as well. The recent election polls showed him neck and neck with Larry Stevens, which didn't provide enough of a lead to stroke his self-important view of himself. He should be dominating the polls ahead of the other man. His campaign manager kept assuring him that the polls conducted by his campaign showed him with a substantial lead but that the false narrative by liberal papers was leveraging the message of a close race to attract readership. Landslides don't sell papers. A tight race was much more interesting.

The Dom could appreciate that. His reality television show, *Mega Mergers*, fabricated a lot of information to make each week entertaining and engaging for viewers. Most tuned in to watch some type of animosity. He'd often kept unpopular contestants, vying for a Cornet Corporation endorsement even though he knew they were deceitful and egotistical. Show them on camera contradicting their own stories, and it was easy to keep the viewers tuning in week after week.

The president pushed his chair back from his desk in the Oval Office and paced the room. There had to be a way for him to use the power of his office to ensure that he stayed a resident in the White House for four more years and any number of years after his second term.

For now, he didn't trust anyone, not even his children. They were well-intentioned but too easily seduced into talking about Coronet affairs to feed their egos. His middle son wasn't the brightest of the three. He had blundered through a number of segments on *Mega Mergers,* and The Dom was forced to give him a script to follow. The scrutiny of the content made his son, Aaron, so uncomfortable that he'd practically stutter through the presentations. The Dom had relegated him to the background and instead let his namesake and his daughter take the lead.

Everyone loved Fiona, and secretly, she was his favorite. Dom Jr. and Aaron didn't share an original thought between them. Dom Jr. had enough confidence to come across as an authority. However, The Dom knew he was closely watching his father for any validation of his actions. The Dom still saw this as a weak move and wondered where he'd failed. *Why hadn't they adopted his killer instincts and ability to manipulate those around them? Maybe they were too much like their mother, a beautiful model who had married him for money and divorced him when the three children were still under the age of ten.*

◼

"What do you mean you weren't charged?" Pam looked at Asher with astonishment. "I don't know. They took me to the police station along with you. We were separated during the processing. They let me make a phone call, and a little bit later, they released me." Asher didn't tell her that he'd called his uncle at the Korean Embassy in San Francisco, who in turn had called an assemblyman representing Oakland, and he'd been released as a goodwill gesture. He'd tried to include Pam, but the embassy hadn't passed on more than Asher's information to the politician.

Asher kept his family affiliation private at the exclusive campus. He didn't believe in boasting about his heritage when it was the accomplishment of others in his family, not his own. He was attending medical school to prove himself to a family with deep pockets and respect in Korea. He wanted to be seen for his own merit.

"What happened to you?" He listened as she outlined the processing and time in the holding cell.

"Luckily, my dad was able to post bail. I don't know what happened to anyone who didn't have someone to help them. I think they end up there until the arraignment."

"Did you get fined?"

"Not yet. That might be part of my sentence. I'm scheduled to go to my hearing, at which time I will enter my plea. From there, it's hard to say what will happen next. My father is getting me an attorney."

"I'm sorry, Pam. I never meant for this to happen to you."

"I know. How could we know?"

"What did they say we did? All I know is we were walking, and then we were asked to sit on the ground."

"According to the information my dad got, it sounds like someone threw a water bottle, and we were at the wrong place at the wrong time. We were the easy target for the person who could have thrown it. I'll never know where it came from. I do know that I didn't throw it, and I'm going to plead innocent."

"You go, Pam! I'm not worried about you. It will all be dismissed, I'm sure."

Pam was beginning to understand her situation and wasn't so sure. It appeared the Oakland Police Department was sending a message to protesters: *Come here, and you'll pay the price.*

Until she'd been arrested, Pam had believed that Oakland was a liberal city with a large Black community, and she would have been safe attending a peaceful rally. She felt the anger and frustration at her situation stirring inside her again. She'd done nothing wrong, but she'd still spent the night in a holding cell after being fingerprinted and processed through the system like a criminal instead of an upstanding citizen. Her father had to post bail on her behalf, while Asher had just received a warning. It also made her angry that several White girls hadn't even been detained on the street.

She thought back to her cellmate's comments. It didn't matter how much White was in her; she was still Black and shouldn't forget it. She wanted to talk with her father to understand the world he lived in. As a young girl, she'd seen a few things that singled her father out as a Black man. She realized now that he'd sheltered her as much as he could. She saw her mixed race as the best of both of her parents. Her mother was outgoing and adventurous. Her father was educated, thoughtful, and caring. He had become a doctor to help people. They were aligned on how to raise their daughter and shared the same life goals. She'd always thought her father viewed the world without the negative consequences of race, but now she wasn't so sure.

She was experiencing firsthand what it felt like to be Black in America, and she regretted that her father hadn't been more open and direct about his experiences. She looked at her phone. It was mid-afternoon, and she knew her father would be with patients. She would have to wait until later in the day to connect with him. She had a lot of questions for him. She was afraid of the answers.

CHAPTER 28

The gear felt more familiar after Tony had completed several weekends of training to enable him to participate as a Texas Freedom Fighter militia member. Initially, the word "militia" made him uneasy. Still, as he learned about the role private citizens had played throughout the history of the United States to preserve their democracy, he was proud to be a member of the TFF. He felt strength and camaraderie when he attended the meetings. It also made him feel better to know he wasn't alone.

The training had been helpful, and as he and Jest rode in his truck toward San Antonio to assist another militia outside the historic Alamo building, excitement was humming between them. Their rifles were stowed in the truck bed with a hydraulic cover, so nothing was visible as they drove. Not that it mattered. This was Texas, and having a gun in your truck was practically a stereotype.

"Erica wasn't pleased about us attending this today. She says she's worried I'm going to get hurt. She thinks that guns and crowds don't mix."

"Did you tell her that our presence is the power in the gathering? Those Black Lives Matter and Antifa fuckers will back down when they see the firepower we have. It's not about using it; it's about conveying that we have the power to halt their activities. No one's going to mess with us. They know they'll be the ones to get hurt." Jest was animated and practically bouncing in his seat.

"Yeah, I told her."

"If she doesn't understand, maybe you need to find someone who does."

"It's not that bad." Tony didn't share that he'd been fighting with Erica a lot lately about his involvement with the Freedom Fighters. They were still having regular sex, and as long as he kept the conversation focused on her videos and followers, he found he could navigate the waters of their relationship. She would understand in time, once the Rainstorm had washed away the efforts of those trying to destroy democracy and the country was restored to its former glory. She hadn't been interested in reading the information he'd found online, and she wasn't interested in hearing it from him either. One thing was certain; she'd come to understand when the prophecies of R were brought to light for everyone to see after the next election. The truth would be revealed.

■

"Crime! Crime was skyrocketing under the previous adminis-tration!" He repeated the word intentionally in his Twitter post to reinforce the message. *"Only I have had the courage to address the insidious influx of criminals at our borders. The wall must be built now! We cannot wait on ineffective MEXICO to pay what they owe so that we can continue towards our goal. We will send them the bill!"*

Instinctively, The Dom knew what resonated with his voters and kept those messages on a continuous loop.

He knew rural America felt left behind. Available jobs were declining, and the towns that had long felt familiar were changing. Gone were the high-paying union jobs of the car industry; fossil fuel was becoming antiquated, and they could see the infrastructure crumbling around them. They yearned for a simpler time, a time of abundance. His critics didn't understand why his base of loyalists continued to support him, but he knew why and leveraged the angst and frustration that many in the country felt.

America was still incredibly wealthy and thriving, but the money flow had shifted. Urban areas, along with the influx of technology, were generally feeling the boom, while rural America was suffering the blows of a cruel fate that felt like a sucker punch. Coupled with the influx of Asians, Latinos, and other nonwhites, it wasn't a big surprise that the shift in traditionally White neighborhoods was sending a message that minority groups were being given an unfair advantage. Affirmative action was seen as creating a pendulum swing that had undermined White men and put them at a disadvantage.

Dom didn't give a shit about saving rural America. He cared about his wealth and power. It was ironic that his loyalists saw him as one of themselves. He considered himself above them, and his opulent lifestyle showed the discrepancies between him and his followers. He knew that was one of the reasons they loved him. Instead of hating him for his wealth, they saw it as something attainable for themselves.

The Dom loved the adoration. Those that didn't give him proper reverence, well, those people would be knocked down and brought to their knees. He would find a way to have everyone worship him.

■

"With the restoration of our great land, there will be a new currency. Have no fear! You can preserve your portfolios by investing in the new notes by converting everything to the cryptocurrency NatCoin. All R nationalists and supporters of Dominic Coronet will be given preference for the conversion by the High Court Banking system, and you can take steps today. There will be long lines at the bank, and a starter supply of NatCoin will make sure you can keep food on your table as the Restoration is established. Be prepared. The Rainstorm is coming. Do not ignore these raindrops. Respect the word. You are being misled. – R."

■

Tony, Jest, and the other Texas Freedom Fighters stood between Alamo Plaza Drive and the historic Alamo. The building was iconic. Tony remembered visiting the site as a grade schooler. He'd learned that Davy Crockett had been one of about 200 people who'd died in February 1836. He'd seen the statue of the tall man adorned in fringed leather attire worn in the 1800s inside the grounds, and the image had stayed with him. The famous frontiersman had been a militia member in Tennessee, his home state, and he had also fought bravely for the freedoms of Texans. Tony would represent him with pride today.

There had been violence on the site almost 200 years ago, but that wouldn't be the case today. They were there to be a deterrent to violence, not incite it. Scanning the line of Texas Freedom Fighters, they looked impressive. The amount of weaponry and camo clothing would make anyone think twice about stepping out of line.

A group of predominantly Black men was amassing on the other side of the courtyard. From his vantage point, Tony could see handmade signs with the messages "Black Lives Matter" and "Let Me Get Home Alive." The one sign seemed ironic to Tony. Of course, they would make it home alive as long as they didn't go rogue. Everyone representing the Freedom Fighters had been trained in how and when to engage. As long as no one from the BLM demonstrators caused problems, it would be a peaceful afternoon.

Several of the Black men on the other side of the square walked toward the line of Freedom Fighters. Tony clutched his AR-15 a little tighter. *What were they doing?* He watched as they approached the line several men away from where Tony and Jest were standing.

"We appreciate you being here."

The comment surprised Tony.

"Thank you. We're here to make sure that there's no disturbance today." Joe King responded.

"We're here to make sure that people understand how Black people aren't safe in the United States the same way White people are."

"Yes, but you know that ALL lives matter, right?"

The young man speaking glanced down before continuing with unwavering eye contact with King. "I agree that all lives matter, but that's not the world we live in today. In the world I live in, I see many people like me being singled out and mistreated, and many are killed just trying to make it home after work. The police single us out, and often times, we're pulled over without cause."

"We are here to protect and preserve," was the calm response by one of the group leaders.

"But we ain't armed. Hell, if I brought a gun here, I'd be dead already. Nothin' like an armed Black man to make a White man's trigger finger itch. Just another reason why I'm here because Black Lives Matter."

"All lives matter."

"Yeah, you can say that, but look around you. How many of you are armed and in full riot gear? Sure, all lives matter. Just some matter more."

"I'm tired of people like you getting special treatment at my expense. I have to work hard. Meanwhile, you get 'affirmative action' when applying for work. That's discriminatory to me."

"That's what you think I got? You're crazy, man. Do you ever worry about making it home safe every day?" The young man gestured to the others around him. "Every one of us has been stopped, detained, questioned, and restricted just trying to move in this world. That ever happen to you?"

"You must have been doing something." Tony could see the nerve on King's neck twitch.

"I find that hard to believe." Tony didn't mean to talk, but he was curious. "Every one of ya have been stopped? That doesn't make sense."

"In White America, you're right. It wouldn't make sense. However, in Black America, that's the world we live in. I'm guilty just walking down the street with dark skin."

Tony had been so focused on his troubles that he hadn't given a thought about the lives the Black men around him faced. *Surely, they had access to the same things he did, didn't they?* It wasn't his fault if they hadn't applied themselves. *Life is hard for everyone. Take a number.*

King spoke in a measured voice. "You ain't the only one stopped by the police. I was just pulled over for speeding last week."

"Were you asked to get out of the car?"

"No, just showed the officer my driver's license and registration."

"Did you get a ticket?"

"Nope. He was a buddy of mine, and he gave me a warning."

"If that had been me, I would have been detained and given a ticket, or worse, taken to the police station."

"I find that hard to believe. You must have been doing something wrong if that happened to you."

"Nope. The only 'something' I did was to be Black."

"My friend would have treated you the same way he treated me."

"You sure about that?"

"Yes, yes, of course." King looked annoyed.

"Maybe you can ask him next time you see him. Ask him how many times he gives Blacks a ticket and how many times he lets his White friends off with a warning."

Tony could hear frustration in King's voice as he replied. "I've known him my whole life. I already know the answer."

"As I said, we're glad you're here. There are sometimes other groups who aren't part of BLM that show up and cause problems. It's good to know you're here to discourage them."

"You talkin' about Antifa?"

"I don't know nothin' about them. I just know some people want to break windows and steal stuff. That's not us."

The young man had been holding a bag. He placed it on the ground. Tony could see it was filled with plastic water bottles.

"It's hot out here, and we thought you'd like some water."

King looked surprised. "You brought us water?"

"Yeah. I know it's not enough for everyone, but it'll help. Thanks again."

The Black men turned. The other two had been silent throughout the exchange, and they didn't say a word as they turned back to the line that delineated their group.

King reached down and picked up the bag with water. "Anyone want one?" The bag was passed down the line in the opposite direction of Tony and Jest. They watched as several Freedom Fighters helped themselves. Others in the line, including King, hadn't taken a bottle.

"Aren't you thirsty, King?" Ralph asked his friend as he twisted off the cap of the cool drink.

"Not drinkin' nuthin' they brought over here. They could have spit in it or something."

"I don't think so, King. I felt the seal break when I opened it."

"If I were you, I'd be thinkin' more about standing the line instead of making friends. No one's gettin' me to drink that water. I'm not giving them the upper hand."

Ralph hesitated as he put the bottle up to his mouth and then lowered it without taking a drink.

"I think he was just being nice."

"Nice, my ass. He came over here to give us a lecture. I didn't do nothin' wrong when I didn't get a ticket last week. At least there are still nice people in the world, and my friend gave me a warning. I've been driving extra careful since then, too. A ticket wouldn't have made a difference."

"Saved you a lot of money, I bet."

"What's your point, Ralph?"

"Just that it was nice of them to bring us water."

"Maybe, but I don't trust 'em anyway."

The Texas Freedom Fighters had responded to a request from another militia group to provide fortification to preserve the historic monument. It was rumored that a large group of BLM and Antifa members were going to ascend on the memorial and decimate it.

The merged militias consisted of various men, mostly in their thirties and forties. Tony was excited and fidgeted slightly, swaying subtly left and right while holding his new AR-15 in front of his body. He had assumed the stance based on his recent training. The Texas Freedom Fighters had met for several weekends with the crew-cut ex-military man who had walked them through the basics. Several in the group had undergone additional training to provide medical assistance as needed.

Tony saw one of the team assisting a man seated on the ground; blood flowed from his forehead. He wasn't sure how the man had gotten injured. So far, the two groups had faced off with each other and most engaged in conversation, both sides curious about the other's intentions. It was different than Tony had expected, and he was proud to be in attendance. It felt good to know he was actively taking a stance instead of sitting on the sidelines.

Erica had pleaded with him not to make the three-hour drive with the other men. He was glad he would be able to tell her how calm and peaceful it had been.

King laughed. "Pansies!"

"What are you talking about?"

"Did you see that group of white vans showed up? They took one look at us protecting the Alamo, and they drove off. It's a good thing we're here!"

"Who do you think it was?"

"Antifa, I'm sure. The Black Lives Matter folks are walking down the street already. They don't have the tactical equipment the same as Antifa. From what I saw, the van guys were equipped, but not enough to take us on!"

Tony could see how things could escalate out of control quickly. It was good that all of the Texas Freedom Fighters had been shown the proper level of engagement to avoid unnecessary excitement. The goal was to remain level-headed and not let emotions get in the way. There was never a reason to fire their weapons first. Words may carry a verbal punch, but unless shots were fired, no one was to discharge their weapons. They were there to protect, not incite. Tony guessed that Antifa had come with a different agenda, and he was relieved to know that they had backed down when they saw their presence. The day was already a success!

The medic was almost done patching up the man with the injury. Tony still hadn't figured out what happened. Maybe he'd fallen on the uneven pavement, considering it was an isolated incident. The medic used a small flashlight to assess the injured man's pupil response. It was amazing how thorough one could be away from a hospital.

The protest in San Antonio lasted almost three hours. A variety of protesters had chanted "Black Lives Matter" while others yelled "Blue Lives Matter" and "All Lives Matter." The variances were drowned out, and "Lives Matter" became the only distinguishable phrase.

Standing upright in one place, covered in tactical gear, was tiring. Tony's AR-15 had felt light when the group first arrived, but as the afternoon sun beat down on them and his stomach protested the lack of food, the weapon felt heavy and cumbersome.

One of the protesters from the All Lives Matter contingent had collapsed, likely due to heat exhaustion. Tony stepped up to help the Texas Freedom Fighters medic while he assessed the vitals of the young man.

Tony was grateful the sun was getting lower on the horizon and people were starting to disperse. It had been a long day, and he was ready for a hearty dinner and a beer or two.

CHAPTER 29

Casey was seeing an increase in hate mail landing in his work inbox. His reporting hit a nerve and triggered a swath of rabid R and Dominic followers. Usually, he didn't click on any links forwarded to him. Still, out of curiosity, he copied one into the search bar on the Whosit online database and discovered this particular website promoting the mysterious R had only been registered for one-and-a-half months. Certainly not long. It was unlikely the originating content provider, but instead, someone leveraging R's popularity to promote their self-interests. Casey switched sites and pasted the URL a second time. According to the Wayback Machine website, which tracked online site history, forty-three percent of site traffic came from redirects.

"Hey, Jerry," Casey called out to a nearby reporter. "What do you make of this?" He quickly shared what he'd found with the other reporter.

"That could mean a couple of things. It could be as simple as people posting links to the new site because they like the content or a change in site hosting."

Casey still couldn't shake the uneasy feeling.

"Any other ideas?"

"Yeah, but you probably don't want to hear it."

"Why?"

"Or...," Jerry looked around and leaned closer before continuing, "this is all a well-planned, integrated series of sites all designed to post the same information in various locations with cross-references to create a validation web."

Casey thought about his interview with the therapist. According to the psychologist, people were prone to remember the negative over the positive as part of their hard coding for survival. Staving off bad things keeps you alive. Applying this theory to the internet and the intricate web of information, one could see how building up a negative narrative, spreading it widely to validate it, and voila, the ideas would get ingrained.

"A validation web? You're beginning to sound like a conspiracy theorist yourself."

The younger reporter continued. "It's simple. You want someone to believe you? Trigger the algorithms. Create enough placements of your information, generate traffic, and the person looking at the screen will trust it because they've seen it multiple times in different locations."

"To what end?"

"God, man, anything really. Want to sell more hair loss cream? Discredit a politician? Or maybe you just like the thrill of creating chaos."

"I get it, but I'm still not sure why anyone would believe such outlandish statements as the followers of R."

"Can't help you there, CK. I never understand what makes people tick."

As Casey pondered the information, he realized that when he read R, he felt he was being served a heaping pile of bullshit. However, R was offering an upcoming change based on correcting wrongdoings, and that was a tasty treat for others.

Respect the word. You are being misled. The closing of each post gave readers the sense that they were part of something big and that the content was reliable. It brought the reader into a sanctum of those in the know.

The Rainstorm is coming. Casey shook his head. *Never underestimate the power of reassurance.*

"Hey, Jerry, what do you think? Is this just entertainment, or do you think it's possible to incite mobilization?"

"I don't know, dude, but honestly, I don't think anyone cares. It doesn't matter if it's true as long as it FEELS true."

"You're kidding, right?"

"Wish I was. Believers will gladly overlook repeated evidence of something not being accurate because of how it makes them feel to believe it's true."

The hairs on Casey's neck were at full attention as the other reporter continued. "They say the internet has something for everyone. Shop 'til you drop, be social, or whatever else your heart desires. It's all there to offer engagement or distraction."

"Thanks, Jerry. I appreciate the sounding board."

Casey was beginning to realize how powerful tapping into human nature could be. Another side effect of trying to tear down lies was the believers would hate anyone for taking away their sense of understanding. Like a person with a heroin addiction who knew drugs were harmful and shot up over and over again anyway. Logic no longer mattered. What mattered was the assurance that the world around them made sense, regardless of how helpless or powerless someone may feel in their day-to-day lives. The messages relayed by

R tapped into their fears and then gave them solutions and hope. The "raindrops" were like heroin—an escape from a world that no longer made sense, a chance to feel in the know and powerful. No wonder his hate mail was increasing. He was trying to take away their fix.

It's a Screentopia. Casey realized the new term conveyed his observations of R followers cherry-picking what they would believe and what they would discard. He could see that the lines of belief were fluid. Show everyone the same story with an array of information and some would accept all of it, while others would believe everything that didn't cross their line of credibility. They didn't stop to think that the entire narrative could be false, just the part that became unbelievable to them.

Was there a network of pedophiles sacrificing children as part of a sex and Satan-worshiping practice with John F. Kennedy Jr. alive and well and about to join forces with the Republicans?

Casey hadn't found any evidence that any part of this narrative was true, so it amazed him that people would believe all of it or accept the part until the prior president's son came back to life. The absurdity of one part didn't negate the probability of the other. Even flat-earthers were gaining traction because they had the internet as a megaphone to promote their claims. Never mind that there were numerous photos from space to show the reality that the world was, in fact, round. The rebuttal was to say the images weren't real, that they had been doctored, and the space landings had been filmed in a movie studio. Casey had been watching shorts on YouTube of an action star he liked only to find out months later that the content had been developed using AI. Artificial Intelligence made it easy to manipulate content, and with a few modifications, AI detection was nearly impossible. Casey had unsubscribed as soon as he learned about the subterfuge, but there were still almost 1.5 million followers who most likely still believed they were watching their favorite star.

Casey stared at his computer screen. He wasn't even sure how to type his following query into the Google search bar. He tried not to laugh at the irony of using the internet to validate the internet. He was trying to figure out how much apathy would tolerate a significant shift in the political landscape. *Could a minority opinion overpower a majority and convert a worldview?*

Casey worried about how many people were seemingly willing to toss aside their democracy on a vague promise of something they believed could be better. Why wasn't democracy valued anymore, particularly since the alternative would destroy the core foundation of the country?

He changed his search query and looked for information on the voting public. If a shift were occurring and there was a growing sentiment that many felt their votes didn't count, he could see why many of them didn't bother to vote. Could a politician or entity take advantage of that apathy? Rallying any sizeable demographic group could swing an election when less than half of the American population chose not to exercise their right to vote. An agenda that did not have popular support could still end up guiding democracy if only extremists decided to vote. Shifts in the Supreme Court and recent rulings were prime evidence of this effect.

Considering how most felt about their rights, ingrained into Americans since birth, it was easy for someone to dismiss their choice not to vote as their personal right. Philosophically, it became a tricky balancing act between individual rights and political duties if the future of democracy was at stake. Would apathy lead to the downfall of the United States, or would it be a group of opportunists relying on that apathy that could alter the very fabric of the country?

The election was only a few months away. Larry Stevens promoted a calmer, traditional platform, while the *Mega Mergers* reality TV star turned president embraced a world of chaos to promote change.

Casey wasn't sure when he'd first noticed a shift in the country's political outlook. In all fairness, maybe he was observing a standard ebb and flow of the political machine with public opinion shifting with the tides. *Surely the current state of extremism creating a division that discouraged any kind of political cooperation—this, too, would change with time?*

Casey had been feeling uneasy for weeks, mainly because he recognized that he was just barely scratching the surface of misinformation. He felt helpless, one lonely reporter swimming through a sea of content, trying to decipher fact from fiction, reality versus entertainment, and looking for the broadest narrative that resonated with the world around him. He'd always known the internet was a two-edged sword, a wealth of information that also came with a plethora of crap—the chain letter gone awry. Threats, scams, and impersonators mixed in with animated gifs of kittens, human failures, and how-to videos. Jerry was right. You can find whatever you wanted on the internet.

The scariest content he had read lately promoted the belief that the United States was a corporation created when the District of Columbia was "incorporated" into the United States. After years of mismanagement and abuse of power, the corporation was now defunct after defaulting on loans, and the country known as the United States of America was about to be restored to its former glory now that the debt-holders were dismantling the corporation. Casey had tried not to laugh when he learned the Pope and the British royal family were the "owners" of Corp USA. Unfortunately, as he dug deeper, he was discovering how extensively the information was being disseminated and believed by a wide swath of the public.

R was stoking the fires and dropping raindrops of information being devoured by a core group of loyalists who took the posts and expanded on them, making their own hypotheses and interpretations. It was nearly impossible to track all the threads to know who was behind the messages.

Casey knew one thing was becoming evident: Anyone could jump into the conversation and add their commentary without any factual substance to reinforce their comments. As he clicked through to a video allegedly of John F. Kennedy Jr. discussing his desire to stay under the radar, then stating that he would be returning to public life when it was appropriate, Casey looked for any resemblance to the young man who had reportedly died years ago. He paused the video and split-screened his view to load a picture of the former president's son and looked for similarities. He couldn't see it. The person in the video addressed the differences by saying the stress of his public past had aged him beyond recognition.

How convenient, Casey thought as he shook his head. How could one expose the truth without becoming vilified by those who still wanted to clutch at the hope of a false narrative? Reporting the truth was becoming an elusive notion.

■

Max pushed open the door of the Oval Office to soothe the ranting president. The Dom was in a full rage with an audience of several of his cabinet members, and the VP had been summoned in hopes of calming that rage.

"Goddammit! This is unacceptable. Don't they know I'm the president of the United States and that they cannot prevent me from leading this country to its former glory and greatness? These simple-minded lifers are clueless assholes that are getting in my way!"

The Dom was referring to the vetoing of his border wall bill. Maxwell knew better than to interrupt the tirade with rationale guidance. He entered the room quietly and watched The Dom pacing back and forth in front of his desk, gesturing into the air to punctuate his comments.

"CRIMINALS are invading our country! FOREIGNERS are taking our jobs! My base will not tolerate this, and we have an election to win. There is no way that I'm giving up the next four years to lead this country to greatness. Lazy Liberal Larry is going to destroy this nation, and I will not stand idle."

The president enjoyed having an audience and was so self-absorbed in his rhetoric that he didn't see the covert glances between his cabinet members. They'd been privy to this type of behavior so many times they'd grown accustomed to the drill. The only question was how long would this bout last? What could they say to sound supportive and dodge an accusation of not being loyal to The Dom and his agenda? There was no way to know if the portly man needed consoling, matched outrage, or suggestions for the next steps. Each observer looked for clues that could give them insights. The first person to speak could be a hero or a traitor. They would be seen as apathetic and weak if they stayed silent too long. It was a no-win situation, and many looked to Maxwell, as the vice president, to take the lead.

Max glanced at his phone. He'd entered the room seventeen minutes ago, and the president didn't seem to be losing any steam. He discreetly sent a message to one of the aides outside and hoped his ploy would work. Within five minutes, there was a knock on the door, and a server pushed a serving cart filled with drinks and snacks into the room. He twisted open the cap of a diet Mountain Dew and poured the cloudy green liquid over a glass filled with ice cubes. He extended the beverage towards Dominic. The president required that any beverage be opened and poured in front of him to ensure ultimate freshness. If too much ice had melted before it reached the president's desk, the whole West Wing would know. The pop of the cap and the release of the carbonated gas accomplished the intended goal, and Dominic reached for the refreshment.

"Got any peanuts?"

"Yes, sir. Right here." The white-gloved server held out a dish with the presidential seal. The Dom scooped up a handful and popped them into his mouth before chasing them down with the diet beverage. The others in the room waited to see if the rant would continue or if the food was enough of an interruption. When The Dom grabbed another handful of peanuts, the tension in the room dissipated slightly. His campaign manager was the first one to speak.

"Mr. President, the latest poll numbers show that your base sees you as strong and delivering on your campaign promises." He omitted that "Lazy Liberal Larry" had inched up two points since the last numbers had been released. He was fortunate that The Dom couldn't be bothered to read anything and instead relied on those around him to distill information into digestible sound bites.

Dominic looked pleased with the information, and Max stood. "Mr. President, I have an idea that might address your concerns. While the funding for your wall wasn't approved, Congress did approve the military budget that was submitted. Couldn't the wall be considered part of our border security, and therefore, the expenses could be included in that bill?"

"Your idea?" The Dom's eyes narrowed as he glared at the vice president. "That isn't your idea, and don't try to take credit for it. I proposed that as part of the budget weeks ago." Max cringed. Of course, the president would want to take credit for any idea that yielded the results he wanted. Max knew if there was any backlash later, the idea would be cast-off to another person to take the blame. It was a tightrope walk daily in the Coronet administration, and it was impossible to gauge the fickle man. Requests could change minute by minute, making it difficult to keep up.

"Of course, Mr. President. I remember." He hated lying, and yet it was the easiest way to deflect criticism and appease the man. He hoped God would forgive him for his transgressions and see the good of his intentions. He would repent his sins by reading his Bible when he returned home. He would pray for his salvation. He would also confess his sins to Nora. She would hold him accountable and give him a pathway for redemption. She would be disappointed in him, but she would forgive him once he'd made amends to God. They both realized that these were unusual times, and they were both being tested by God. Maxwell was pretty sure that Dominic Coronet had landed in the most powerful position in the world by selling his soul to the Devil. Every day, the vice president's actions and resolve were being tested by both God and Satan.

Secretly, he hoped that The Dom wouldn't be re-elected in a few weeks. He wanted to live an honorable and devout life. The Dom was a constant reminder of how far he'd veered off his path. Many days, he didn't recognize the man he'd become, and the anxiety he felt entering the Oval Office or attending rallies to boost the president's power made it almost impossible to sleep at night. There had to be a way to save his soul and his political career—the easiest way he could see was with Dominic Coronet out of the Oval Office. He would have to be patient and count down to the election. That was his only hope. He knew he would survive politically after the chaos of the Coronet administration was behind him. He didn't want to wait another four years for that to happen.

■

Pam stood beside the attorney her father had hired and faced the judge. The judge looked directly at her. "I want to make sure you understand the severity of these charges. While everyone is afforded freedom of speech, it cannot come at the detriment and peril of those around you. There were more than one million dollars of damages the day you attended the protest. While I recognize that it is easy to get caught up in the emotion of a large gathering, that does not condone disruptive behavior. Do you understand?"

Pam nodded.

"How do you plead?"

"Not guilty."

"Did your attorney advise you of all your options related to your plea?"

Pam nodded again.

Her attorney had advised her to plead "no contest" since she had no prior arrests. She would likely be assigned community service hours, and that would end the proceedings. The prosecuting attorney, a young Asian woman appointed to the case, had offered twenty-four hours of community service in lieu of a trial.

Pamela's attorney said he was willing to take whatever action she wanted and that community service was a good choice: No jail time and no fines.

"I'm not guilty. I'm worried about the impact on my medical school applications."

"The charges will be dropped to a misdemeanor, and medical schools will see you as committed to a cause."

"The only way *not* to have this on my record is to plead 'not guilty.'"

"Yes, but you'll run the risk of a jury finding you guilty, and then you could have bigger issues than a few hours of community service toward a misdemeanor."

The system was flawed. *How was it that she needed to negotiate the correct way to plea when she was innocent? Shouldn't "not guilty" be the logical choice, with justice prevailing in the end?* Her attorney had advised her otherwise. "No one wants to go to trial; the time and expense, along with the risk of a harsher sentence—most opt for the plea deal."

Pamela was adamant that she do whatever was required to be found innocent. Fortunately, her father had supported her choice. She knew it was costing him a lot. "It's only money, Pammy. We'll make sure that this sorts itself out." Now, facing the judge, she wasn't so sure, but she clung to the belief that justice would prevail.

"The court accepts and records your plea of 'not guilty.' The county clerk will set your court date for a trial." The judge tapped the gavel on the wooden block. Pam hoped she was doing the right thing. She'd just given control of her life to a group of strangers.

CHAPTER 30

When a videographer approached Leon about his video quality, the older man scoffed, saying that the content was what was important, not so much how it looked. However, as he saw his followers dropping off when others started spreading the word of R, he pulled out the email introduction and hired someone to help him. Not only had his viewing numbers jumped again, the number of subscribers had increased as well. He shouldn't have underestimated the importance of the image in addition to the content. Marketing himself wasn't something that came naturally to him.

The person he'd hired had even set him up with accounts on other platforms. It had surprised Leon to learn how much money could be made by creating content on a variety of channels. The initial payments he'd received from ad revenue connected to his channel had been a welcome surprise but weren't going to make him rich. Now that he was starting to receive sizable payments, it didn't take long to recoup the fees paid for the assistance. It was nice having someone else take care of the details, and whenever he had a question, he could pick up the phone. The videographer didn't look much older than twenty. Leon couldn't figure out how someone so young had learned so much about computers. He was still afraid of what would happen if he pressed the wrong button.

A large number of people were searching for meaning in the world. R was offering those insights, and Leon was pleased that he was an early adopter of the information. It gave him a level of credibility that newer R followers lacked. He'd been there since the beginning, and he'd been deciphering the raindrops for anyone interested in the gospel of R.

He hoped that one day, R would make himself known to at least his original posse of evangelists. Leon had his suspicions about R's identity, and he'd bet money that it was Dominic Coronet at the helm. Leon's video proclaiming The Dom as R was among his most watched posts. The president certainly had a wealth of secure data at his fingertips and could disseminate any information he determined the American people deserved to know.

The sound of an alert pinged on his machine, and he looked to see what the message relayed.

It couldn't be. Really? The Dom had just retweeted one of Leon's posts. Leon gasped for breath as he clicked into the site. The excitement made him want to jump up and scream so the whole world would hear.

The Dom reads my content! The president must be R, and his retweet was a direct confirmation that he was being recognized for his efforts by R himself! The repost started a cascade of likes and subscribers on his channel as The Dom's mega base engaged with his content. Leon was sure this was going to boost his income even more. He'd almost fallen off his chair when he received the first payment for several hundred dollars. Now, he was receiving thousands each month, and he'd stopped looking for work in a town with a sparse job market. He'd never made so much money in his life, and he saw it as yet another sign that he was ordained to do this work. He wouldn't stop until everyone knew the truth.

Leon printed the retweet from the president's personal account, and he'd pick up a picture frame the next time he was in town to look at it framed on his desk.

"Prepare for the Rainstorm, or you're going to get wet." R was The Dom; he was the chosen one. Leon could feel it in his bones.

◼

Brad's commanding officer was pissed.

"How did your body camera footage get blocked?" The officer with over two decades on the force was seething. "Do you understand how fucked up this is?" The elders in Whites had shown Brad Restore a variety of ways to mask the camera feed. It was unlikely that the camera footage would be looked at unless something significant happened. The elders had said that eliminating the feed would protect him.

Those who have not been enlightened will judge your actions. You are executing God's plan, but laws enacted by the misguided could be used against you.

Brad looked at his supervisor directly and shook his head. "I don't know what happened. There was so much going on that day. Maybe the camera malfunctioned due to the commotion."

"You think I'm a fuckin' idiot?" Spittle was gathering at the corner of his boss's mouth. "Nine out of ten times when the camera doesn't work, the officer has fucked it up. Why would you fuck up your camera?"

"I didn't." Brad wasn't going to give details. He'd been coached on how to respond. "It's gotta be something with the feed, or it got damaged."

"This is bullshit. You're just lucky I don't have any way to prove that you obstructed the feed, or you'd be on probation in a heartbeat."

Brad waited a moment. "Can I go now?"

"You better hope there are no future issues with your camera operation."

The threat didn't concern Brad. He'd continue to manipulate the video feed. *What would they do to him? Fire him?* They'd have no proof. He was protected. He had to execute God's plan, and he wouldn't be able to do that if he were sitting at a desk.

■

The Dom scanned the sea of faces before him. They looked eager and attentive, and he smiled. "Friends, we are watching the Liberal Left attempt to destroy our great country. They are willing to fling open our borders and allow any and all immigrants into this country. Criminals and those looking for a handout from the world's greatest country are leading the pack. Do not allow this shameful behavior to continue."

Cheers erupted around him, and he paused, enjoying the animation in the room. Signs with his name filled his view, bobbing in the sea of people before him.

"I'm asking for your support at the polls! The only way we can stop this destruction is to stand firm. We must fight to maintain our rights. It is imperative that we don't let these illegals steal from us. You will see crime rise if Lazy Larry is elected."

The Dom loved to use nicknames to erode confidence in his opponents. Referring to Larry Stevens with any formality wouldn't help his cause. Calling him lazy would subconsciously stick with voters when they were in the voting booth. He was amazed that no other politician had leveraged this tactic before he ran for office. He was showing them how it was done, and it pleased him to see other Republicans follow his lead, albeit not with the same finesse he'd honed for years while developing his corporation and reality television show.

"Don't let the liberals take your voice. Be heard! Show your support! I value your loyalty!" Dom knew that if someone came at him, he would knock them down verbally, discredit them, and use whatever other tactics were needed to weaken them. It made him invincible.

The rally cries around him reminded him how easy it was to push buttons to get a result. He was transcending president and becoming a God. He would rule the world.

The Dom stepped down from the podium. He felt exhilarated. It was his last rally before tomorrow's election. Based on the thunderous applause and packed auditorium, he was convinced he couldn't lose. His concern from earlier in the day was a faint memory as he basked in the energy of the room.

Lazy Liberal Larry was an old-school politician who hadn't seen the tides turning to sound bites and showmanship. He was an archaic dinosaur. The American people, the true nationalists of the United States, didn't want big government—they wanted a show. Politics were boring to most; something happening without much attention, a big yawn fest when listening to the arguments on the House floor. It was the small snippets of information that sparked a response. Trigger a few hot buttons to create a feeding frenzy that was fun to manipulate and even more fun to watch.

The Dom understood the power of creating a hidden villain to be able to rule the world. As long as he kept everyone fearful of what lurked in the dark shadows, it was possible to manipulate them to hand over their rights in exchange for promised security. His wish was their command. He could make them so fearful they wouldn't want to leave their homes. No movement meant no protests, and no demonstrations meant public peace and order.

Spoon feed people what they wanted to hear and they would be loyal for life. Dom still laughed about his tax bill that passed two years ago that primarily benefited those in the country's upper echelon. All the members at the top got a fifteen percent tax cut, accounting for billions of savings. At the same time, the middle class greedily gobbled up an extra deduction that only padded their pockets a few hundred dollars. The math didn't add up, but the promise of a tax cut, no matter how small for the bulk of the country, allowed The Dom to minimize his tax contribution by more money than he could spend in a lifetime.

I wonder if I can waive taxes for the president? The thought flashed through his mind. He had his sights on world domination, and that would take deeper pockets. After he was elected, he would find a way to bury that in a bill and give himself even more power. He would crush his competitors through trade deals and strong-arm tactics. He'd offer military assistance abroad in exchange for loyalty and could pull his support at any time. If anyone or any country tried to limit his power, he would crush them. Winning the next term was all that was needed to position him for his broader expansion of power.

As one of his first steps, after he was sworn into office for a second term and while his popularity ratings were high, he would remove the term limit imposed in 1951 by the 22nd Amendment. It required three-quarters of the state legislators to enact, and if The Dom were correct in his calculations, at least that many states would put him in office.

He knew that the liberal states located in the Northeast and the West Coast wouldn't support the change, but he didn't need them. Middle America was going to elect him. Once he was in office, it would allow him to establish himself as their leader for more than the next four years. Some of his followers were even calling him their prophet, ordained by God to restore America. He laughed. He never felt constrained by the moral compass of the religious zealots, and he had never been God-fearing in his life. He knew that God was used as a device for control. That played out throughout history time and time again. Hell, even his VP was "God-fearing," and look how much The Dom had controlled the other man who saw himself as one of God's disciples. *That poor schmuck Maxwell Hovick had lived his life of piety, and what had it gotten him? Nothing.* He was a great example of how playing by the rules had minimal reward, but bending the rules or ignoring them completely could yield so much more. The Dom held the president's office while Max was relegated to the second chair. He had waved a carrot that the presidency could be Max's if he were patient and became a loyal follower. Max would find himself waiting for an opportunity that would never come. The Dom wasn't to give up his seat in the Oval Office any time soon.

The Dom's campaign manager met him at the bottom of the stage steps. "Excellent. A perfect final performance before the election."

"We will win tomorrow!"

"Even though we couldn't make it to Pennsylvania or Georgia for one last push, you have extensive support in both states. Based on the election results four years ago, you should have no trouble securing their votes."

The Dom nodded. "What about the Midwest? Texas and Arizona are important for us, too."

"Fortunately, you were able to visit Houston several months ago, and Arizona polls are showing you ahead."

"Good." The Dom smiled. "Any last-minute dirt we can release anonymously on Lazy Larry?"

"We can post something again about one of his aide's claims of sexually inappropriate behavior twelve years ago, although there's no evidence that it's true." The campaign manager felt compelled to add the disclaimer.

"Who cares if it's true?! If you have a person who swears there was bad behavior, push that live! That will give us an upper hand, and if he's innocent, it will all be revealed after the election when it will be too late. Find a way to get that information throughout the media cycles. We need to amplify the message that Stevens is the WRONG choice."

"I'll take care of it." The campaign manager pulled his phone from his pocket. "Let's get you to Air Force One."

CHAPTER 31

The Dom had no patience for the morning briefings, so he tapped out a few Twitter messages while waiting for the room to clear. "Secure your future." "Be sure to vote for me tomorrow at the polls." "Four more years!" "Don't halt the progress we've made on the wall!" "Don't let others steal your future." "Your vote counts."

There had been a significant uptick in absentee ballots since the previous election, and Dom wondered how easy it would be to stuff the ballot box with ballots sent through the mail. He knew that each state had to certify the results of their elections, but he was still unclear on the process. It would be too easy to manufacture fake ballots and return them en masse. Usually, he wasn't paranoid, but the latest poll numbers showed a shift in support between him and Lazy Liberal Larry. It was hard to believe that voters were interested in supporting the weak candidate when Dom was on the ballot.

His campaign had leaked the story of the intern from twelve years ago, but it seemed to be having the opposite effect of what they expected. It would have come across with more credibility if it had just happened. At the final hour, it was perceived as a feeble attempt to discredit a politician with over three decades of untarnished experience.

After the briefing in the Oval Office ended, he summoned his campaign manager. "There has got to be something else we can do to deflate the liberals' campaign."

"At this stage, we have to sit tight. We can do more damage than good."

Patience was not a strength Dominic embraced. He started pacing around his office. Sitting still was impossible.

"Sir, don't worry. By the end of tomorrow, you'll be re-elected and positioned to lead this country for another four years."

"If that doesn't happen, it'll mean something's wrong. The polls show me ahead." He tried not to sound anxious, and yet he felt uneasy. He couldn't shake the jitters and started pacing again.

The campaign manager hesitated. "May I suggest that you enjoy a nice lunch? I'm sure the chef can prepare whatever you'd like."

The Dom had a better idea for taking his mind off the election.

"Can you arrange for the girl that was here last week?"

"Of course, sir. I'll make sure she's here within the hour."

■

Cynthia Liu, the prosecuting attorney for Pamela Jackson's case, had just received the body camera footage of Officer Bradley Taylor. Unfortunately, a shadow obscured the replay, making it impossible for her to determine who was involved in the skirmish and precisely what had happened.

How did we get this far? This should never have reached the arraignment stage. She felt frustrated at being put into this situation. She'd trusted the officer's report as sufficient evidence and an accurate report of the situation. She chastised herself for not being more thorough. A heavy caseload and a lot of pressure from the city to control crime was part of the reason she'd slipped up.

It was her responsibility to ensure that criminals were held accountable for their crimes, but from what she could tell, Pamela Jackson didn't fit into that category. Looking at her file, the lawyer could see the young woman was a pre-med student at Stanford with no prior charges. It seemed highly unlikely she was an agitator. *Why had she been singled out of the BLM protest and charged?* She looked at the bail amount, and even that seemed excessive.

Liu shook her head. She wasn't sure how she could proceed in the courtroom without looking foolish. She wondered if she could get Pamela to agree to community service instead of a trial. It wouldn't hurt her to contribute a day or two cleaning up the trash along the roadways, and it would solve the problem that Officer Taylor had created. She hadn't crossed paths with the police officer before this case, and she pulled up his employee listing on the internal server. This wasn't his first transgression. She also read about his suspension after discharging his weapon that killed an unarmed teen. He'd been allowed to return to work because internal affairs had determined the officer had reason to believe the teen was armed.

Why had she chosen a legal role in Oakland County? She should have pursued corporate law or some other nonconfrontational practice. Drafting contracts and protecting corporate assets seemed more appealing these days. Considering her sub-par pay compared to her classmates and an overflow of criminal cases across her desk, she began feeling jaded at thirty-seven. She was tired of seeing the riff-raff funnel through the court system.

Returning her attention to the case file, she saw that a hired bulldog attorney was representing the young woman. This wasn't going to be easy. So much for a public servant assigned to represent the student. At the hourly rate Hugh Schmidt charged, he would happily take the case as far as it could go, even if it conflicted with his client's best interests.

Unless Hugh was a family friend, it would appear that Pamela Jackson came from a wealthy family. *Was she trying to lash out, hoping to get love from her parents?*

Cynthia looked at her watch. It was almost noon and if she left now, she should be able to cast her vote at her polling location about twenty minutes away. She'd meant to request a mail-in ballot that would have made it easier to vote, but she'd been consumed by work, and now she would consume precious time making sure her vote counted.

■

"Don't lose sight of your power! You can control your future destiny. Don't be a whimpering coward. Join the forces of the Restoration Movement to preserve our country for generations to come. Today is the day to vote for your future. Vote for Dominic Coronet! The Hollywood elite faction committing crimes against our society has been held accountable through the trials in the High Court Tribunals. The day of reckoning is approaching. The Dom will lead us! You are being called to rise up to reclaim your power. Respect the word. You are being misled. – R."

CHAPTER 32

"You're watching Fox News, your place for accurate and up-to-date information on the election results. The polls are closed on the East Coast, and counts are starting to come in. Dominic Coronet is leading in Georgia, North Carolina, and Virginia." The news anchor looked directly toward the viewing audience. "There's no surprise that Dominic Coronet is leading in these states. Larry Stevens is ahead in Massachusetts, New York, and New Jersey."

The young blond anchorwoman sitting next to the fifty-year-old White man chimed in, "Stay tuned for more information as the night progresses. We'll be the first station to declare the winner of the presidential office!"

The Dom looked at the screen. He focused less on what they were saying and instead on the blue and red banners showing the percentages for each state. The red bars that represented his party were getting traction. He leaned back into his chair. It wouldn't be long before he could put his next plans into action. Picking up the remote control, he displayed several news stations on the numerous screens around him. He kept the volume turned up on Fox but muted CNN, NBC, CBS, ABC, MSNBC, and several other cable news stations.

For now, The Dom was alone in his private quarters and would leave for his election night celebration in an hour or two. He had a lot to celebrate. The red bars were surpassing the blue ones on each screen, and with only 7% of the cumulative count tallied, it would be a long night. He didn't have concerns about the remaining 93%. He believed the early trend was a good indicator that the Oval Office would be his for years to come.

■

Larry Stevens slid out of the black Town Car that had taken him to his election hub for the evening. Inside the gymnasium, his campaign had set up large screens and tapped into live feeds of election parties around the United States. A bar in Boston, a school in Texas, and a church in Georgia were a few of the groups being included throughout the room with a two-way connection that kept both sides informed of the others' activities.

His wife, Linda, exited the car after him. He reached his arm around her back and helped her forward. He felt a wave of gratitude as he looked her in the eyes before they started their walk to the building entrance. They were used to the flashbulbs and camera clicks going off around them.

Linda smiled a genuine smile that creased her eyes, showing the lines of age around her face. Larry thought she was still beautiful and counted himself a lucky man. He was there mainly because of her sacrifices and willingness to put her needs aside to support her husband. When they'd met at the University of Chicago, neither of them had ever thought they'd be where they were today. Larry had political aspirations and had only embraced a more significant dream of the presidency after he'd been in office for several years. It was the way to make the most significant impact.

"Larry! How are you feeling tonight?" one of the reporters outside the arena called across the crowd, his voice penetrating through the commotion swirling around them.

"Great!" Larry made a thumbs-up gesture with his free hand and smiled. The cameras clicked, and the lights flashed. This could be the photo splashed across newspapers and online news sites when he won the election. If he lost, the image would be obscured in the archives. Larry pushed the thought aside. There was no room for negative thoughts. He'd spent a career to get where he was tonight, and the polls, while close, showed that the office could be his. Now, it was just a matter of time. They'd cast their votes in the morning before a sea of reporters, and with the West Coast polls closing soon, they'd done all they could. They would win.

■

Maxwell watched the banner scroll across the bottom of the television screen on Fox News, displaying the percentage of votes counted by state. Large screens had been placed throughout the venue for easy viewing. His wife, Nora, stood by his side. The race between Dominic Coronet and Larry Stevens was too close to call. Now that all the polls were closed, it would take hours before the final count had been confirmed. Max turned and saw Dominic Coronet standing in the large ballroom at his hotel in Washington, D.C., where they had converged to announce their victory. There was a hum around the room that was a blend of optimism and anxiety. The Dom started pacing, proclaiming his victory. "We're ahead in the polls, and we've won this election."

Max wasn't going to contradict the older man. He also didn't mention that the polls aggregated on fivethirtyeight.com showed a different story. While some certainly favored the current president, the majority were more favorable towards Larry Stevens. It would come down to which candidate had been able to mobilize people to vote.

"I don't trust the liberals tasked with counting votes. We know they would stoop to low measures to make sure the votes tally the way they want for their candidates to win."

The harried campaign manager was trying to stroke The Dom's ego. "I'm sure you've won. Look, Virginia just declared you a winner!"

Dominic roared. "That's what I'm talkin' about!" He smacked the campaign manager on the back. Max was pretty sure the younger man would welcome the time after the election to catch up on sleep. His hollow eyes and dark circles conveyed how little sleep he'd had in the months leading up to the election. It must be a thankless job trying to guess The Dom's quick shifts in temperament.

"We always knew we wouldn't carry California and New York. However, there are a lot of people in middle America that see you as their president. You've got this."

Max hoped the campaign manager wasn't promising something he couldn't deliver. The vice president thought back to the rally he had led in Georgia. It had been a tough group.

The news channel reported another state's results. Groans could be heard around the room as Illinois voted in favor of Stevens. Max placed his hand into his wife's and squeezed it gently. They looked at each other and silently conveyed their hope the night would end favorably for all in the room. While they knew it would be difficult catering to the president's whims for four more years, it beat the alternative. The Dom would not take losing gracefully.

■

Larry and his running mate, Sheila, stood on the stage built on the large gymnasium floor in his hometown just outside Madison, Wisconsin. They had selected the site to watch the election results for a multitude of reasons. Returning to the school he'd attended before leaving for college and launching his political career connected him to his roots. It also conveyed his stance on the importance of education while juxtaposing the other side's opulence and overindulgence. They were the candidates for the everyday person in the United States. Linda was nearby, supporting her spouse.

A projection screen at the back of the stage displayed a map of the country and was being updated in real-time as the votes were counted. Wisconsin was already filled in with blue to convey the state had elected their brethren. Sheila's home state of Iowa was also blue. If either state had not supported their own, it would have been a terrible sign for the outcome of the evening. Electoral College votes were displayed in the lower corner, and it was still too early to predict a winner.

Larry scanned the room and saw the familiar faces of his team who had worked tirelessly to promote their agenda. As he stepped to the podium, he smiled with appreciation.

"Hello, everyone!"

Cheers erupted, and Larry could see many election signs waving in the air.

"The night is still young, and we have many hours before we'll know the results. I am confident that we will prevail at the polls. We have been truthful in our campaign. We have shown the American people that we are here to represent them and to improve their lives."

The stage vibrated with an energetic response. Larry paused and enjoyed the hum around him. "I want to express my immense gratitude to everyone who has committed themselves to getting the word out to their communities about our agenda. While it takes strength to lead, a powerful leader understands that they are only empowered because of the dedication and loyalty of those around them. You have given me your support and helped build the foundation of our success!"

Larry looked directly at the camera positioned to capture his campaign headquarters activities for the world to see. "I want to thank every single person watching tonight who cast their votes and supported our campaign. I am here to lead our great country for the next four years, and we will make a difference!"

The room was filled with thunderous applause, and Larry relished the moment with a measured beat after years of being in front of an audience. He knew instinctively how long to wait before continuing.

Just before he was about to speak, the voice of his campaign manager crackled in his earpiece, and he smiled. "I have just learned that Illinois has reported our win!" He gestured to the screen, and the production team changed the state to blue to coincide with his wave. The Electoral College count increased by 20 in his column.

The group inside the gymnasium started whooping their approval, and as Larry looked at the screens around the room, he could see the joyful reactions of those celebrating remotely. He looked up to the large canvas tarp stretched overhead, filled with balloons and confetti that would be released to celebrate their victory.

It was going to be a great night. Larry could feel it in his bones.

CHAPTER 33

The Dom tried to bury his rage. It was not the right time to be seen reacting to the results flowing in. The fucking Electoral College count was displayed in the lower corner of most of the reporting stations. He couldn't believe there was still a question about whether or not he was the winner of the election.

Michigan had betrayed him. They had voted for that schmuck, Stevens. The state had adored him four years ago. There had to be a mistake.

Several larger states still hadn't confirmed their final counts, and while other smaller states were still up for grabs, their contributions wouldn't sway the outcome. Dom needed Pennsylvania, Arizona, and Georgia to declare him the winner. Their collective power would keep him president. He did a mental calculation. He wouldn't need Michigan's measly 16 Electoral College votes if he carried most of the remaining states yet to declare a winner.

His campaign manager approached The Dom with a drink in hand. *This wasn't a time to drink alcohol. What was the man thinking?* He was showing his weakness. Stress wasn't a reason to drink; it was the time to keep one's wits at full capacity. Dominic was relieved that he wouldn't have to deal with this man again after tonight. He'd been effective and communicated well throughout the election, but if he'd done his job correctly, The Dom wouldn't be looking at the screen conveying a tight race. It should have been a landslide.

"You're fired."

The younger man looked shocked. "What?"

"You heard me."

"The campaign is over. You can't fire me. The job is done."

"Oh, yes, I can. I want you to know what a piss poor job you did. You're fired. We should be watching a landslide, but instead, we're watching this shit. We'd already have confirmed the win if you'd done your job."

"We will win."

"Regardless, you are weak. Get out of my sight. I don't want to see you again."

The Dom turned and stepped toward the podium. His wife, Melanie, and their young daughter, Heather, stood nearby.

"It's just a matter of time before we receive the votes needed to win. We know I will continue as your president. I am the best man for the job, as evidenced by the last four years! No one has done more for this country. I have fortified our borders with a new wall. I have reduced taxes and kept the economy strong. I have imposed trade tariffs that favor our country. No one and I mean no one, especially Lazy Larry Stevens, could have done a better job."

The room erupted with cheers and applause. The group had arrived with frenetic energy and hummed with an amplified vibe as they waited for results. The president knew how to bolster the crowd. The Dom also knew that the news teams in the back of the room were reporting and making sure the American people were informed that he was the one in control, even if the votes had not been fully counted. The polls might be closed, but he could still preach his message.

■

Jamiel turned off his television set around 11:00 p.m. when it was evident that the election results wouldn't be confirmed until the morning. He was tired after months of being barraged with political content. He'd done his part and cast his vote earlier in the day.

He read the pros and cons printed in the published voter guide submitted by advocates for each side. He'd gone online, weighed the information he'd found, and cast his vote as best as he could. He also knew that Larry Stevens was the better candidate for the country regardless of how much trash talk the other side spewed about the veteran politician.

Black history showed that many had been denied easy access to voting and historically required a literacy test to vote. Jamiel wondered what would happen if voters had to pass a test that outlined the basics of domestic and international politics. *How many people really understood what the Constitution stood for and the cause and effect of legislation? The Dom had railed against NATO, but how many voters in the United States even knew what NATO was and why it existed?* Climate change was another topic with ignorance rearing its head throughout news stories and political rhetoric. When he'd been in South Carolina months earlier, he'd seen a sign that said the only climate change was the shift between winter, spring, summer, and fall.

The Dom had started his campaign based on his history as a successful businessman and had said he would self-fund his campaign. That had subtly shifted to taking donations from individuals interested in supporting his candidacy and ultimately expanded to companies with their own agenda for his campaign. Casey had shared information with Jamiel that showed how the campaign funds were allocated. It amazed both men how many people in the United States didn't care or see a conflict with the donations. Many still thought The Dom was fully funding his campaign even though the required quarterly fundraising reports showed a flow of millions to the president's campaign.

Apathy had thwarted several emolument clause complaints. Jamiel hoped that apathy wasn't going to destroy the democracy he valued. It was flawed, as shown by the need for movements like Black Lives Matter, but at least he was afforded the right to vote, the right to assemble, and a right to representation, even if it wasn't perfect. After he kissed his wife goodnight and turned off his bedside lamp, he looked up at the ceiling. *Was the country at risk of losing its democracy?* The thought did nothing to help him fall asleep.

■

Casey had invited a group of fellow reporters to his apartment in Georgetown to watch the election results, pig out on burgers, brats, and chips, and be prepared to fill in their headlines for the next paper run. The group had been consuming Diet Coke, Sprite, and Fanta, but someone had finally opened a beer around midnight. They'd wanted to be sober, but as it was becoming evident that no victor would be declared for hours, Casey used the magnet-backed bottle opener attached to the front of his fridge to pop the top off a cold bottle of Samuel Adams beer. It wasn't his everyday choice, but having beer named after one of the Founding Fathers on an election night with his co-workers seemed fitting.

"The Dom must be shitting his pants right about now." Jessica from Lifestyles voiced what they'd all been thinking. "I mean, he was so damn cocky this past week. Kinda nice to see him not handed an easy win."

Casey suspected that most in the room had cast their votes for Larry Stevens if they'd even voted. It still amazed him how many Americans didn't exercise their right to vote. He saw voting as a tribute to those who had been denied the right to vote by a country founded on a patriarchy that often excluded Blacks, Native Americans, Asians, and women.

His laptop was open, and two articles had been written: One to push live if Stevens won and the other if Dominic Coronet was elected for four more years. The team had vetted both with their editor. It wouldn't take long to add final details and post it to the internet as well as send it for physical printing as soon as a winner was declared.

The team huddled at Casey's apartment were just a small number of *The Nat Times* writers assigned to report on the election. Others had assembled at various locations to push snippets and commentary live, both on *The Nat* website and across the paper's social media feeds. It was possible to have a presence in the news even if television broadcasting coverage ruled throughout the election.

Several reporters drifted home, and Casey, along with two others, drank a few beers and hypothesized about the news being reported. They'd toggled between a few, including Fox, CNN, and MSNBC, but had finally settled on the BBC feed out of New York City.

"Man, I hope this is done soon." The statement by Jerry, one of the newer writers at the paper, conveyed a sentiment that extended beyond the late hour and summed up the roller coaster ride of the past four years. It was well documented how disruption had played a role in the Coronet administration. It would be nice not to cringe daily when reading or reporting the news.

■

Leon stared at his computer. He couldn't believe the reports. *How had Larry Stevens amassed so many votes?* R had confirmed that The Dom would be the next president in his posts. Dominic Coronet was a prophet, and the High Court Tribunal had appointed him as the chosen one destined to lead the country back to greatness.

He looked at the BeWarned.com website, but R had been silent for the week leading up to the election. His last post hadn't indicated that he'd be going dark. If he were right and R was Dominic Coronet, it made sense that there were no recent posts while the president focused on affairs of state. However, now Leon wasn't too sure about R's identity. Regardless, he knew R had a security clearance with enough clout to see the information restricted for an elite few.

Could R have been caught by the dangerous elite? The thought both scared him and energized him. If R had been discovered and abducted, all of his posts would be a testament to his role as a true nationalist of the United States. He was a hero. He had spoken up when others had been afraid to speak out about the atrocities going on behind the scenes of the country.

With several tabs open in his browser, Leon pressed reload over and over again, hoping to see a post from R on the BeWarned site. It distressed him that there was no message, especially now, while it was so critical. *Was there a strategy to the close results?* Leon suspected there were people brighter than him, ensuring the preservation of their society. If there was one thing he'd learned during his time following R, the truth was not being reported by mainstream media. It made sense that the talking heads of traditional news sources had been bought and paid for by those wanting to control the dialogue. With the elimination of the Incorporated United States of America, those who had enjoyed being in power were being hobbled, and the saviors of the country were taking their place.

Leon was confident R would post again soon. There was no way he'd been shut off from the world. He would know how to remain protected. The Rainstorm was coming, and with it, there were a lot of future raindrops to decipher. Leon still had important work to do.

◼

It was three in the morning when Larry Stevens opted to leave the high school gymnasium. The counts were still being tallied. Many people had already slipped away, exhaustion taking its toll on those who had been pushing tirelessly for the finish.

Nothing good comes easily. The message instilled in him at a young age by his mother was proving true once again. Earlier in the evening, his instincts told him he was the winner, but Dominic Coronet was proving to be a pesky candidate.

Larry felt tired as he'd watched footage from the Coronet Corporation hotel where The Dom had ensconced himself for the evening.

"The liberals are trying to STEAL the election. The polls have shown my popularity! I am your president and will continue in my office for the next four years!" The Dom didn't sound like a desperate man clinging to the last hopes of being re-elected. While there was still a slim chance the votes could turn in Dom's favor, that window was slowly being shut. Larry was superstitious enough not to assume anything. Cautiously optimistic without cockiness was his best bet.

Larry slid into the Town Car next to his wife, and they rode in silence to their hotel. Both were exhausted and without a definitive answer for a victor, it was easier to stay silent than to voice either hope or reassurance.

"There's no telling when the remaining states will report their results. Let's try to sleep." The two navigated the hotel suite, well-orchestrated movements of a couple married for decades who still shared a bed and bathroom.

CHAPTER 34

The Dom returned to his private quarters in the wee hours of the morning when it was evident that his victory wouldn't be announced anytime soon. So much for the extravagant party they had planned at the Coronet Corporation District hotel.

He'd flipped on the television at 6 a.m. and rotated around the news channels, looking for updates.

CNN was the first to predict Larry Stevens as the new president, using exit data as their rationale.

How dare the news report that he did not have enough Electoral College votes to secure the presidency!

The Dom almost threw the remote at the screen but caught himself, reminded that if he broke the screen, he wouldn't be able to stay informed.

What states had betrayed him? Why did the alternate news think that he'd lost? He knew he was the winner. No one was going to take the Oval Office away from him. It was humiliating to think that he hadn't been able to receive enough votes to secure a second term. Only losers couldn't hold onto their office. He wasn't a loser.

He flipped the channel to Fox News and watched for any contradiction of the information being reported on CNN. Fox had always been good to him, and he knew they would say he was the winner.

The wall of screens in Dominic's private chambers were all tuned to an array of news channels. The splattering of red and blue on all screens did not give him comfort. There should have been an abundance of red representing his party. He didn't like seeing all the blue allocated for the liberal hack, Larry Stevens.

The Electoral College votes for each candidate were displayed on most of the screens, and the commentators on Fox were making predictions about the states that had not been called. Pennsylvania, Arizona, and Georgia were still undeclared, and they represented enough Electoral College votes to tip the scales to keep Dominic in office.

The Dom had retreated to his chambers to be alone, watching the results. He'd barely slept through the night and instead had installed himself in front of the screens, sending tweets throughout the night.

Early declarations for the Coronet campaign came from Republican strongholds of Texas, Florida, and Ohio, providing almost one-third of the Electoral College votes he needed to win. The Dom's tweets were positive and energetic:

"The results are strong all over the country. THANK YOU!"

"I will be making a statement soon to celebrate a big WIN!"

As the Electoral College votes were levied into Larry Stevens's column and threatened his lead, Dominic became more desperate. Losing was not an option. There was no way that Larry Stevens was going to take the White House away from him.

Twitter provided a release to his frustration: *Last night, I was leading, often solidly, in many key States, then, one by one, they started to magically shift as mysterious ballot dumps were counted. VERY SUSPECT! Is this the last gasp of the Hollywood elite trying to retain power?*

A new dump of Mail-In ballots. Why are they so skewed? This is a last-gasp effort by the Left and their power of destruction.

We are up BIG, but they are trying to TAKE the Election. We will never let them do it. Votes cast after the Polls CLOSE are not valid! We will PREVAIL! Lazy Liberal Larry is not a leader. I AM the president!

Dominic obsessively watched the screens with his phone by his side. Fox News was still optimistic about his win, and he retweeted one of their favorable takes on his campaign.

He did a quick mental calculation. California, a mass of Electoral College votes, would go to Stevens. Dom didn't need those granola-munching, hippie-dippies anyway. It wouldn't matter if Larry Stevens got more of the undeclared smaller state votes. It was the more prominent states that mattered. Pennsylvania, Georgia, and Arizona were poised to give him the remaining count he needed. It was hard to be patient.

One by one, he watched several of the remaining states switch between blue and red. He ticked up a few, and Larry Stevens secured several others. It was coming down to the wire. It was a much tighter race than The Dom wanted to acknowledge. His advisers had warned him about several polls leading up to election day, but he had brushed them aside, stating they'd been done by liberal publications. "That's a false positive for Stevens!" had been his response, but now he began believing they had more merit. It was essential to crush the competition, not cower away in the corners. He needed to get out of his bathrobe and face the world.

Stepping away from the bank of screens, he showered, shaved, and selected one of the most expensive suits in his closet. Usually, he had a valet assist him, but he'd banished everyone from his inner sanctum and preferred to dress without the pampering today. He would bask in his glory once the results were finalized.

Stepping back to the alcove of screens, he glanced at the vote. "What the hell?" Georgia and Arizona had reported blue. *Why had he stepped away?*

Picking up his phone, he tapped a response on Twitter: *Mail-in ballots are statistically flawed in their count versus votes cast at polls. This indicates there is rampant fraud! Mail-in ballots need to be verified! Prepare to fight to ensure this election isn't STOLEN!*

The two candidates were neck and neck.

Larry Stevens had slept a few hours with Linda by his side. He knew she was awake, attempting to breathe in an even, measured count to project calm in their bedroom. As he sat up, she turned and placed her hand on his thigh.

"We've come a long way, and you're a winner to me, no matter what happens."

He picked up her hand and kissed the inside of her palm.

"We're going to the White House, I'm confident."

He reached for his phone on the bedside table and quickly scanned his texts before opening one of the news apps. No congratulatory emojis or high-fives. It was safe to say the election was still up in the air.

He randomly picked one of the news sites, knowing they all would be reporting the same information. A lot had happened since they'd stepped away from the news feed hours before. He was just a few votes away from being declared the winner. Nervous energy and excitement pulsed through his body, and he left the bed.

"Dang, Linda, we got Arizona and Georgia!"

"I knew you were going to win!" The creases around her eyes showed her sincerity.

"Looks like Pennsylvania is going to determine this race." Internally, he voiced a silent thank you to his campaign manager, who had encouraged him to campaign in the state within the past week.

"You've got this." His wife pushed the blankets aside.

"Don't be too sure about anything. They're called swing states for a reason!" Larry had tirelessly committed himself to the potential voters that would secure his place in the Oval Office while not taking the tried-and-true blue states for granted. Dominic Coronet hadn't appeared in Georgia but sent his VP instead. The results were evident as Larry looked at the blue box on his phone screen surrounding the state tally.

"Don't worry about getting up now. Try to get some more sleep. It's going to be a long day." He urged his wife to stay in bed. He knew she hadn't slept much, and he'd prefer a little privacy as he paced the adjoining living room of their suite.

It had been a fitful night fueled by anticipation, uncertainty, and exhaustion from a grueling campaign push leading up to election day. Larry moved from the bedroom of their suite to the open area that included a couch, desk, and small kitchenette. He brewed some coffee and flipped on the television to watch as the election results continued to be reported.

He looked at his cell phone again. Numerous messages and calls had flooded in. Without a victory to declare, he decided to ignore the device. Instead, he flipped through the cable and local channels on the hotel television, looking for any updates that would determine his fate for the next four years.

It felt like the quiet before the storm. The evening prior had been full of ups and downs, fueled by adrenaline and caffeine. He tried to push his frustration aside, disappointed that it hadn't been a landslide and that he was forced to wait longer for the results.

His campaign manager had assured him that the mail-in ballots were still being counted. They would likely contain a more liberal voting base. The Republicans catered to citizens of Middle America who generally showed up in person to vote, while the Democrats were usually found in metropolitan cities. The residents on the two coasts opted for the convenience of sending in their votes—not an exact breakdown of demographics, but enough to give Larry hope for the outcome. There had been many elections since the results had been too close to call on the same day votes were cast. With the sun rising on Wednesday morning, the senator wondered if he'd know by the end of the day if he were the next president or if the count might take longer.

Dominic Coronet's image flashed on the television screen, and Larry stopped scrolling channels, curious what message the current president would convey.

"I am the president of the United States today and for four more years!" He was broadcasting on his favorite network, Fox News, and it didn't surprise Larry that the reporter did nothing to interrupt the monologue. For anyone just tuning in, it sounded like a declaration of victory, and yet, in the lower corner of the news screen, the Electoral College tally still showed that the race had yet to be called.

■

"This just in! Pennsylvania has reported their election results, and LARRY STEVENS HAS WON THE ELECTION!"

The Dom watched the array of screens in front of him change, flashing a victory for Stevens. Anger flared, and he picked up the universal remote, flinging it toward the wall. The control made contact with one of the displays, and it shattered the screen into a spider web of cracks before dropping to the floor with a thud. The news feed still played behind the splinters of glass.

"It's NOT possible!" He looked around the room for anything to help him release his anger. He saw a wooden chair with a padded seat, most likely an antique from a predecessor. He grabbed the back and started assailing the screens. There was no way he was going to lose his place in the White House.

The sound of breaking glass, along with electrical pops and hisses, prompted him to strike the screens repeatedly until the wooden chair wobbled apart. Every screen was dark.

The Dom dropped the tattered remains of the historic chair and collapsed into the leather armchair he used when viewing the informational wall. There had to have been a mistake. He picked up his phone and pulled up his Twitter account.

There is rampant fraud in this election. Follow the ballot trail, and you'll find padded voting, including dead voters and ballots cast after polls closed.

We will certify the results with every state that shows election irregularities.

We will prevail.

The phone on his desk rang. He hesitated before picking it up but decided it was better to own his narrative as early as possible.

"Mr. President, we are being asked to concede to the Stevens campaign." Max Hovick was on the other end of the line.

"No fucking way. I haven't lost. I'm not conceding to anything."

"Mr. President, Larry Stevens has both the popular vote and enough Electoral College vote to confirm his win."

"NO! Didn't you fucking hear me? I'm not a loser. There needs to be a recount. I KNOW that there is voter fraud, and I've won. This is a manipulation of the vote to drive me out of office. I'm not going to bow down that easily. They want me to bend over and take it. They can fuck themselves."

The Dom slammed down the handpiece of the phone and wondered why landlines were still peppered throughout the White House. It just went to show that too much in the U.S. government was old and outdated. He still had too much cleansing to do before leaving office. He wasn't going to go down without a fight.

■

"Do not believe what the false news narrative is telling you. The election results reported by the false news establishments after the elections yesterday are the last grasp of power by Satan-worshiping elites who have controlled the government for too long. They know the power that our savior, Dominic Coronet, has to hold them accountable for their wrongdoings. Do not stand idle while they unjustly try to take the position in the White House for the next four years. Respect the word. You are being misled. — R."

Leon sighed with relief as he read the post. R was fine. He hadn't been abducted or thwarted in his mission to send the critical messages to save the democracy. Leon prepped his home studio and prepared to record a new video. Clearly, he had a lot of work ahead to ensure that The Dom was sworn in as the true election winner. Those trying to alter the outcome and deny The Dom his rightful place would not prevail. They could try to alter history, but they wouldn't be able to if people like R and Leon were there to spread the word, the truth. The Dom won the presidential election, and Leon didn't care how many Electoral College votes were displayed on his screen, which showed otherwise. R had foretold the future. The Dom was a prophet. The future of their democracy was being held hostage by the evil hiding in the shadows.

CHAPTER 35

How could Dominic Coronet consider himself the winner of the presidential election? All evidence showed that he'd lost, fair and square—sore loser.

Pam looked up from the news feed on her tablet as Asher entered the Stanford Cafe. The warm summer days had been gradually disappearing now that half the semester was behind them. November days in Palo Alto were beautiful. Clear skies and air turning crisper. The weather on the south peninsula of the Bay Area brought cool mornings and temperate afternoons. This was her favorite time of year. She'd adapted quickly to the northern part of the state, grateful to leave the heat and smog of Los Angeles behind her. The two locations were worlds apart, and she recognized how fortunate she was to be at the elite school pursuing her dreams.

"Whatcha reading?"

Pam slid the iPad over to her friend, and he scanned the headline.

"Don't worry. The Dom will have to admit he lost sooner rather than later. This should be behind us soon."

"I don't know. It's been three days, and he still hasn't conceded. Cries of voter fraud."

"There's no evidence of fraud. He'll have to face the truth soon."

Pam sighed. She hoped so. She wasn't sure why it surprised her that, in losing, The Dom continued to behave as if he were a winner. She could hardly wait for January when Larry Stevens was sworn in, and the country could return to normal.

∎

Brad Taylor didn't need to follow politics. He had sworn an oath to Whites Restore, and the elders dictated his role in the organization. They had told him to vote for The Dom even though they'd warned him that California had been lost to those in liberal cities like San Francisco and Los Angeles. The large populace didn't represent those outside of the two metropolitan areas. Other chapters of WR were located in parts of the country that could be saved. The cleansing was coming. The Restoration was near.

In parallel, Brad had been reading R's posts, and he knew the Rainstorm was coming. To Brad, it was just semantics. The Rainstorm was the Restoration. Back to 1776. Back to the strength of White men. Those with inferior lineage would be guided in their ascension.

The current gathering of Whites Restore was animated. Various conversations rippled around the room. "We have feet on the street outside the election offices in Georgia, Arizona, and Pennsylvania."

"The Dom has called for a public count of votes. It seems that some election offices have something to hide. They are trying to conceal the fraud and irregular ballots."

"I saw pictures of large boxes of ballots being dragged in after the polls closed. There is so much corruption evident in the election."

"ATTENTION, attention! We are calling this meeting to order." The elder who led the chapter stood at the podium. "Someone, please ensure that the meeting room is closed. Our session today requires diplomacy and discretion. This is a critical time for our mission. We must prevail in cleansing society, and we cannot make mistakes now that could thwart our cause."

A new member sprung from his chair and looked up and down the hallway before closing the double doors. "All clear. No one outside."

"Good, good. Thank you. Let us begin."

An hour later, Brad emerged from the church building, excited about his role in Whites Restore. Great things were about to happen. He had been given guidance and knew his direct orders would be coming soon.

■

The Dom had replaced the wall of television screens in his personal chamber. The maintenance staff, sworn to secrecy by NDAs, had been discrete in the removal and installation. He had all the screens muted except Fox. The morning show hosts were discussing the theft of the election and Dominic's determination to recount ballots.

Picking up his phone, he dialed into the station and was quickly patched into the anchors on the air. "I've just been informed that the president of the United States is on the line. What a privilege to have you join us today, sir."

The Dom muted the volume on the television and watched as the banner scrolling along the bottom of the screen informed viewers he was on the air.

"Breaking just for you!" The Dom paused for effect. "We have put out the word to voters throughout the United States to report irregularities at their polls on election day. We've received numerous messages about the tricks used to cast illegal votes for Larry Stevens."

The news anchor nodded, and Dom continued. "I'm asking everyone watching today to do their part as nationalists and contact the Elections Irregularity Hotline with any information that highlights the rampant fraud occurring in our nation. I am the president of the United States, and I will rightfully retain my position for the next four years."

He stopped himself from adding "and beyond." That would come in time. For now, he had an office to secure, and his bigger plans would unfold in due time.

■

"Can you F'ing believe this guy? The election was three days ago, and the count was completed with Larry Stevens declared the winner, but Dominic Coronet won't concede. Who does that?" CK had a job to do, and The Dom's actions weren't making it easy.

"I guess he wants to go out with a bang." Jerry tried to console him. "It really shouldn't be surprising. His entire presidency hasn't been normal, whatever 'normal' is."

The internet had lit up with a rampant flow of misinformation.

"I wouldn't worry about it, CK. The process will prevail. Maxwell Hovick will confirm the results at the Capitol at the beginning of the year, and the House will record the tallies. Regardless, The Dom will be out of a job in January."

"As far as I'm concerned, I will sleep better at night without him in office. This has been a shit show for the last four years." Casey was tired of the drama, the attacks, and the discrediting of everything he showed up to work each day to protect. It had taken more of a toll than he'd realized until the recent election put Larry Stevens in office, and he'd been able to relax. However, his tension and anxiety were returning now that The Dom wasn't giving any indication of stepping down.

Freedom of speech. Whether or not you like the message, news reporting still required checks and balances. Facts were facts, and Dominic Coronet had lost fair and square. Just because he didn't want to leave the White House wouldn't suddenly change a fair and just process.

"Man, you can't make this crap up. Who would have thought he wouldn't concede?" Jerry was animated, fueled by coffee and youth.

"I guess I should have seen that coming after reporting his term for the past four years." CK shook his head.

"Any chance he's right? That the election was taken from him?"

"Highly unlikely. Each state has a process for ratifying the results. There's too much scrutiny to try to manipulate the voting counts. Even if there were some elements of fraud, he would need a massive quantity of votes to have been miscast to alter the outcome. Historically, that has never happened. Inappropriately cast ballots have been a handful, not hundreds of thousands."

"What about the voting machines? Couldn't they be hacked?"

"Sure, that's possible, but there's no evidence of tampering." The Dom had attacked the manufacturer on Twitter, accusing the company of fraud. "From what I can tell through my research, to attack the company that produced the machines isn't going to make The Dom any friends."

"Still, Casey, many people who voted for him are crying foul."

"Ironic that he called upset voters when he won four years ago sore losers, but today, he's turning the tables and saying he was wronged."

"Fortunately, he'll be out of office soon enough. Hopefully, Stevens can restore a sense of calm and rationality in the country."

"Yup, I hope that, too. I miss the presidential protocols with a sense of decorum."

"I don't think The Dom even knows what those words mean."

"Lucky for us, come January, we won't have to worry about Dominic Coronet again."

CHAPTER 36

"The Dom needs your assistance. He is calling on all nationalists to come forward to defend our great land. There is rampant voter fraud, as evidenced in Georgia, Pennsylvania, and Arizona. The corruption needs to stop. The Dom won the election, but the Hollywood elites and pedophiles are trying to deny his rightful place in the White House. He is the true leader of our great land. He is the president! He is the only one who can continue the work of the High Court Tribunal to restore our democracy to 1776. Do not let them take your country, your voice, and your democracy. Anyone who tries to tell you otherwise is believing the false news narrative. Trust me, I am on the inside and know the behind-the-scenes work being done around the clock to bring back our democracy. Respect the word. You are being misled. – R."

■

Leon felt the ups and downs of the past month. The first snowfall of December had covered his yard. As he looked out at the white expanse, he reminded himself that The Dom would retain his office next month, and things would settle down again. There was a flurry of activity on Discord. The

Dom had taken legal action to ensure votes were counted accurately, eliminating the ballots miscast in Pennsylvania, Arizona, and Georgia. These states, he said, had been the most heavily corrupted by fraud.

Steam from his coffee rose from the mug he held in his hand, and he welcomed the warmth of the beverage as he took a sip. He turned from his kitchen window and returned to his laptop, careful not to upset anything as he placed his mug on a coaster. Now, it was more important than ever before to get the message of R out to the world. While he'd amassed a significant following and had been surprised at how much money he was receiving because of his number of views, he knew many in the United States were unaware of the darkness lurking behind the scenes. It was essential to restore peace, eradicate evil, and reestablish order.

He had prayed for God to help him, and the assistance had come in a way he'd never expected. His compensation from YouTube enabled him to devote all his time to deciphering raindrops and spreading the word. Technology had its benefits. He didn't know how to set up the AdSense account in the YouTube partner program, but his tech-savvy IT hire knew what to do.

The more videos he made, the more money flowed into his accounts. This change in his life since his job had been eliminated was a win-win situation: Spreading the doctrine of R, promoting the prophet status of The Dom, and filling his days. As Leon thought about the prior year, he'd found a purpose in the world. He was part of something significant.

He converted his latest royalty payment to NatCoin. His crypto account had grown steadily since he'd started funneling funds into the online account. He looked at the large, unopened cardboard box in the corner of his office that contained the survival meals he ordered months ago. It wouldn't hurt to order another six-month supply now that he could afford it. He supposed he should hide it somewhere in his home. With the Rainstorm imminent, it would expose those that were prepared and those that weren't. It was probably a good time to buy a gun, too.

■

Casey had never seen anything like it. The sitting president of the United States had lost the election, both by popular vote and Electoral College votes, yet he refused to concede. Instead, he was calling the election results tainted and said there was evidence of foul play.

All fifty states had their own election rules and regulations, and manipulating the votes would have been difficult. Ironically, Dominic Coronet was only concerned about the fraud in the states that had narrowly swayed to Larry Stevens. *That was convenient. How was it that only those states were suspect, but all the ones with a cushion of votes in favor of The Dom were legitimate?*

Casey had been watching message boards and reading the emails sent on behalf of the Coronet campaign. It surprised him how many people were willing to believe the accusations made by a man who appeared to be a sore loser.

Casey had never thought about it before but was learning the benefits Dominic Coronet received by not conceding. He could still solicit donations since he hadn't bowed out of the campaign. The latest email from the Coronet campaign that had landed in his inbox fifteen minutes ago was urging subscribers to donate to fund the investigation into supposed fraud. Casey read the small print, which disclosed that large portions of the donation could be routed to a leadership PAC, Save Our Democracy. Digging deeper, he found very few restrictions on those donations, and they could be used in any way the campaign desired.

His general practice was to subscribe to both party's email campaigns to see how the candidates viewed and conveyed their policy plans. Casey hadn't realized how insightful it would be to understand the variances between the two men who had pursued the position in the Oval Office.

While Larry Stevens was old school and used a team-building voice in his emails promoting unity within the party to achieve his agenda, Dominic Coronet had a very different message: scare tactics with warnings that "the liberals are destroying our democracy," pleading for action by stating "only you can save America," along with a promise of exclusiveness with "donate today to receive a limited edition signed photo." Casey could see how unsuspecting readers could believe that the election fraud was real and that Dominic Coronet was working on their behalf to restore democracy. However, Casey, after speaking with the psychiatrist on cult indoctrination, could see a different objective of the Coronet campaign — one that padded the pockets of the president and allowed him a wide array of freedom to leverage donations.

When had party lines become so entrenched that the members of one party saw the other as the enemy? Didn't they know the danger that posed to the very fabric of the country? Traditional news outlets like *The Nat* were being denounced as promoting false narratives. Now, the voting process in the United States was under suspicion. *If the Republicans could create distrust and doubt in voting validity, what would happen during the next election? Would it be easier still to discredit legitimate results?*

Casey had reviewed the audit process in the three states in question with what The Dom called "rampant voter fraud." Nothing indicated that there was misconduct. A recount had only found a variance of three votes in Arizona, seven in Pennsylvania, and two in Georgia. There was nothing statistically relevant to toss out the results and nothing even close to the number of votes that would have been enough to shift the results from Larry Stevens to Dominic Coronet.

Casey felt fear prickling his neck hairs. *If Dominic Coronet could generate millions in donations post-election, what else would his followers be willing to do?*

■

Larry Stevens was frustrated. "What can we do legally to get the Coronet administration to start the transition process? That he hasn't conceded yet and is still spreading lies about the results is unacceptable!"

Larry had assembled the framework of his cabinet and a group of loyal aides who had been by his side for years. "It's unprecedented, for sure. We can't get any traction at the White House even though the General Services Administration declared you the winner."

Larry kept his choice words for The Dom to himself. It was time for him to be a leader and for Dominic Coronet to step aside. The Dom's claims of abundant election fraud without evidence continued to damage both political parties, leaving each frustrated; one side looking for a smooth transition while the other looked to expose election fraud to recognize their candidate as the victor.

Larry listened to his staffers. "He hasn't conceded because he can still fundraise as a candidate."

"Leave it to him to figure out how to continue to milk the system."

"He's raking in a ton of donations spreading these lies."

Larry focused on the end game. "This should be behind us after the inauguration. Let's do our best to unite the country. Transitioning will be easier as soon as Congress ratifies the Electoral College votes." Just a few weeks from now, this delay would become just a hiccup in his presidency that was poised to do great things. Larry was confident of one thing: Dominic Coronet was a lame duck whether he liked it or not.

■

"The Hollywood faction of elites have been hobbled, and they are grasping at the last bits of power they believe is in their control by trying to manipulate an election that is not theirs to win. Dominic Coronet is the rightful holder of the presidential office. There is widespread ballot tampering and manipulation. There is proof that votes were cast using the names of people no longer alive. Their good names were smeared after their deaths, pulled into a quagmire of deceit to stuff the ballot boxes by those who are trying to defraud the government. There is only one way to stop this abuse of power. The Rainstorm is close at hand. It is time for you to step up and show your allegiance. For those to know you are a disciple of R and a supporter of Dominic Coronet, you must show the sign. The sign of R. Do not reveal yourself too soon, or we will give the corrupt the upper hand. Follow the message boards and threads of those who manage the raindrops, and you will be guided. Respect the word. You are being misled. – R."

CHAPTER 37

Pam wasn't sure why, but her case was dropped. The judge cited "insufficient evidence," though they'd seemed to have enough to detain her, require bail, and schedule an arraignment hearing when she was arrested.

"The court has determined, based on her solid academic standing as well as this being a first offense, that it will no longer pursue the charges against Pamela Jackson." She knew she should be relieved, but it angered her that she'd been put into this situation when no one else around her had been treated the same way. She tried not to use "being Black" as a barometer in her day-to-day activities, but this was feeling a lot like she'd been singled out. The White students that were part of her group and even Asher, an Asian student, had come out of the situation unscathed. Pam had to endure the night in a prison cell, heckling from other inmates and a lack of privacy. She'd had to defend her rights after a White police officer had singled her out.

The anger she'd felt that day sparked inside her again and consumed her with a slow burn that she tried to push down. She couldn't talk to her mother about it; she wouldn't understand. Her father was busy trying to save the lives of those struggling with kidney disease. She'd find a way to deal with it on her own.

■

No one in the Oval Office wanted to broach the subject of conceding the election. For weeks, even after multiple recounts and many dismissed legal cases that lacked substance, it was becoming apparent to most in the room that The Dom had lost the bid for a second term. Max and others in the Coronet Cabinet watched, mostly in silence, as The Dom paced behind the large oak desk.

"Arizona is going to find the votes in the recount that show I'm the winner!"

No one wanted to point out that even if that happened, the eleven Electoral College votes still wouldn't be sufficient to bring the Coronet numbers over 270.

"Pennsylvania found some abnormalities, too," the portly man continued. The recount only shifted the vote by twelve. With millions of ballots cast for both candidates, it was statistically insignificant and certainly not enough to get The Dom over the threshold to declare victory.

The cabinet members and advisers in the room didn't see the sense in committing political suicide by arguing with The Dom. His tenure in the Oval Office might be ending, but that didn't diminish the power he wielded over their party. Over the last four years, many had erred by disagreeing with The Dom and seen their positions eradicated. The Dom had changed the game, forcing the party to be an "all in" group versus the party of years past that allowed for a range of conservatism throughout the ranks.

"We're finding proof that the voting machines have been set to tabulate votes for Larry Stevens when they were cast for me." The Dom pressured Fox News, a network that had seen the value in being a direct conduit to the president for the past four years, into siding with his claims. The Dom used multiple channels to stoke his party and urged their involvement to sway the election through his social posts. Max was amazed that The Dom was even beginning to believe he'd won. The thought of losing was too painful to acknowledge.

"Yes, yes, I saw the newscast this morning." One of the beleaguered advisers stepped forward, grateful for a chance to support the man in front of him.

"Gentlemen..." The Dom started and then caught sight of the one woman in the room, "and Julia. Your loyalty is not going unnoticed. You will be rewarded in the coming years. Your dedication to me and the administration will preserve our power to bring greatness to the country. It is our moral responsibility to do what is right to propel the country to greatness."

Some in attendance had been with him from the beginning, while others had replaced administration members whom The Dom had fired throughout the years for not being loyal and dedicated to their leader. "You know your place is based on your demonstrated commitment to the Coronet agenda. Do not disappoint me."

As the group disbanded and gradually filed out of the room, Dominic mentally assessed each one. There was bound to be one Judas in the group, and Dom was pretty sure he knew who it was: Maxwell Hovick. Whether he knew it yet or not, Maxwell, as vice president, could stop this corrupt power grab by Larry Stevens when the Senate was scheduled to ratify the election results in early January. The Dom would make sure the VP understood his duty and responsibility not to hand over the reins of the country to Stevens. The Dom slapped the top of his desk. *Larry Stevens will not sit in this office.*

■

Who do you notify if you find evidence of an upcoming coup orchestrated online and encouraged by the president of the United States? Casey was popping Rolaids as if they were candy. The information was in front of him, in plain sight. Facebook, Discord, and Reddit boards were firing out messages calling for action, calling for people to partake in the Rainstorm. R raindrops were splashing across social platforms. Casey couldn't tell how far-reaching the messages were. One thing was certain: a disgruntled group of people were descending on Washington, D.C., to take a stand outside the Capitol Building when the election results were certified.

Casey popped his head into his editor's office. "Got a minute? I need your help." It didn't take long to share his findings.

"Are you sure these posts are real?"

"I cross-checked as many of them as I could find. There are many posts out in the open about mobilizing a network of nationalist militias to ensure that the election certification is halted. They believe the election was manipulated by a Hollywood faction pulling strings behind the scenes. The integrity of the election officials has been questioned. There have been numerous recounts and pressure to reverse the results. Dominic Coronet refuses to concede, and is even encouraging people 'not to give up the fight' to halt the certification."

Casey's editor flicked the tablet, scanning various posts, including a disturbing Discord server titled "Rainstorm." He scrolled through the "Meet Me at the Mall" announcements, highlighting the flurry of online activity. After a minute, he handed it back to the reporter. "We should report this. Better safe than sorry."

He picked up the phone and dialed the number for the District of Columbia's police force. After identifying himself to the person on the other side of the line, the editor was transferred to the internal communications team.

"Who do I have to talk to about a threat to the city?"

"You can tell me, and I'll pass it on." The seasoned professional provided details and sent a follow-up email with supporting links.

Casey had taken a chair opposite his editor's desk. "What about the FBI?"

"Good call. I bet they already have this on their radar, but it won't hurt."

Thirty minutes later, the two men had disseminated the information to various officials. "All we can do now is hope there's enough time to barricade the Capitol Building."

"Surely, they can respond quickly. The election certification is in two days. That should be ample time to secure the streets."

"I'm sure everything will be fine. There's always a group of people disappointed that their candidate didn't win. I've never seen anything dramatic happen."

"I know, but this seems to be on a grander scale and much more organized than anything I've seen in the past."

"We've done our part. We researched and validated the information before passing it to the authorities. It's in their hands now."

Casey couldn't believe that it was almost five in the evening. The day had been consumed by research and alerting officials. "Care to join me for a drink?" The editor nodded. "I could use something strong right about now."

The two men made their way to the ground floor of *The National Times* building.

"Do you own a gun?" Casey wasn't sure why he asked his manager that question.

"No. I've never felt the need before today."

"Me neither, but this could get ugly fast."

"I know. There's no way that Dominic Coronet is planning a coup, is there?"

"I've been able to track communications from various militia groups, but nothing tied directly to the president's office."

"What about his Twitter feed?"

"So far, he's talked about the Rainstorm coming, but there are no real specifics."

"Yeah, my guess is this is just a small group of disgruntled folks with a large megaphone. We're in good hands with local authorities. There's no way that the results won't get certified."

"I hope this is the roar that goes out with a whimper." The two men raised their glasses. "I'll drink to that." Casey motioned to the bartender. "Keep 'em coming. Thanks!"

■

"Maxwell Hovick, as the vice president of the United States, has the power to uphold the true results of the election. Fraudulent voter activity in a variety of states will be revealed. However, time is ticking toward the election ratification at the Capitol Building in Washington, D.C., as the elites in power try to close the door on recounts that will reveal the false reporting of election results. Too many politicians voted into office to represent you, believe the false narrative, and plan to confirm the results. Dominic Coronet is the true

president. He will keep his rightful place in office if nationalists like you, along with Maxwell Hovick, do the right thing
and not stay idle. Tell your representatives you will not lie
down to this travesty. The Rainstorm is coming. Anyone who
does not heed the storm will show their lack of nationalism
and their brainwashing by those in the old guard of government. Respect the word. You are being misled. — R."

CHAPTER 38

"Dominic Coronet is our savior! The prophet sent by God!" The Whites Restore elder was animated as he led the weekly meeting in the church meeting room. "The Dom is our president and will eradicate the remaining wrongdoings against our country while he's in office for the next four years."

The older White man with thinning hair continued. "Dominic is asking for our help. He has asked us to rise up and prevent this travesty from unfolding. We need to mobilize!"

Brad watched with excitement. He wasn't sure what he could do, but he was confident the elder would guide him. "Members of Whites Restore throughout our nation are going to help divide and conquer! Those who are unable to travel will guard our interests locally. Those who can should go to the Capitol to show our support for our president when Congress tries to certify the Electoral College vote next Tuesday."

The group applauded.

"Maxwell Hovick will stop the certification! We will be there to support him."

"Hear, hear!" Others in the room echoed their approval.

"Fellow Brad Taylor."

It surprised him to be called by name, and he almost stuttered as he replied. "Ye... s... Right here." Brad waved his right hand briefly, and the elder nodded.

"We would like you to lead the charge in D.C."

Brad swallowed, trying to find his voice. *Why was he being chosen?*

"You have police experience and will validate our presence in the Capitol."

"But..." *How did he articulate that he didn't have enough for the airfare?* After paying his rent a few days earlier, he'd been left with $347, which had to last him until the end of the month.

As if he were a mind reader, the elder continued. "Whites Restore will sponsor your ticket in exchange for you being our emissary. We encourage everyone who can to join Fellow Taylor. Everyone else, I'll assign a task for you locally."

Brad felt a sense of pride being a member of this fine group. He would support the cause of Whites Restore. He knew he was getting closer to God. He looked down at his arm and wondered how much whiter his skin could become. He was close to ascension. He wasn't afraid to die. When he did, he knew he would be elevated to sit by the side of God.

■

"After midnight, mark a letter R on your front door. This will show your allegiance. This will also become your uniform. Be sure to wear something that shows your alliance and loyalty. Be sure to protect yourself. Ideally, wear a helmet with a red letter R on the front. If there's no R on a home or on a person who crosses your path, they are the enemy. Wear a bulletproof vest and arm yourself. Some are going to want to destroy you to preserve their own sick and twisted ways. The pedophiles and sex traffickers need to be held accountable. They do not understand the breadth and reach of the followers of Dom Coronet and R. We are no longer willing to stand idle while the country is being destroyed. Rise up and reclaim what is rightfully yours. Squash and destroy the sinners ruled by Satan and force them to the depths of Hell where they belong. Do your part to restore Heaven on Earth and the chosen country of God! Respect the word. You are being misled. – R."

■

Tony, Jester, King, and Ralph were in their regular booth at Whataburger. Their previous involvement at the Alamo had energized them, and now they were being called to provide a presence at the capitol building in Houston.

"I wish I could go to D.C.," Ralph lamented his circumstances. All four men were financially shackled and prevented from being able to travel to the nation's capital.

"R says our presence is just as valuable in our local communities, too."

"Yeah, but it sounds like a real shit show is going to happen in D.C., and we should be there to keep the peace."

Tony chimed in. "Texas is my home and heritage. I'm glad I can be here to protect Houston."

"Hear, hear!" King raised his diet soda. "I'll drink to that. It's not a beer, but it'll do."

They spent the rest of their lunch discussing the logistics for defending the local capitol building in the morning.

Tony wondered if Erica would be supportive of his efforts.

They'd been drifting apart, and he hoped their relationship would return to normal once Dominic was sworn in as the president for a second term. She'd been angry at him for his involvement with Texas for Freedom. Her family was from Texas, too. She should see the value in what he was doing. He hadn't mentioned the troubles at home to the men at the table. It was better kept to himself.

■

"The time for mobilization is NOW. Tomorrow, Congress will formally accept Larry Stevens as the next president of the United States. This is wrong. He is not the winner, even though false news channels report his win by 1.2 million votes. It is time to act. If you are able, travel to Washington, D.C. Do not fear. If you are not able to descend on the Capitol, it is possible to show your strength at home, either at your state capitol or in your neighborhood. You are not alone. The majority will stand to show their strength and demand their vote be heard. Dominic Coronet is the rightful occupant of the White House. He will be given the opportunity to lead us for the next four years. The Rainstorm is coming! Respect the word. You are being misled. — R."

Leon read the post and decided that he could travel to Washington, D.C. Two years ago, he had been struggling with unemployment, but today, he was respected for the role he was playing in promoting the truth for the world to hear. He could show his support in person. There was no reason he had to stay at home.

■

"Erica, you need to wear this." Tony held out a T-shirt with a large letter R on the front that he'd made with silver duct tape.

"Are you nuts, Tony? Do you hear how crazy this sounds?"

"I love you and don't want you to get hurt."

"How is wearing this shirt going to protect me?"

"It shows your allegiance to R."

"I'm not a follower. I think it's crazy; some whack job from who-knows-where on a power trip to see who they can manipulate. He's probably going to laugh when he sees how many people he can get to wear a stupid T-shirt."

"He speaks the truth. He's communicating from within the government and warning us of the faction's attempt to remain in control of the government."

"Look, Dominic Coronet lost the election. I know you don't want to hear it, but he lost fair and square. There's no evidence of election fraud."

"That's what the faction wants you to believe. They want you to be obedient followers and allow them to take the election away from the true winner."

Erica grabbed the T-shirt and threw it on the couch. "Tony, I don't even know you anymore." Tears filled her eyes, and she tried to push down the sadness as she saw the future of their relationship dissolving before her.

"Hey, hey, it's OK." Tony pulled her into his arms and stroked her blond hair. "You don't have to wear the shirt. Just promise me you won't go outside tomorrow. I don't want you to get hurt."

"What's happening tomorrow, Tony? I don't understand."

"Maybe nothing, maybe something. I just know that we need to reclaim our past to create our future."

"What's wrong with what we have now?"

"It's a lie. It's all built on a lie. It's time to restore the truth."

"What's the truth, Tony? Tell me. How do you know it's true?"

"I read it online. I did my own research. I can show you."

"We've been having this same argument for months now. I don't trust the sources you're reading online. It doesn't FEEL right."

"It FEELS right to me."

"That's the problem. I don't know how we'll ever find common ground again."

"What are you saying?"

"You're not the man I fell in love with. He's been replaced by a gun-purchasing, militia-joining, crazy person."

"I'm not crazy. I'm fighting for our future."

"Not our future. Your future. The future you THINK will exist, but I know in my heart it's a fallacy. You're fighting for something that doesn't exist."

"You need to read the posts. Then you'll understand."

"This makes me incredibly anxious."

"That's why I'm telling you everything, so you don't have to worry. There's no need to be anxious. A beautiful change is almost here."

"At what cost, Tony, at what cost?"

"What do you mean? There's no cost to believe."

"You're going to find you paid a price you weren't expecting." Erica sighed. "Be careful what you wish for, honey. You might just get it."

"I want to retain our history and restore our democracy."

"How do you create a revolution?"

"This isn't a revolution; it's the Restoration."

"Call it whatever you want, but you're going to find that you were fighting for something completely different than what you're actually going to get."

"How can you say that?"

"It's because you're fighting for an anonymous poster."

"No, I'm not. R has been very upfront about who he is."

"Really? That's why you know exactly who it is?"

"Many people believe it's Dominic Coronet himself."

"Do you hear yourself? 'Most people' are guessing who R is. I'll bet you that R is no more than an opportunist who likes to see how far they can manipulate people."

"That's not true. R is a nationalist! R is preserving our rights and our liberties."

"Honey, follow the money. Who benefits by you believing the election was rigged? Who is making money from you embracing these stories?"

Tony shook his head. He didn't know how anyone was making money off of his beliefs.

"You've been convinced that we don't even have democracy right now, and you're willing to fight to restore it."

"The democracy was dismantled when the District of Columbia was INCORPORATED into the UNITED STATES OF AMERICA." Tony hadn't meant to start yelling, but she was poking at him and questioning his intelligence. He was smart. He'd done his research. He wasn't so easily duped into a false narrative.

"Please, Tony, listen to me. 'How do you create a revolution?' You do it by telling people they don't have what they are entitled to. If you live in a democracy, nothing needs to be restored. But if you're being told that your democracy was stripped from you illegally, you'll fight to restore it, right?"

"That's what I've been telling you."

"I know, honey, but what if that's not true? What if we still have a democracy and the election wasn't rigged, and Larry Stevens is, in fact, the next president of the United States?"

"We've been trained to defend and to defend only. We're not here to initiate a war."

"I know, I know, but PLEASE, don't go tomorrow.

"I have to show my support for our country. I have to do my part to keep our democracy."

Erica stopped trying to reach her boyfriend. She'd lost him to the prophecies of R.

CHAPTER 39

"We are among you, and no one can tell us apart. The followers of R and The Dom know that democracy is being restored. Those who are not believers will be shown that their willingness to toss aside their great democracy is at their peril. You are either one of us, or you are against us. If you are against us, you are against democracy. The Dom has the power to restore our country. Do not lose sight of his greatness. Only he can preserve our democracy by removing the corruption from within. He has not sold his soul to the corrupt and the greedy within our government. R has shown us the way."

Leon felt like a messiah, bringing the messages of R and The Dom to the disciples, ready to follow the lead of their great president. He knew he couldn't save everyone in the world, but he knew he had the power to save those in the United States willing to listen. The Restoration Rainstorm, as he liked to refer to it, was building power and momentum. R was a true nationalist. R understood the movements behind the scenes and was selfless in risking his security clearance to spread the word. Leon was tired of being misled. He was tired of the world being controlled at the expense of people like him. He was finding his power on YouTube, and his followers reminded him of his pivotal role in restoring the intentions of the Founding Fathers. He turned off the video recording after preparing his message for the day. He would take a little time to edit the digital file and then push it live before leaving for Washington, D.C., for the Rainstorm tomorrow.

■

"This afternoon, Congress will attempt to ratify the stolen election by confirming Larry Stevens as the next president. Maxwell Hovick, the vice president of the United States, can refuse these false election results. If he stops this confirmation, we will know Hovick respects the word. His actions will show us if he is the enemy standing in the way of the Restoration. Remember, the elites are not going down without a fight. Dominic Coronet is the prophet sent by God to preserve our great country. Larry Stevens and the big government elite will strip you of all your rights. Our democracy is at risk. Do not let it fall into the hands of the corrupt. Check the message boards for ways to mobilize to protect yourself and your future. Whether you are in D.C. or demonstrating in your hometown, the Rainstorm is here. Respect the word. You are being misled. — R."

■

Tony tucked the sign with the large letter "R" into the window facing the street and pulled the curtains closed so Erica wouldn't see it. She wouldn't wear the T-shirt he'd made for her, so he had to make sure their home was clearly marked as a household dedicated to the prophecies of R and Dominic Coronet. He needed to know he'd done everything to keep her safe.

The posts outlined how those without an "R" in their window or on their clothing had been led astray by the unlawful leaders of their country. Nationalists, like Tony, were being called upon across the nation to help the U.S. military branches with weeding out the traitors to the nation.

It was early in the morning. Soft hues of pink and blue were cresting on the horizon. He was dressed in the camouflage shirt and pants he'd purchased months earlier, with a knife strapped to his leg. A handgun was inserted into a compartment in his bulletproof vest. Tony picked up the AR-15 that he'd outfitted with a scope and ensured the extra magazines filled with ammunition were added to his kit. He didn't expect he'd need to use them, but it was insurance that made him feel confident in his role today.

Houston's City Hall building was located on Bagby Street; he was meeting Jest, King, and Ralph nearby on Smith Street before they made their way to meet up with the other Texas Freedom Fighters. They were among numerous militias around the United States that Dominic Coronet had encouraged to join forces. They would help prevent the wrongful winner from being sworn into office later that day.

Texas had voted for Dominic Coronet and would be casting their Electoral College votes en masse to keep the president in office. However, other states had been infiltrated by massive voter fraud, and Maxwell Hovick had the power to stop the certification as the vice president of the United States.

The chat rooms had been clear. The vice president would stop the certification of the Electoral College votes, or if he refused, it would become evident that he had been corrupted. He would stand trial at the High Court Tribunal if he were a traitor. Tony wasn't concerned about that. He was sure the

VP would show his allegiance and dedication to the administration he'd been a part of during the last four years. He was bound to take appropriate actions to ensure that he retained his position as VP. He would also be rewarded with the opportunity to run for the coveted role of the president of the United States after Dominic Coronet's second term ended.

Tony tucked his cell phone into one of the vest pockets, along with a battery pack, to ensure he could charge his phone throughout the day. His cell phone was his link to information, and the message groups could convey actions needed based on how the events unfolded. He read the latest Discord posts to the group for all Texas Freedom Fighters to access. He also clipped on a walkie-talkie for immediate communication with the group.

"We are honoring our duties today. We are restoring our democracy and ensuring that the thieves of our country's rights will be held accountable."

Another post followed. "I have an extra vest if anyone wants to borrow it. DM me directly. More information will be shared shortly. Turn on your notifications and stay in the loop."

Their core group could communicate with the radio, and they all would be able to tap into the broader narrative on Discord, WhatsApp, Messenger, and texts sent directly to their cellphones.

Tony had left Erica sleeping. She would likely sleep until ten or later after staying up late to finish one of her videos. He debated about kissing her goodbye but knew she'd be angry if she woke up and saw him dressed in his tactical gear.

He closed and locked the door to their first-floor apartment before making his way to the parking spot in front and sliding behind the wheel of his truck. He looked at their picture window and confirmed the sign was legible. He saw other neighbors had added signs to their windows as well, while others did not have any indication of their allegiance.

R had talked about how followers were everywhere, interspersed with those who did not believe. R said those who had been duped by the corrupt leadership were blindly following an archaic oligarchy that was about to be toppled. It was their fault for not heeding the warnings and not acknowledging the world for what it was. Dominic Coronet was the rightful president, and those who didn't see the truth were destined to be pulled down by the lies they embraced.

The certification of the election results was scheduled for 10 a.m. Eastern Time, and the Texas Freedom Fighters would be deployed to their positions outside the Houston City Hall an hour before the proceedings began on the East Coast. They would hold their positions and ensure a peaceful transition when Maxwell Hovick stopped the proceedings. It was going to be a good day. It was going to be a day that would make him feel proud.

◼

"Max, here's your chance to do the right thing and keep us in office for the next four years." The Dom was coaching his vice president. He was very good at reading others and instinctively knowing what message would motivate their actions. While Maxwell had never really shown Dominic that he was motivated by power, the president had assumed the VP had a desire for the desk in the Oval Office. He knew the man considered himself a moral, God-fearing citizen, and The Dom knew convincing Max he was doing God's work would be the most substantial leverage.

Max fidgeted. "Sir, with all due respect, I haven't seen any evidence that supports not certifying the Electoral College vote today."

"The states are still counting mail-in ballots and performing recounts to ensure the votes are tallied completely and accurately. I just heard today of another county in Pennsylvania that had accepted votes from people that were dead. Last I checked, no one has been able to cast a vote when they're buried six feet under!" He watched the man for any indication of support.

"You know, Max, you were my first choice for vice president. Do you know why? I'll tell you why. It's because I knew you were a man of principles. You were a man who would always do what is right, what is needed to make sure we can deliver the best for the American people. I wanted you on my ticket because you are a God-fearing individual who knows God's will prevails."

The Dom wasn't particularly interested in religion, but he knew how to turn up the dial to speak to the likes of Maxwell Hovick. As far as The Dom was concerned, the church was just a distraction from his golf game, and yet for others, like Hovick, it was a place that provided rules for individual behavior and a code of ethics.

Sorry bastard! He doesn't even realize that he was a weakling in his life. The Dom scoffed at Hovick's tendency always to consult the Bible and his wife for guidance. *The dumb fuck had a chance for greatness.*

"By not certifying the vote, you'll ensure we can continue promoting our agenda. You'll be putting the true winner into the White House." He could see uncertainty cross the other man's face and he didn't like it. *How could he make sure that*

Maxwell Hovick would take the proper steps in the following hours to ensure he stayed in office?

One thing was sure. He had a contingency plan. There was no way he would let the next four years slip away from him. Once he secured his rightful seat, he would make sure that the term wasn't his last. There was still a lot to do.

"I trust you, Max, to do the right thing. You will be an emissary of God!"

CHAPTER 40

The drive to Washington, D.C., was just over four hours. Leon had never left Pennsylvania, not for any particular reason; he just hadn't had any desire to leave the town where he was born and lived for sixty-two years. Others might have a desire to travel, but Leon was content to stay where he knew everyone, even though the population had been shifting lately.

Today was different. R had posted that the Rainstorm was coming, and while he was prepared to weather out the storm from his home base, he also heeded the call of Dominic Coronet and R to travel to the nation's capital.

Since the night of the election, the country had been divided on who the actual winner of the presidential race was. Dominic hadn't conceded. The privileged elite were pushing Larry Stevens on a traditional timeline, but Leon knew that the final results would reveal the winner was The Dom.

He looked at the gas gauge and decided to fill the tank before he started the drive south. He had half a tank but didn't want to find himself in an undesirable area when the gauge was low. He had packed extra clothes and placed them in a grocery bag stashed in the footwell of the passenger seat. He was nervous about the trip, not sure what to expect, but he knew it was imperative to show his support for his president.

The Dom's latest messages on Twitter encouraged everyone to stay focused on a positive outcome for the results. The Dom and his supporters would reveal his rightful place in the White House. "Don't give up. The fight for our future depends on your support! Do not let the elite few take the election and give the office to the traitor Larry Stevens."

Leon merged onto the main road leading out of town with a renewed sense of purpose. Ever since he'd found the postings of R, he'd found his calling. Looking at the dashboard clock displaying 5:02 a.m., he did a quick calculation. He should arrive in D.C. by 9 a.m., just before Maxwell Hovick would denounce the certification of the election results. The Dom had to stay in office. R had shared the news that the election had been rigged. Leon felt it in his bones. Dominic Coronet was his president, and he'd ensure it stayed that way.

■

King, Jest, Ralph, and Tony walked through Sam Houston Park toward city hall. Parking was almost impossible, with many protesters descending on the area that housed the city government buildings. While it wasn't the Texas capitol building located in Austin, the men had felt it was important to stay local and protect their city from any disturbances that might arise during the upcoming events of the day. R had warned for months that the Rainstorm was coming, and the internet was flooded with posts proclaiming that today was the day.

R had proclaimed the Rainstorm would be nationwide, not just confined to Washington, D.C. The men felt like they were part of something historic and significant. They were there to defend democracy.

Tony looked at the area of the park that used to house the Spirit of the Confederacy statue that had been removed. He marveled at how far he'd come since that day he'd driven by the park and acknowledged the loss of the statue. He had been so frustrated, yet now he felt powerful and in control. His history was not going to be destroyed. His country would not continue to be undermined by a small faction of elites operating for themselves. He would play an essential role in restoring the country to the proclamation written centuries ago by their forefathers and ending the rampant corruption. The government had grown out of control, and restoring power to the nationalists fighting for democracy was imperative.

As the group exited the park and turned on Bagby Street, they found other Texas Freedom Fighters amassing between city hall and the Annex Building across the street. Groups of protesters were joining the gathering, and Tony saw many of them wore the letter "R" on their jackets or shirts.

A young blond girl walked by him wearing a pink sweatshirt that read "Love is the Answer," her hair pulled up in a ponytail. He wondered if she were a follower of R. *Wouldn't she wear something with the letter designation?* He had taken the time to put duct tape on the back of his vest, as well as an R on the right thigh portion of his pants. This way, he was identifiable from the front or back.

The group appeared to be a mix of people; some were carrying signs that said, "Larry Stevens is the Rightful President," while others proclaimed, "The Dom is Da Bomb," "Dominic Coronet is MY President," as well as those directly challenging the election results like "Voting Machines Can Be Programmed to Lie."

Tony had cast his vote for Dominic Coronet, as had everyone he knew around him. Texas was a Republican state, and The Dom, although not a political lifer, had done a lot to advance the party. To the south, the border wall was being built to ensure the illegal flow of immigrants would be thwarted. He'd passed a tax bill that had positively impacted Tony's paychecks, and he was charismatic. It was easy to be on board the Coronet campaign trail. Tony still couldn't understand why anyone would have voted for "Lazy Larry," who didn't have much to show for his years in a political office.

The people milling outside city hall started to fall into two groups: One encompassed the Texas Freedom Fighters and R cohorts standing in front of city hall, facing the Annex Building. Across the street were those who appeared to oppose their gathering. Tony saw them as people who had been duped into believing that Larry Stevens should be sworn in as the next president of the United States. They had been misled by the evil faction trying to thwart democracy.

It was still early in the morning, and the activities at the Capitol Building in D.C. would begin soon. Tony saw the girl in the pink sweatshirt again across the street, accepting a sign from another demonstrator. She tipped it up over her head, and he could see the slogan, "I voted for Larry. I voted for Democracy."

She couldn't be much older than her early twenties. Tony wondered how she'd opted to believe the false narrative being shoved down their throats by the Satanic Left. *What had made her think that the election had been fair?* Dominic Coronet had already shown that he was the rightful winner. Pennsylvania, Arizona, and Georgia had miscounted the vote, and the request for a recount was still underway. He'd seen the videos of ballots tossed in garbage bins behind the election offices. Many others had come forward to validate the fraudulent activity by officials wanting to pad the voting to swing the results for their candidate.

"You want some coffee?" Jest nudged Tony, bringing his attention back to the group.

"What? Oh, yeah, sure. Black, two sugars."

"You got it. Want a Danish, too?"

Tony had eaten a bowl of cereal while leaning against the kitchen counter before he'd left his apartment. He'd consumed it quickly, which had done little to address his appetite.

"Sure. If there's a bear claw, I'll take that. Want some money?" He reached into his pocket for his wallet, but Jest waved him off.

"I got you, man. We'll work it out later."

It took a while for the bearded man to return, carrying a tray with four coffees and a bag filled with pastries. "Man, the line was out the door." He dispersed the items, and the four men huddled while they ate, having animated conversation between bites about their presence in the square.

Tony took a big bite of the pastry covered in slivered almonds and washed it down with his coffee. Erica would have scolded him for eating "empty calories," but it tasted good and was satisfying. He crumpled the paper bag and tossed it, along with his empty coffee cup, into a trash bin on the corner and returned to the group. More people were arriving, and he saw a white Sprinter van pull up to the intersection. A group of men wearing military-style attire exited, armed, and outfitted similarly to the Texas Freedom Fighters.

"Hey, I think that's another militia supporting the cause. I recognize one of them from our training." King nodded toward a large man carrying a rifle who emerged from the nearby vehicle.

As the hour for the certification in Washington, D.C., neared, more people were amassed, many carrying weapons openly. The two-way radio connecting him to the other Texas Freedom Fighters crackled on his belt as if on cue. "Remember our training. We do not initiate; we are here to respond if anything gets out of hand. I repeat, do NOT initiate. Watch your message apps and listen for updates on this channel." Tony recognized the voice as the retired military colonel who had conducted the safety training.

There wasn't much to do except stand and create a defensive line. Others around him were holding their rifles. Now that his coffee was gone, Tony moved the strap of his rifle to bring it forward, and he held the cool metal. He felt a wave of excitement. The Rainstorm was about to bring about the resolution he'd been reading about for months. Dominic Coronet was the leader prepared to make sure that the United States remained a democracy. The Hollywood elite and Satanic worshipers controlling things behind the scenes were going to find out that today was a day of reckoning.

■

Losing two days in the Oakland Police holding cell served as an incentive to join more protests. Black Lives Matter rallies were continuing around the nation, and her experience shed additional light on what Blacks in her community faced every day. She knew she had to step up and fight for the rights Blacks had not been easily afforded before or after the inception of the United States of America.

Recently, she'd been researching her family tree. It was easy to trace her roots through generations of her White ancestors. On her father's side of the family, it was hard to find any information before the Civil War when most Blacks in the South were slaves. It was nearly impossible to know what part of the world her ancestors had been abducted from when they were tossed onto a ship and brought to the "New World."

She knew she should be studying for her upcoming physiology exam, but she was distracted. Nothing had been the same since the protest and court arraignment. It was hard to be laser-focused on her medical studies when she had so many unanswered questions.

The rallies were gaining momentum, getting traction from a wide array of attendees. She joined Asher, and they navigated their way to San Jose. Pam didn't have any interest in returning to Oakland soon.

The energy around her was palpable. Many gathered were carrying signs and chanting. Police had barricaded the street to allow the throng of foot traffic to pass. Officers dressed in blue were scattered along the river of metal gates. Pam was relieved they were dressed as usual, not in combat gear. She was optimistic the day would go well.

It surprised her to see so many people coming out in support or protest related to the election. She'd opted to join Asher and would have stayed home if she had realized how much the rally had been subsumed by the groups waving signs for the election. Some in attendance supported Larry Stevens, while others, wearing clothing with the letter R, seemed to be there to "Stop the Robbers!" Pam had been hearing a lot in the news lately about how the Coronet administration was trying to promote a narrative of thievery and deceit related to the election, but nothing she'd read supported that claim. She wondered what the letter R signified, but before she could pull out her phone to type a query, Asher directed them toward an opening in the crowd. She'd google it later.

She looked down at her black sweatshirt, chosen because of its message. The large white letters "BLM" were splayed across the front. She was proud to be at the event supporting marginalized Blacks in the United States.

CHAPTER 41

The newsroom was a flurry of activity. Casey saw his editor leave his office, a harried look on his face. "Casey! It's not a Rainstorm, it's a shit storm. The D.C. police and the FBI didn't take our alert seriously. I just got off the phone with them, and they said that everything indicated that it wouldn't be a big deal today, just a few disgruntled people."

When Casey had unlocked the door to his apartment building three blocks from the Capitol the night before, he'd seen many out-of-town people overflowing from the pub down the block. *Nothing like mixing alcohol and a bloated sense of purpose.* He knew they were there to protest the certification, but he hadn't expected what was unfolding on the screens scattered around the newsroom.

There was pure chaos on the mall, and an angry group of protesters, many carrying weapons openly, moved outside the perimeter of the Capitol Building. The letter R was emblazoned on many jackets, shirts, and flags. A makeshift noose had been erected outside as well.

"If you can, get down there and assess the situation. Take anyone available with you. It looks like strength in numbers is the name of the game today."

Casey looked up from his computer monitor and nodded to his editor. He had seen the simple barricade outside the steps of the grand building on the way to his office, and now he wondered how long it would be respected. Security guards and police officers were visible on the other side, but nothing compared to the fortified groups that Casey could see throughout the crowd. This had the potential to take a dangerous turn.

"I'm on it." Casey turned to the others in the room. "I'm heading to the Capitol. Join me if you can." Four other men and one of the women in the room stood and moved toward him. Casey didn't want to be sexist but was nervous about Ashley joining them. It could get rough, and he didn't want her to get hurt. He swallowed his thoughts and nodded as they joined him by the elevator bank. She was an adult and capable of making her own decisions.

"This could be dangerous. It looks like a mob mentality is brewing. I want to make sure you all know what you're getting into." They all had been watching the newscasts and had seen the gathering expanding.

"We got you, CK. We're here to report the news. I'm not sitting at my desk for this one." Aaron, a stocky man with glasses and thinning hair from the sports desk, expressed the sentiment of the group.

The elevator bell rang, and the doors slid open. The group stepped inside the empty chamber and pressed the button for the ground floor. As the car dipped lower, Casey could feel the nervousness emitted by the team.

Traffic was blocked off, and navigating the streets proved slow, with the mass of visitors who had descended upon D.C. The reporters opted to take the Red Line and emerged from the public transportation terminal into the group swirling in the streets. Casey had seen numerous marches before, but there was a frenetic pulse today, unlike any others he'd attended. He was surprised to see how many people were openly carrying weapons; it was more than a little unnerving to see the extent of firearms in plain view.

The reporters huddled to devise a game plan now that they saw what they were facing. They decided to split into two groups, one to work the perimeter from one side of the Capitol entrance and the other to stay on the other. They were armed with cell phones and one photographer per group. Casey paired up with Jerry and a lifestyle photographer named Thomas, while Aaron, Ashley, and Zack banded together.

"Let's create a group chat to communicate." After aggregating the team's numbers within his iPhone's message section, Casey sent an initial message. He heard the various pings around him as the message was received, and everyone nodded that they received the text.

Casey moved his messenger bag strap to cross his body to allow for ease of movement. The three turned toward the expanse of lawn ahead of them and started to traverse to the other side. Casey saw lots of clothing and flags depicting the letter R. He knew from his research that the gospel of R had been gathering a following, but until now, he hadn't realized how extensive the outreach had become. He thought R had a fringe following, nothing like the group he saw before him.

He and his editor had alerted the authorities the day before based on posts for mobilization, but nothing had indicated it would be this scale. One man wore a jacket with a silver R made with duct tape on his back. Others had purchased items with the letter R more formally displayed. One man's shirt read, "*R is a Nationalist. He is our Prophet.*" Casey hoped this was just a skewed reflection of R's presence by his followers concentrated in a single area. If this was what was being mobilized throughout all fifty states as the posts had implied, this was way scarier than Casey had realized.

"What the hell is R?" Thomas commented on the sea of attire around him. The question from his colleague made Casey hope that meant that R was still a fringe movement.

"Good question. No one has been able to determine who R is, but part of the population has adopted his messages as a sign that the United States is about to be restored to its former glory."

"Former glory? Like what? Slavery and women without the vote?"

"The opinions vary. R leaves 'raindrops' that various individuals and groups interpret across the web."

The three men flanked the crush of people, uneasy about being engulfed in the swarm around them. They were there to observe and to report, not to join the protesters.

"How have I not heard of this?"

"The latest poll says that about 35% of people in the United States are aware of R. It's still a minority representation, not a widespread popular view. I'm not surprised you haven't heard about it. I only know about it because of my research into the extremes of the internet."

"Should I be worried?"

"I don't know. There's certainly an R presence here, but I have to believe it doesn't extend to the bulk of the country."

"So, they're harmless?"

"Well, they seem heavily armed. They're only dangerous if they find a way to mobilize."

"You don't think this is mobilization?"

"Yes, of course. We alerted both the D.C. police force and the FBI yesterday after seeing lots of activity on message boards about the Rainstorm that is supposed to happen today."

"Rainstorm?"

"Yes. Followers take the clues, called raindrops, sprinkled onto the internet by R, and they see it culminating with a Rainstorm that will restore the U.S. to former power and glory."

"This is the rainstorm?"

"From what I can put together, yes. The FBI and D.C. police assured us that their intel didn't give them reason for concern. They said we were overreacting to the posts."

"I certainly hope they're right."

The ominous feeling he'd been pushing down returned as Casey scanned the area. This wasn't going to end well.

■

Maxwell stood in the atrium of the Capitol Building. As the vice president, it was his role this morning to ratify the votes for the president-elect of the United States, Larry Stevens. Dominic Coronet had advised him to reject the votes and declare Dom the winner. Max knew this was pure folly and the last attempt of the man to stake claim to the office he would have to depart later in the month.

"There's no evidence of voter fraud." Max had tried to reason with the portly man.

"That's bullshit, and you know it. Georgia only had to find a few more votes, and we'd have carried that state. Too much fraud goin' on there. I know they destroyed ballots that had been cast for me. More than the amount they claim I lost by."

"Even so, you still would have had to carry Arizona and Pennsylvania."

"At the very least, we have to delay the ratification."

Max had no intention of arguing with the president. The petulant man had refused to concede and still wanted to believe he had a claim to the office. The VP had visited the swing states after the election to observe the recounts and hadn't seen anything that would cause concern. It would just be a matter of time before they could confirm what Maxwell already knew. Larry Stevens had won fair and square.

His cell phone vibrated in his pocket, and he pulled it out to make sure there had been no last-minute adjustment to the day's schedule.

Dominic Coronet was in rare form and posting on Twitter.

"The election was stolen by the communist liberals trying to destroy our democracy!"

"Fight for our nation!"

"Nationalists, stand for your rights, your freedoms!"

"The Rainstorm has been looming on the horizon, and you must act!"

"Do not let your rights and freedoms be taken from you!"

Maxwell read the messages and shook his head. The following tweets sent a shiver down his spine.

"If Maxwell Hovick fails to correct the wrongdoings instigated by a fraudulent faction stealing the election, he is a traitor! The VP is either with us or against us. He is an enemy of the people if he does not declare me the rightful winner of the election."

The Dom had been stoking emotions and keeping them in a frenzy. Max was sure it would die down once he ratified the election results. It wouldn't take long for things to return to normal. He could consider his presidential run in four years without being shackled to the unhinged man currently occupying the White House.

■

"Fight for our Constitution and our democracy! This is not a time to be complacent!" The Dom hit the send button, and the message was displayed for his millions of followers to see.

The Dom composed another series of tweets. "My Number Two is about to reject the vote tally being submitted today. Max Hovick will secure the rightful outcome of the election. Lazy Larry has rigged the election results, and we won't let him get away with this crime." The Dom smiled and leaned back in his chair, propping his feet on his desk in the Oval Office. There was no need to pack. He was in his home.

Watching the gathering being broadcast over his news feeds, he was pleased with the turnout. There had been many gaps in the mall when he was inaugurated four years earlier, but there wasn't a patch of grass to be seen today. His followers had mobilized at his request, and as soon as the news announced that the vote had been cast for The Dom instead of Lazy Larry, he could make the changes he wanted.

His phone vibrated beside him, and in unison, he could hear pings, bells, and alerts echoing across the sea of screens before him. The Dom had hoped it wouldn't come to this. Maxwell Hovick had shown himself to be a current-day Judas. He had failed his only responsibility that morning. The Dom would trigger his personal army. The platform developed by R had given him the megaphone he needed.

"Maxwell Hovick has betrayed us. He accepted the Electoral College vote. He is a traitor who has been misled by the corrupt trying to take the election from the rightful winner. The Rainstorm is here! Fight for your democracy! Fight for your freedom! Nationalists, you are being called upon to help restore peace and justice! For too long, the elite have tried to rule our country and strip away the Constitution. Today is the day we say No More!" The Dom recorded the brief video and posted it across his social channels. He'd tapped into a group of followers hungry for acknowledgment, and for over a year, he'd been grooming them for mobilization.

It didn't take long for the video to trigger his network. The Dom looked at the array of screens in front of him. Many protesters outside the Capitol could be seen consulting their phones, and cries rang out throughout the group. "Hovick is a traitor! Find him!"

The Dom felt elated as he watched the crowd surge forward and could feel the shift. The movement forward was like a wave washing against the shore, ready to cleanse the system.

CHAPTER 42

Casey and his team wove through the crowd. It appeared to be a mixed group, with some protesters carrying signs that proclaimed Coronet the winner and those who supported the Stevens win.

For the past two months, The Dom had been stoking the fire of his base, and he'd called them to assemble today. Casey was relieved to see that the attendees were under control and commingling. He hoped Maxwell Hovick would finish his certification soon, and then the gathering would disperse and release their hopes to overturn a fair election.

Casey looked at his phone—10:28 a.m. The vice president should be accepting the Electoral College votes that secured the path for Larry Stevens to be sworn into the office of the president. As he moved closer to the Capitol Building, he saw the line of barriers installed in front of the historic structure. Several D.C. police officers were positioned on the other side. There were many people milling around, but no one was attempting to breach the line.

Casey had an uneasy feeling. Many of those around him carried visible firearms even though D.C. had no open carry laws, and it was unnerving to be this close. He wondered about their intent to use the weaponry. *What prompted them to carry? Wasn't this a peaceful protest?*

He looked at his phone again. 10:32. *Surely, the results were recorded by now?* As he returned the phone to his pocket, the air around him was filled with a cacophony of pings and beeps. The screens lit up in a sea of technology as those in the vicinity consulted their phones. CK wasn't sure what it meant. His screen remained dark, and yet many around him had just received something in unison. "Maxwell Hovick is a traitor!" A large man about thirty feet away yelled. "He didn't reject the certification."

Casey's fingers trembled slightly as he located the Discord app on his phone and looked for the "Meet Me at the Mall" channel announcements to see if he could learn what was happening around him. It didn't take long to find what had been posted.

"Soldiers! We are the defenders! We have trained and prepared for the day we would need to step up and protect! Today is that day! We are ready to guard our country and the president of the United States! R has shown us the way. The Rainstorm is upon us! Find Hovick and make him pay for his transgression!"

A chant rose in volume: "Traitor, traitor, traitor..."

Someone with a megaphone yelled, "Charge!" and Casey watched in shock as the group around him erupted into a mass movement toward the entrance of the Capitol Building.

People surged around him as he tried to keep his ground and stand in place, along with protesters who supported the Stevens win. The rest mobilized and pushed forward.

"Shit, CK, what the fuck is going on?" Jerry looked terrified.

"I'm not sure yet, but let's get away from the entrance." The reporters tried to navigate the throbbing crowd and move to the perimeter of the mall. Casey saw a man nearby, pushing forward, holding a rifle across his chest, using it like a battering ram.

"Move it, people! We have our democracy to protect!" His face was red as he yelled, and Casey dodged away from him to make sure they didn't come into contact.

A group of college-aged students nearby started screaming, their words unintelligible in the melee that had erupted with war cries and anger.

Casey's ears were ringing. The reporters managed to push their way to the sidelines, stunned to see the group engulfing the entrance to the building. Breaking glass could be heard, with both cheers and sounds of dismay. The few police officers were massively outnumbered but tried to keep the crowd at bay, standing behind the few barricades surrounding the building. Casey ducked instinctively, losing visibility of the scene except for those running around him. It was chaotic.

His team had managed to stay near the periphery. Thousands of people were on the mall, and it was impossible to know how far-reaching the discontent was within the group. CK looked around for any spot that could give him more visibility. History and news were being made in real-time.

He saw a metal trash bin nearby and motioned to his group. "Come with me!" As he reached the container, he pressed on the wheel brakes to make sure it was locked in position. "Help me close the lid." The three flipped both sides of the split top, and the pieces clanged shut as gravity pulled the heavy plates down. "We should be able to get a better view on this." The three worked together to climb on top of the bin. Casey tried to ignore the stench inside of rotting food and wet cardboard. He didn't have the luxury of looking for a more sanitary perch. Fortunately, the metal lid supported their weight, and the three watched in horror.

Casey pulled his phone from his pocket, fumbled to unlock the screen, and realized his hands were shaking with adrenaline and fear. He accessed the camera app and started to record a video, holding his phone as steady as he could while zooming the lens to get the best possible view of the Capitol Building's entrance.

"This is Casey Kiel with *The National Times* newspaper. I am here today to report on the Electoral College vote. Minutes ago, when it was learned that Maxwell Hovick ratified the election results, the crowd erupted into the scene you can see unfolding in front of you. Up until today, Dominic Coronet has claimed the election was rigged despite there being no proof to support his allegations. His supporters appear to be mobilized to contest the day's proceedings."

He paused, unsure what else to say, as he watched the attendees surging forward. He also wasn't sure his commentary could be heard over the commotion around him. Thomas had put a zoom lens on his camera and was taking pictures of the scene. Casey stopped his video and called his editor. "Hovick ratified the election results, and the people here aren't pleased about it."

"OK, be safe, but get that story!" His editor was screaming to be heard. The two spoke for a minute longer, and Casey hung up, knowing they were watching an unthinkable event in his lifetime. *What had happened to the country? Why was there such a divide? The election had been held, and people had voted, but the results were being questioned for the first time in history.* A chill went down his spine.

If you question your democracy, do you have one at all?

∎

"Stand down!" Tony heard the yell further down the line from where he was standing.

"Stand DOWN!" The crowd across the street started surging toward the city hall building, and tensions were high. He brought his rifle up to his shoulder and was prepared if something went awry. The protesters on the other side of the street near him did not appear threatening, but he kept his rifle raised anyway.

He could feel his heart pounding. He tried to recall his training from several months ago. It had seemed so simple and straightforward that weekend, but he wasn't so sure now, facing a group that was moving with many armed demonstrators.

"Stand DOWN!" could be heard again, and angry retorts were hard to distinguish. Tony looked to Jest, King, and Ralph; the three men had also raised their rifles.

"What's happening?"

"I don't know." Jest was the first to respond.

"Some A-hole advanced toward our fortified line, but I don't think he's armed." King was closest to the area where the yells were originating.

A popping sound filled the air, and it took a second to realize it was a gunshot.

A woman screamed, and the group erupted in movement.

Tony couldn't see who had initiated the gunfire.

"BREACH, breach, breach!" crackled over his radio. "DEFEND the perimeter!"

The four men moved closer to create a human barrier, and they scanned the crowd moving toward them. A man they'd seen exit a van half an hour earlier was holding an AR-15 similar to the ones that the Texas Freedom Fighters were holding.

"Fuck this shit. I'm not getting shot today." King pulled the trigger, and Tony saw the man from the van drop to the ground.

"What the fuck, King?! What are you doing?"

"You heard the radio. There's been a breach. It's us or them, and I'll be damned if it's going to be me."

The additional gunshot triggered a reaction, and Tony saw a young Freedom Fighter fall to the ground, clutching his thigh. Tony could see blood beginning to seep through his pant leg, and he tried to move to help, but more gunshots rang out.

"WAIT! STOP!" Tony didn't know what triggered the response, but he knew the chance of controlling the mass of people would become unlikely in a matter of seconds. If anyone else fired their weapon, it would cascade into full-on warfare.

Further away, Tony could hear more shots being fired, and he jumped behind the low wall that flanked the city hall building and squatted down, seeking some protection from the surging crowd. Other Freedom Fighters followed suit, some propping their arms on the low wall to stabilize their weapons.

Screams and movement created confusion. A large man was rushing towards the government building; adrenaline kicked in as Tony pulled the trigger. It had been instinctive, and he'd done it without thinking. As he watched the man's body twitch before falling to the ground, Tony felt sick to his stomach. He had come to defend his history, his rights, and his freedom, but nothing had prepared him for how it would feel to shoot another human being. His stomach heaved; partially digested pieces of almond pastry spewed to the ground along with stomach acid and bile.

"LIE DOWN! On the ground, NOW!" Several Freedom Fighters had moved to the street and were forcing people down on the ground.

The group was moving in all directions. Some were running away, but those advancing were still posing a threat to the fortified line that the Texas Freedom Fighters and supplemental militia members had established. Police presence in the park was minimal since the main department was several blocks away. Sirens could be heard as law enforcement descended onto the scene.

His radio crackled again. "To the followers of R, you are prepared to fight for your freedoms! Anyone who is not aligned with the truth of our nation and ready to restore our democracy is a traitor in alliance with the corrupt. Remove the filth and unfaithful from our country. Nationalists need to rise up for our sovereign rights! The Rainstorm is NOW!"

Tony watched in disbelief as those around him, empowered by R, surged forward.

Brad scaled the front of the Capitol Building with ease. His police training and youth gave him an advantage. He reached down and assisted several people in climbing the face of the building. He wasn't there as a police officer. He was proud to represent Whites Restore as well as R. He wore the shirt openly, excited to see so many others displaying the moniker as well.

He'd never been to D.C. before, and while the Capitol Building was iconic and an image he'd seen numerous times, he didn't know anything about the interior. He'd received a text moments before that had conveyed the news that Maxwell

Hovick had accepted the Electoral College vote, effectively paving the way for Lazy Larry to be sworn in as the president of the United States later in the month. Hovick was a traitor. R had posted about the rampant fraud and said there was proof that the election had been rigged. Dominic Coronet was the true winner and should be entitled to continue his presidency.

Brad was going to find that son of a bitch turncoat and make sure he paid for his duplicity. *How could he consider himself a true nationalist if he wasn't even willing to stand up to the corruption of the election?*

Brad saw the older man he'd helped up the facade of the building and stepped in pace with him. "Come with me!" The two started opening office doors. It wouldn't take long to find the traitor.

■

"This is awesome!" Leon exclaimed out loud to no one in particular. He wasn't the most athletic person, but he'd been helped up the front of the Capitol Building by demonstrators around him, and the crowd was surging into the entrance of the building.

On the veranda, he turned and looked at the mall; the expanse was filled with a sea of people. They were his comrades. They were there to represent the truth! The elite and power-hungry selling their souls for the demise of democracy were to be held accountable for their wrongs.

Leon looked around the interior with awe. History was being made in addition to being restored. He was there to reinstate the foundation of the United States by removing the ones standing in the way of greatness, the ones that were denying him of his rights and giving his power, his freedoms, to the brown people in his neighborhood. He wanted to feel safe and to have value again.

The interior of the building was throbbing with activity as many of the protesters were trying to find their way into a building they'd never entered before. "Over here, over here!" voiced a group of men in camo clothing, many holding rifles, with one man holding a United States flag. Another was waving a banner with the letter R.

Leon felt pride as he watched the letter flapping on the fabric. He had helped R share the word. R would go down in history as a great nationalist who had risked his life and security to let those in the world know of the wrongdoings.

"You, come with me!" A tall blond man wearing an R shirt beckoned Leon. The two moved forward and opened doors. Most lead to empty offices of Representatives.

"What are we looking for?"

"That traitor, Hovick. Asshole had one job to do today, and he didn't do it. Time to pay the piper." They turned down the hall and saw more offices.

"Fuck this. Where's the area they meet to discuss laws and shit?"

"Upstairs?"

Leon had entered on the far-right side of the building. He suspected they needed to reach the center of the grand structure.

"Let's try over here." They ran, stopping with awe as they entered the rotunda of the building, gazing overhead. They were standing under the dome. Leon was amazed at the site. He'd never been this close to anything that embodied his country so iconically.

The blond man pushed forward. "Come on, old man. We don't have time to waste. That asshole is here somewhere." Leon decided not to say anything about being called an old man. He guessed he was, compared to the younger man, but he still had a lot of life in him.

They found a stairwell, and the blond took the steps two at a time while Leon tried to keep up. Some demonstrators stopped to take selfies of themselves in front of a flag or other historical markers.

"This is what I'm talking about." The doors to the large chamber were open, and a group of protesters were already inside. It was impossible to navigate further.

"He's here! We found him!"

Shots rang out around him as Secret Service agents stood their ground, protecting the vice president. Leon instinctively crouched down as he watched men on both sides fall to the ground. The Secret Service detail was outnumbered, and they were not able to defeat the mob. Soon, the shots subsided as the agents were eliminated.

Cries rose from the interior, and Leon watched as a scared Maxwell Hovick was dragged from the room. He almost felt sorry for the man. He'd liked him throughout the four prior years. He'd always been a constant in the Coronet cabinet. *What the hell had happened? Had he been a traitor the whole time?*

"Let me go! Let me go!" Hovick struggled to free himself, but the group of men carrying him overpowered his efforts.

"Let's get this traitor outside and show the world what happens when you betray the United States of America!"

Leon and the blond followed, having arrived at the pinnacle of history.

Hovick was squirming, trying to break free. He lost his shoe as he was dragged down the steps. Leon picked it up; the leather was smooth, and the sole was barely worn. Nothing like the athletic shoes Leon wore until they fell apart. He'd felt bad for Hovick, but holding his shoe, he was reminded that Hovick wasn't like him. He was one of the power elites that was destroying the democracy.

The angry mob pushed forward, and Leon noticed that others were being carried outside. The Democratic minority leader and several others were being hauled down the steps along with the vice president.

They stepped out to the veranda overlooking the mall. The person leading the group yelled into a megaphone: "Hang 'em high!"

Cheers from the immediate gathering around them erupted, and Leon watched as a large rope with a noose on one end was tossed over a makeshift structure. *Who had brought rope? What was going on?*

The blond man stood by his side.

"It's about time we reclaimed our history and cleansed this world of its filth."

Leon watched as Maxwell Hovick was knocked to the ground with a blow from a rifle butt. Several men lifted the unconscious man, and several others fitted the noose around his neck. There was some blood seeping from over his left eye and a bruise starting to bloom.

"What happens to traitors?! They pay the price! The laws of the United States have deemed that a traitor's transgressions are so great that the punishment is DEATH!" The megaphone amplified the message, and it sounded uneven and tinny.

Those gathered cheered.

"Maxwell Hovick, by certifying the false election results today, you showed yourself as the traitor you are. You have betrayed the office you swore to uphold when you took your oath four years ago. You will be recorded in history as a traitor!"

Hovick looked groggy and tried to speak, but his voice was drowned out by the chanting around him. "Traitor, traitor, traitor!" "Death, death, death!"

Hovick's body was hoisted above the group. His legs flailed in the air before finding stability on a chair. His eyes darted back and forth. His mouth opened and closed as he fought for air to speak, the noose around his neck also impeding his voice.

"Help me, help me! This is wrong!"

"You need to pay the price for your wrongs!"

The man with the megaphone stepped forward and kicked the chair. Maxwell Hovick's body dropped. Leon was close enough to hear his neck snap.

The crowd cheered, and Leon felt a lump in his chest. He'd never witnessed the killing of a man before, and even though he knew that R had predicted the need for violence to restore their democracy, seeing it firsthand was shocking.

Two more hanging stations had been erected, and the man with the megaphone called out their crimes. "You will pay the price for your wrongs!" Another chair was kicked out from underneath an elected official, and then another.

Cheers filled the air. The blond man next to Leon was smiling. "Well, old man, justice has been served today. These traitors are ascending to be closer to God. The cleansing of the race is here. We are being enlightened!"

CHAPTER 43

Tony observed an unsuspecting group of people get mowed down. Most were unarmed. *How had this happened?* The Freedom Fighters, all proponents of R, had been approved to move forward and eradicate anyone who did not share their beliefs.

It was becoming clear to him now why the R signs had been so vital. Today's response wasn't about being reactive to defend; it was about exerting one dogma over another group and forcing compliance. You were either a follower of R or not. He hoped Erica was OK and that the violence was limited to the area around him. He tried to call her, but she didn't answer.

King and Jest had gotten separated from Tony and Ralph. He looked for the young man who had been by his side. It didn't take long to find his lifeless body. Blood pooled underneath him, and his eyes were vacant. He'd fallen defending democracy, and the prophecies of R. Tony reached down and closed his eyes, sadness washing over him. *How had this happened?* He looked around and saw an array of lifeless bodies scattered on the street. The young blond girl with the pink sweatshirt was among the dead. "Love is the Answer" was splattered with bloodstains that were starting to dry a deep brownish red. A pool of blood around her was still wet and sticky. Tony threw up again, this time mostly stomach acid with a few stray bits of food. Most of his stomach contents had been eliminated with his first expulsion.

"Hey, there you are, man!" Jest, followed by King, moved toward him. "We did it! We have upheld democracy. Respect the word!"

"Come with us. We're securing the area and making sure that no other uprisings occur. We are here to support Dominic Coronet and R!"

"What happened?" Tony was still trying to piece together what had triggered the morning's events.

"Didn't you see the messages?"

"No, everything seemed peaceful, and then it wasn't. I didn't have time to look at my phone." He hadn't thought to look for messages when he'd tried calling Erica. Reaching her had been his top priority.

"Maxwell Hovick did not halt the certification of the election, and he was hanged outside of the Capitol in D.C."

"Wait, what?"

"He was a traitor to the nationalists and the presidency of Dominic Coronet."

"I don't understand. He's part of the Coronet administration. Why would he certify the false election results?"

"He was a traitor to The Dom. The militias on-site in D.C. defended our democracy. Dominic Coronet will remain as our president."

■

"Dammit, I'm the commander in chief of the military. When I say gather all the generals, I mean gather all the generals!"

The Dom had been pacing his office, watching the crowd surge forward into the Capitol Building on the large screen in his office. He was animated and excited. His plans were falling into place.

He thrived on chaos. Hovick had actually done him a favor. It would have been smoother if Hovick hadn't ratified the results, but as The Dom watched the protestors constructing gallows and hanging the top officials, he realized he had something even better. The group was sending a loud message: Dominic Coronet WAS their president. There wouldn't be a long-drawn-out deliberation in the courts on how to set a new precedent if Hovick had declined to ratify the results. Now Dom could use the system and make his changes without hindrance.

His aide entered the Oval Office and instructed The Dom to join a video conference. He was pleased to see the top commanders in the country on the screen.

"As the president of the United States, I'm invoking martial law. Every military base and personnel are to be deployed to keep order."

One of the older Generals shook his head. "I don't understand, sir. The unrest is isolated. There is no reason to deploy all bases."

"It is imperative that we control everyone throughout the country. Surely, there will be those who will respond on both sides. It is not a time for civil war!"

Others on the call murmured their support.

"I want a military presence everywhere. Await my further instructions."

"With all due respect, sir, you have not consulted us."

The Dom snapped in annoyance, "Why must I consult you? If you cannot be loyal to your posts, I will accept your resignations. You're either with me or not."

The group showed a shocked surprise at the outburst. "Mr. President, I'm merely suggesting that we establish a War Room to work strategically. The goal is to ensure that civilian lives are not lost, and we curb this outburst from escalating."

The Dom pondered for a moment. He needed the military to support his claim to office. He would be able to determine the men's loyalty if he had them close at hand.

"Yes. A War Room makes sense. We will meet here. However, no one will take action without consulting me first. We will control the response."

He exited the screen and picked up his phone. Now that the U.S. military was being deployed, he would blend the forces with his personal army.

■

The Whites Restore elders in California set up a scrappy sniper station on the rooftop of an abandoned building in San Jose that provided enough coverage as well as a bird's-eye view of the gathering below them.

The crowd was a blend of R followers, Dom Coronet supporters, and a bunch of pesky BLMers. The elders were convinced there was Antifa and additional riffraff in the group as well.

The morning had been uneventful, and they were considering packing up the arsenal they'd carried to the roof, bored that their presence wasn't needed. R had told them of the Rainstorm, yet nothing was out of place. Maxwell Hovick must have rejected the election results by now.

The dozen men dispersed along the building's edge agreed to leave when a series of pings and beeps reverberated as the text messages were relayed to their phones. "*The Rainstorm is upon us! Fight for democracy! The enemy is among us! Find them and remove them.*"

The highest-ranked elder yelled to the group, "The Enlightenment is here! Cleanse the filth from society. You know what to do!" Metal clicked against the brick wall as the men brought their rifle sights up to eye view. Shots filled the air, and the assembly below, peaceful seconds before, became a swarming mass of screams as people tried to scatter.

"Pop." "Pop." "Pop."

Those without a letter R or Dominic Coronet branded clothing were quickly weeded out of the crowd using the crosshairs of a scope, and it didn't take long before there was a pile of bodies lying on the ground.

"We are enlightening the fallen for faster ascension to GOD!" The senior elder was animated as he changed the cartridge of his AR-15. "Dominic Coronet is our savior!"

∎

"Generals, it is a long-held practice that members of our communities are here to support the country. Militia groups have been formed to protect our lands since before the Constitution was enacted. Many brave men have stepped up today to defend!" The Dom was pacing the War Room set up down the hall from the Oval Office, gesturing with animation.

One of the military leaders at the table sighed. "But, sir, with all due respect, the troops we've deployed are trained and positioned to retain order."

"Yes, but there is a support group that should not be ignored! Many have been trained by ex-military personnel. They are vital for maintaining control. Ensure that all your military personnel are instructed that militia members wearing clothing supporting the messages of R or with my name are on our side. They should not be detained. They are to be free to patrol the grounds to protect!"

"But sir..."

"Don't 'but' me, general!" The Dom looked at the group. "I appreciate your expertise, but these are unique times. These are times when we need support beyond those that have been deployed. We have a group of citizens who are dedicated to the preservation of my presidency, and they will not be detained or deterred!"

"Mr. President...," another general started to speak.

"If you're not a Loyalist, you don't need to continue."

"I was going to say that our military is easy to identify in the field. They all have uniforms that convey who they are. These militia members... you're saying they're dressed as a paramilitary?"

"Yes, you must be deaf. I just said that."

The general tried to control his response, aware that the president needed coddling. "Respectfully, sir, I'm just suggesting that mistakes could be made. It will be easy for detractors to disguise themselves as members of these militias and to cause problems."

"Trust me, these supporters know who are in their ranks, and it would be hard to deceive them. It is imperative that your men recognize them for their contributions. Make it happen!"

Dominic Coronet strode from the room.

CHAPTER 44

The alert over the loudspeaker of the PA system at Cedars-Sinai Hospital was calling all available doctors to the emergency room. What had started as a quiet morning performing rounds and connecting with his patients had been disrupted by an unusually high number of sirens wailing outside. Jamiel finished with his patient and stepped into the hallway. A flurry of activity of nurses, aides, and even hospital administrators swarmed around him. "Hey," he called out to one of the nurses, and the young man stopped briefly. "What's going on?"

"I don't know. Maybe a gang war. All I know is we're being inundated with patients mostly suffering gunshot wounds."

"Gunshots?" Jamiel thought about the areas neighboring the hospital. Beverly Hills to the West, the Hollywood Hills to the Northeast, and West Hollywood, a trendy, gay-friendly neighborhood that flanked the hospital to the east. These weren't traditional turf war areas.

"Yeah, we're taking overflow in addition to our patients."

Jamiel wondered how many people were impacted. *Was it the work of a single shooter? Why was Cedars handling overflow? It wasn't exactly close to the traditional gang infiltrated neighborhoods of the greater Los Angeles area.*

After thanking the younger man, he turned down the hall, his leather dress shoes barely making a sound as he traversed his way to the emergency admitting area he rarely visited during his days at the hospital. He was shocked by what he saw as he pushed through the double door divider that bridged the main hospital wing with the ER. A frenzied staff was trying to assist the hundreds of people that had surged through the doors. The floor had streaks of blood distributed by the wheels of the gurneys. People were moaning or screaming, while others lay silent, their injuries so severe they had gone into shock or were unconscious.

Jamiel had done some work in the ER during his studies, but that had been decades ago, and this was different than anything else he'd ever seen.

"Doctor, we're so glad you're here." An agitated nurse with a badge indicated she was at her regular post. "Try to help us determine who needs immediate care, who can wait, and who we can't help."

"Can't help?"

"Some of these wounds have done too much damage. We need to focus on saving the lives we can, not focus where our efforts won't count."

He scanned the immediate area, trying to determine the number of patients.

"Here, take this, you're going to need it." She thrust a box of disposable gloves towards his chest. "We're tagging people with a 1, 2 or 3." She showed him the process for marking each patient's ranking. She leaned in closer and spoke softly so as not to be heard by those around her. "One's need immediate attention, twos are next, and threes are the ones that won't make it."

How was he going to make proper assessments? It had been a long time since his residency.

"Start with this hallway."

Jamiel pulled on a pair of gloves and stepped to the first gurney, discovering a variety of bullet wounds that had entered and exited the body. He could only feel a faint pulse, and the patient's breathing was shallow. He noted the number 3 and stripped out of the gloves, leaving them on the side of the rolling bed, and then moved to the next person.

Jamiel was exhausted after spending hours tagging people. He could imagine the surgical staff was overwhelmed as well. It was an all-hands-on-deck moment with a flood of people being brought into the packed hospital. There were no beds. Many people had suffered injuries from gunshot wounds; others had been trampled in a frenzy of panic throughout Los Angeles.

He left briefly to check on his patients who also needed his care and to grab a drink and sandwich from the vending machine in the hallway. When he returned to the ER, he saw men dressed in military garb standing at the entrance to the ER. He assumed they were part of the National Guard, but then another man joined the men in camouflage clothing. He noticed there was no insignia, and the clothing looked like it had come from an Army surplus store. The man did not appear to be part of the formal military presence, and he started assessing each person coming through the doors.

"Bring this person in for treatment."

Jamiel watched, trying to understand the rationale when another person was turned away.

"You're not welcome here." Jamiel overheard the man speaking.

He walked toward the door. "I'm a doctor in the hospital. What are you doing?"

"I am here to make sure the followers of R and our prophet Dominic Coronet get the attention they need. Anyone who is not a true nationalist is not to be treated."

Jamiel looked at the man in front of him. "We assess need based on medical procedures. Are you a doctor?"

"I don't need to be. I've been given my orders. Only those who are followers of R and supporters of Dominic Coronet are to get treatment."

"We treat everyone who needs help."

"Not anymore."

"According to whom?"

"Dominic Coronet himself. If you don't like it, you can take it up with the president."

Jamiel stopped trying to have a conversation with the man. Instead, he turned to go behind the nurses' station and picked up the phone to call the hospital administrator.

The phone rang twenty times before Jamiel hung up. That was unlike the staffing office. He redialed the number to make sure he had the correct extension. After seven rings, someone finally answered.

"We have someone down here turning away patients."

"We'll have to get back to you. There's someone from the military in our office dictating our behavior."

Jamiel hung up the phone and looked to the entrance. Too many people were being denied admittance. He maneuvered to the back of the hospital to an exterior door and stepped outside. He'd never seen anything like it. Thousands of people were on the street; many were helping those who were injured, and many were trying to queue for the ER.

Movement was slow. Jamiel suspected that there were military posted on most of the streets around him. He could hear the voice over a megaphone nearby. "Please go to your homes. The Dom will address the nation tonight at 7:00 p.m., and all will be revealed. The United Republic is here."

Jamiel felt a ball forming in the pit of his stomach. Gone was the elite neighborhood. The followers of R. had taken it over. He returned to the interior of the building. It was better for him to help treat the people he could.

■

"World Resources is redirecting your query."

Casey read the screen with disbelief. He was trying to access *The National Times* website, but the familiar home page would not load. The streets outside were chaotic, and CK was attempting to report on the activities they'd witnessed at the Capitol. Protesters had overrun the building, and his team had witnessed the horrific hangings of top officials. His cell phone signal kept going in and out, and the team of reporters had pushed to return to their office in hopes that the internet connection would be more robust.

The page that loaded proclaimed the victory of Dominic Coronet.

"The United States of America has been restored, and corruption has been eradicated! It is the beginning of the United Republic!"

A video started to play. A talking head of Dominic Coronet filled the screen. "Nationalists! You have done your part and stood up to the corrupt and bankrupt individuals who have held the reins for too long. We have successfully trampled down the opposition and restored our democracy." The portly man spoke with animation.

"Those who came to fight this transition have been eradicated. Militias across our land have stepped up to support our troops and protect our rights, our human rights. I am the rightful leader of the United States of America. We have restored our lands to the proud and loyal."

Casey watched in disbelief and confusion. What had happened to *The National Times* site? "If you are watching this video, you have tried to access a site that has been deemed a threat to our democracy and dedicated to undermining our freedoms and liberties. The site you tried to access has been eradicated. You will be able to get information on this page and sites redirected to World Resources URLs in the days and weeks ahead. We will no longer tolerate misinformation being spread about our great nation."

World Resources… it sounded familiar. Where had he heard about the organization? CK remembered the information from months ago. World Resources was the agency that had received the 170 million IP addresses from the DoD that had been moved to an LLC in Louisiana by Dominic Coronet's administration. It didn't take long to deduce that the IPs were being used to funnel legitimate sites to the message that Dominic Coronet wanted to control.

Casey typed in the URL for *The Nat Time*'s competitor in New York. It redirected to another World Resources link. The same video of Dominic Coronet began to play. He checked the code and confirmed that the two sites were pointed to different IPs. The reporter continued to type traditional reporting website URLs into his browser window, and each linked to a different World Resources IP.

Why use different IPs for the same info? The answer came in a flash. *This way, servers wouldn't be overloaded, and Dominic*

Coronet's message would be played without interruption. Casey didn't know how far-reaching the ramifications would be, but he was pretty sure he was out of a job.

■

Tony replayed the video of the scene outside the Capitol Building. It had been recorded two weeks ago, and the images had gone viral. Tony watched in dismay as he saw Maxwell Hovick hanged along with several Representatives. The crowd proclaimed they were traitors of democracy and killed them for their treasonous acts.

What happened to having a trial of one's peers?

Dominic Coronet had declared martial law and demanded a curfew of 9:00 p.m. Texas Freedom Fighters, along with other militias, were given the responsibility to patrol the streets to ensure peace, along with members of the military from bases around the United States. Tony still wasn't sure the extent of activity that had occurred the day the Electoral College votes had been ratified, or at least attempted to be ratified.

The internet was spotty and intermittent. His Facebook page appeared to be heavily censored, and it seemed only his private group comments for Texas Freedom Fighters were consistently delivered. About two-thirds of the Twitter users he followed no longer existed.

Erica's channels still played on YouTube, but anything related to the news or recent events was stripped from the site. Erica hadn't been able to upload any new content during the days following the "Restoration Day."

When he tried to visit several news sites, he received a message that World Resources had determined the site was an enemy to the country by spreading falsehoods against the United Republic. The only news was directly from the president, who was replaying the video of Hovick's death to convey his victory and to minimize any civil unrest. "Those who betray our country betray themselves!"

Tony still couldn't get the lifeless body of the young girl wearing the "Love Is the Answer" sweatshirt out of his mind. The image haunted his dreams. Her death seemed senseless.

Every day when he woke up, he learned of additional changes being implemented "to maintain peace and protect law-abiding citizens." He still went to work and fixed plumbing issues around Houston, but seeing armed guards on many street corners was unnerving. There were also occasional roadblocks, with guards asking where he was going. The Ready, Set, Flow logo was insufficient information to identify his business. He was often late for jobs because of the checkpoints, and when he arrived at various homes, the people he met had a harried look about them, probably not much different than his own.

There were also videos circulating online of police and military members in standoffs with citizens upset with the current situation. Houston was quiet, eerily quiet, for a city heavily armed. Fear was ever present as it became clear that the rules were changing.

Tony had joined Texas Freedom Fighters to protect democracy and his state's history. Observing everything around him, he had a sinking feeling that his actions had helped destroy the very thing he'd been fighting for: freedom.

R had been silent for days. *Maybe those posts were being censored as well?* R had predicted a Rainstorm would come to restore the country to the prior days of glory. What he had predicted was a different type of "rain." This was all about promoting the "reign" of Dominic Coronet, not the good of the United States and the citizens who had supported the man in the White House.

"Respect the word. You are being misled." The words took on a new meaning. The truth had been right in front of him the whole time. *You are being misled.* Unwittingly, Tony had been a pawn in the destruction of the United States of America. His intention of preserving the democracy he'd known his whole life had destroyed it instead. *How had Erica been able to see the truth in the messages?*

For now, they were still together, linked in an attempt at normalcy in an ever-changing landscape around them. He hadn't told her about the man he shot outside city hall. He still saw images of the man's body dropping to the ground and blood pooling underneath him. It played out in his dreams, and he could not escape the images in his mind, playing in slow motion, highlighting every detail of the moment.

As a member of TFF, Tony had been elevated to Watchman, a guard position to patrol at night, looking for any breach or rebellion against the United Republic.

There were still many unknowns with spotty internet connections and censored websites. The new state media conveyed a mishmash of information, mostly touting the praises of Dominic Coronet and declaring his electoral win.

The president had been sworn into office near the very location where Maxwell Hovick had lost his life. No one knew what had happened to Larry Stevens and his wife. No one discussed the absence of the other presidential candidate. Fear was palpable, and armed guards posted throughout cities across the U.S. commanded adherence to the curfew. Those who voiced any opposition disappeared without notice.

Rumors were rampant, and Tony could only imagine what was true and what was false. There was no narrative that he trusted anymore. The only thing for sure was he hadn't gotten what he'd been fighting for, and he hoped there would be a way to correct his wrongs someday.

CHAPTER 45

"Brad Taylor, you are hereby acknowledged for your bravery and fortitude on the steps of the nation's capital. You have ensured the proclamations of Whites Restore are being honored, and our great nation is being cleansed."

Brad lowered his head as the Whites Restore elder looped a medal around his neck. The large metal disk acknowledged that he had fought courageously to help the Restoration Movement, ensuring that Dominic Coronet could lead the United Republic to greatness. The elders also commended him for helping inferior filth transcend closer to Heaven.

"Today is a great day in the history of the United Republic. Whites Restore has been granted militia status as part of the martial law imposed by Dominic Coronet to preserve peace. We are part of the new army. We are tasked with keeping the peace. We are controlling the destiny of our children and their children. We will no longer take a back seat on the bus when it is the rightful place of Whites to ride in the front. There will be no more transgressions against our race. We are the chosen. We are the elite. We are the powerful."

Brad looked down at the medal and smiled. He had followed directions and been rewarded. He had found his place in the world and in the United Republic.

■

Pammy and Asher had barely escaped the scene in San Jose when things started going south. They'd heard gunshots and didn't wait to discover why. They'd started running and ran for blocks before wheezing to a stop somewhere east of the demonstration.

"What happened?"

"I don't know," Pam said, "but we need to get home."

"I agree. Let me get a car."

"From here? That'll cost a fortune."

"Don't worry, I've got it."

"Asher, you can't afford that. Let's try to make it to Caltrain."

"I said I've got it." The young man tapped a message on his phone, and seven minutes later, a black Town Car turned onto the street and stopped in front of them. A driver stepped from the front, walked around, and opened the passenger door of the limo. "Sir."

Asher slid into the interior, and Pam followed suit before the chauffeur closed the door.

"This isn't an Uber."

"It's my uncle's car."

"What's your uncle's car doing in San Jose?"

"I promised him I'd let the driver stay nearby in case something happened again, like in Oakland."

Pam had heard about Asian families' protectiveness toward their sons, but this seemed over the top.

"Who's your uncle?"

"He's the Korean Ambassador to the United States."

"Wait, what? I thought you said your father was a school teacher in Korea?"

"He is a professor at a university."

Pam had to shake the image of grade schoolers from her mind. There was more to Asher's background than he'd shared.

"Your uncle works at the Korean Embassy in…" Pam wasn't sure what location to name.

"San Francisco."

"Anything else I should know?"

"My other uncle is the Prosecutor General of South Korea."

"So, your family is well-known in Korea?"

"In South Korea. We thought it would be best if I didn't advertise my affiliation, and since our last name is common, it would be unlikely that anyone would make the connection."

"Why are you attending these rallies?"

"Asians face similar discrimination around the world. I wanted to do something on my own without my family's influence."

"So that's why you weren't charged after the Oakland incident."

"There was concern about diplomacy between our countries if I were detained. I tried to get them to release you, too."

Pam didn't know how to respond. It frustrated her that there had been so many inequities that day, like the White girls who weren't even arrested. Learning that Asher had been released without charges because of his family's political connections in San Francisco seemed unfair when her father had to post $10,000 bail on her behalf, not to mention the need to appear in court and enter a plea. She still didn't know why the charges had been dropped. *Had Asher's family had any influence on her case?*

As Pam leaned back in the leather upholstered seat of the Town Car, she realized that nothing was simple. Each community, race, nation, and the world has layers of hierarchy. There will always be the haves and the have-nots. She was one of the lucky ones, but as she looked out the window as the car maneuvered through the crowded streets of San Jose, she wondered about those on the street. *Weren't they entitled to the same life she was afforded? Not everyone could be a doctor because of their aptitudes, but couldn't everyone be given a chance to be something, anything in the world? Was that why there was so much fear and political unrest in the country?*

She was grateful she'd escaped the eruption of chaos in San Jose before either got hurt. She tried not to think about the other protesters who didn't have a luxury car waiting in the wings. The news of the destruction of the democracy she'd known her whole life wouldn't be fully evident for several more days. She was going to have to navigate an entirely new set of rules.

■

Leon had traveled back to his hometown in Pennsylvania. There had been multiple checkpoints along the way. He'd been waved through as soon as they'd seen his R attire. He had been in D.C. for the historic Restoration! He'd been a part of securing the democracy that had been given up over one hundred years earlier. The Pope and Royals could no longer stake a claim on his country!

It would be exciting to see how the country was being restored. Several days later, he pulled into the parking lot of his local grocery store and scanned the spaces for an opening. *Why were there so many people shopping for groceries in the middle of the afternoon? Even though he'd lost his job over a year ago, didn't most people work during the day?*

He was able to wedge in between the cart caddy and a small compact car. When he entered the store, many shelves were bare, and people were snaked in a queue waiting for the register, with carts overflowing with groceries.

"What do you mean my card has been declined? I have a lot of credit that I haven't used."

The clerks looked haggard. "We only can accept NatCoin."

"Nat, what?"

"NatCoin. All other payments have been disabled."

"How do I get NatCoin?"

"Dunno. It's a cryptocurrency or something like that."

Leon overheard the conversation and smiled. If only the shopper had listened to his YouTube channel, they would have been prepared. Leon had been promoting the acquisition of NatCoin for over a year. He had an app on his phone that let him access his shares. He could buy whatever he wanted in the store today, while others would have to wait for their money to be converted.

CHAPTER 46

"You have been identified as a person associated with spreading falsehoods about our great nation and the president of the United Republic. This is your High Court Tribunal trial to determine if you are guilty of crimes or were an unsuspecting pawn used by the prior establishment to promote their incorrect narrative. How do you plead?"

Casey sat in a chair, facing a man in a black robe. He had pounded a gavel on a wood block to start the proceedings. However, there was no one to represent Casey. It was unlike any court experience he'd observed in the past, with a guard blocking the door and the judge-like figure the only person of authority in the room.

"I'm sorry, I don't understand what I'm being charged with."

"As a prior employee of *The National Times* newspaper, you were assigned to report information in direct conflict with the truth of the United Republic. Did you convey this information knowing that it was inaccurate in an attempt to create the destruction of our democracy, or were you unsuspecting in the way your prior employer used you to disseminate information?"

Casey wasn't sure how to answer. He had done his job well, yet the question was designed to establish his faithfulness to the new order. Answer one way, and he would likely be imprisoned or executed. Answer as an unsuspecting pawn and know he'd sold out for his self-preservation.

What would his life be like in the United Republic? Would he be able to orchestrate change from within? He'd have to try.

"I plead not guilty." The words almost stuck in his throat. He tried to push down the shame he felt by lying about his prior role and the pride he'd taken reporting for a Pulitzer Prize-winning newspaper.

Dominic Coronet had already stripped the government structure that Casey had known his entire life, proclaiming that he was removing the toxins from the United Republic. Instead, he inserted his followers into a new structure. Congress no longer existed. Elected officials from each state had been given a chance to embrace the Coronet regime or were relegated to a long list of traitors. Initially, some officials had stood up to the coup initiated by Coronet. However, when public executions showed the peril of taking that route, many toed the line. They swore their allegiance to the man who had stolen the presidency and the country by mobilizing a personal web of militia members across the United States. With the proclamations of R, Dominic Coronet had seized the opportunity.

It was impossible to know if R was truly a government insider, but Casey was confident that the online messenger's goal was to create chaos. R had cast doubts and laid a foundation for Dominic Coronet to step into the role of savior. Maybe it had just started as a joke to see how gullible people would be, or perhaps it had been carefully orchestrated to topple the government and the United States as he knew it. Casey would never know. He hoped at least his plea would give him a chance to fight in the future.

"Evidence supports that you were a knowing participant in your prior role. However, this court can also see that your superiors manipulated you. Your editor pleaded guilty and was executed yesterday. He swore of your innocence."

Casey tried not to visibly cringe when he heard the news. His editor had been a good and fair man. To know he had died standing up for his beliefs made Casey squirm at his plea. He knew he wouldn't be able to do anything if he were dead, and he made an internal pledge to his prior manager that he would avenge his death. It might take the rest of his life, but he was determined that he'd live long enough to make a difference, that he would survive to work to restore the nation he loved and had his allegiance, not this United Republic sham of democracy touted by Dominic Coronet.

■

Casey was appointed to the desk of the new United Republic newspaper, which had taken over the offices of *The National Times*. He could tell he was being closely monitored, and he was spoon-fed the articles he could write—*censorship at its finest*.

"The Dom has restored peace and order throughout the United Republic. Traitors of the United Republic have been thwarted in their attempts to disrupt the peaceful proceedings of the government headed by Dominic Coronet. The High Court Tribunals are processing cases daily, and reporting channels are being put in place to allow anyone to alert authorities of traitors in our midst."

CK wanted to scream at the inaccuracies of the story. He knew from navigating the streets around him that there was still chaos with fear palpable in the air. He suspected he was assigned to the new United Republic paper to give it credibility. Still, he was sure there were many who would know that it was a manipulated propaganda vehicle to promote the Coronet Commission. The term "Cabinet" had been replaced, along with other changes to the government structure. There was no longer a vice president. The Dom had dictated a structure that eliminated a leadership hierarchy below his position. "Maxwell Hovick was a traitor to this country. We will not risk another transgression and have eliminated the position of vice president."

Casey was still trying to assess the situation and tapped into an underground rumor mill churning out an abundance of information; however, it was impossible to know what was fabricated and what was true. Internet access was intermittent, with extensive redirects to United Republic URLs highlighting the importance of being careful what was typed into the search bar. It was easy to deduce that he was part of a propaganda machine with no supporting merit. Anything could be imagination or fact. Casey looked around him and wondered if anyone else believed in what they were doing. *Had the people who responded to the call for the Rainstorm gotten the world they desired: To be watched under the threat of being shot?*

From the posts he'd seen and reported to the FBI before the coup, it looked like his worst fears had come true. It was evident that Dom Coronet had mobilized the militias around the country to become his personal army. Their presence was heavily seen throughout the country. Self-funded, gun-toting

"Nationalists" had provided another layer of protection for Dominic Coronet and had been triggered online by the mysterious R.

The spider web of support had responded to the call for battle on the ratification day. Instead of confirming Larry Stevens as the next president, Dominic Coronet had empowered the militias to perform a cleansing of those not in support of the incumbent.

Casey still wasn't sure how far-reaching the support had been, but he doubted it accounted for most of the country's population. Dominic Coronet had declared martial law, invoking the powers of the military of the United States for his beck and call. Rumors were prevalent that anyone who objected was being court-martialed. The Dom was calling the shots now, and anyone who didn't toe the line would be weeded out and punished quickly.

CK popped a few antacids. The stress was tearing at his gut. He was hopeful that in the coming weeks, he would find others of like mind, and together, maybe they could find a way to rise up against the dictatorship forming around them.

■

The president of the United Republic, Dominic Coronet, looked at the expanse of lawn outside his office and smiled. R had served him well. He had convinced a large swath of people that they didn't have a democracy, created an acceptance for change, and he'd done it openly.

Stupid dumb fucks didn't stand a chance. The whole messaging system had been easy to manipulate. It started with a few simple posts on obscure message boards, and the algorithms did the rest. Those looking for meaning had clutched onto the belief that the prophecies were true.

Pick a villain or a group that would be easy to despise and hard to pinpoint, and the ball was set in motion. The Hollywood echelon became victims of their own privilege. On one hand, members of the elite dismissed the information as conspiracy theories with little or no substance. On the other, most people didn't care but thought the elites should be taken down a peg or two. People disgruntled with their own lives didn't mind disrupting the lives of others if they saw them as having something they couldn't have. They wanted to level the playing field.

Militia members had learned one by one about R as they yearned to defend their communities and the history they feared was being threatened. The Dom had not created the machine. He'd exploited it. He had thought the election was his, and the surprise loss had worked in his favor. It gave him a shortcut to his endgame by giving him the power to dictate. He was free to rule the way he wanted. He kept fears escalated and watched people fall into line, willing to follow whatever rules were necessary to stay alive.

He had a large following willing to do his dirty work. Many were eager to show him their allegiance. Some liked chaos and being contrarian. The Dom didn't particularly care why they supported him. He used them for his gain.

He had the power and the position to make the world his. It was just a matter of time. The United Republic would become the new world order.

ACKNOWLEDGMENTS

Writing is a solitary activity, and it's easy to get caught up in the world a writer creates, but it's the people in my day-to-day life who make it possible to write, revise, and finish a novel. I am not alone in this process.

Thank you to my agent, Bill O'Donnell, who is unwavering in his support and dedication to ensuring my work is ready for the world.

This book required research and I appreciate the insights of Dr. Luis Folan for hospital procedures as well as information from a militia member who chose to remain anonymous.

Thank you to my two editors, Margaret Beegle and Christina Howell, who provided valuable feedback.

Special thanks to Sağnak Taşırlar, who devoted hours to reading, re-reading, and editing the book. His feedback made the book stronger. I value your unwavering commitment to helping me publish.

Thank you to Nitin Garg and Angi Orobko for their emotional support. Also, thanks to Amie McCracken for the interior book design and Quinton Maki for technical assistance.

Lastly, to my extensive writer network, particularly in Munich, who listen, support, laugh, and play with me as we journey through our projects. Here's to success for us all!